Prai

MW01179189

"They say that in life, the goal is not to live together – but to create something that will. In *Mocha Madness*, the second in its series, Pashmina extends her creativity to new heights, and again we are absorbed by the trials and tribulations that life offers, and strength that must endure. A must read!"

~ *Lorraine Hahn former anchor CNN and CNBC*

"*Mocha Madness* is a thought provoking and uplifting book about the bonds of friendship. Pashmina brings you right into the lives of her characters and through these characters, she shows you the importance of friendship, and of living life in the moment. The three women the book is centered around are a richly diverse group from different races, cultures, spiritual beliefs and walks of life but together they find what they are missing in each other. There is much laughter, thought-provoking ideas, tender moments and great joy in this series! I can't wait for the final book in the trilogy!"

~ *Judy O'Beirn, International Bestselling co-author of*
Unwavering Strength *series*

"*Mocha Madness* by Pashmina P. discusses the crucial elements of being humans as we age. The trials and tribulations that we face in life appear to morph in its state and depth as we grow older; but we don't have to fall victim to our circumstances. When we look at our lives in awe and wonder, much like a child at play, we tend to find that the obstacles before us are merely tools for us to gain a better understanding of ourselves. Let the aunties in "Mocha Madness" take you on a ride in the complexities of being human, and how we can all learn from one another to overcome our own challenges, to expand and grow ourselves. Another wonderful tale by Pashmina. Definitely a must read as a follow-up to *The Cappuccino Chronicles*."

~ *Joanne Ong, International Best Selling Author of*
The Sun Within: Rediscover You

Mocha Madness

Pashmina P.

Published by
Hasmark Publishing, judy@hasmarkservices.com
Copyright © 2017 Pashmina P.

First Edition, © 2017 Written by Pashmina P.

Disclaimer

Permission should be addressed in writing to Pashmina P. at
pashmina.p.writer@gmail.com

Editors
Sam Strozzo, samstrozzo@gmail.com
Lex Maritta, lexmaritta@gmail.com

Cover and Book Layout
Anne Karklins, annekarklins@gmail.com

ISBN-13: 978-1-988071-65-7
ISBN-10: 1988071658

Dedications

I would like to dedicate this book to my mom, my two amazing sisters, and my brightest stars – my two beautiful daughters. Stars shine bright when we know we are diamonds... #WomenEmpoweringWomen... keep soaring...

My husband – keep making my soul giggle; your support for me on this journey shows me how an incredible friendship gets stronger with time.

My step dad, you have been on this journey with me endlessly, and it is going to just get better and better. Thank you!

To my extended family, thank you for always making me smile. You are delightful.

My friends near and far: you are always in my heart and never many oceans apart. I can't wait to celebrate with so many of you... very soon.

Acknowledgements

Thank you to my family, keep rockin'.

Thank you to my friends, thank you for always making me feel like family.

Thank you to Sam Strozzo, my editing partner and friend. Thank you for always being there on my literary journey... "*#movingtothe seaside.*" Your friendship and remarkable insight into writing is truly a gift. THANK YOU!

Thank you to Sonika and Naveed for helping me move through this journey.

Thank you to Judy O'Beirn and her amazing team from Hasmark for believing in me and being on this journey with me. It has been such an exciting ride. You are indeed my "book family."

Thank you to Dharaglobal Co. Ltd., and CEO Willian Reis de Souza, *www.dharaglobal.com* – You are an incredible sponsor, and your belief in me has humbled me as an author. Thank you for being on this journey with me.

Thank you universe for allowing me to pursue my dreams. Let's keep this amazing ride moving and soaring...

Author's Note:

This is a work of fiction. Names, characters, places and incidents are either the product of the author's imagination or are used fictitiously and any resemblance to actual persons, living or dead, event or locales are entirely coincidental.

I want to thank everyone who has supported me throughout *The Cappuccino Chronicles* journey. Firstly, my family – the greatest inspiration of all. Next, for the endorsements from Lorraine Hahn, former anchor for *CNN* and *CNBC*, as well as Judy O'Beirn, International Best Seller of *Unwavering Strength*.

The journey as a writer has been challenging as well as extremely enlightening. Without jumping into the unknown, you will never know how far you can succeed. As I continue to write, I feel as so many of us do—that the sense of storytelling is indeed a part of my DNA, and I am growing alongside the characters I have created.

Inspiration comes from a variety of sources, and my family has been one of my biggest motivations on a journey I adore. Never stop doing what you love to do, as it will always come back to you in a magnitude you never understood. Never look back, always enjoy the present moment, and know that tomorrow is never promised to anyone. When success surges towards you, you will know how you got there in hindsight... keep moving forward and love what loves you back. It's all in the stars.

Table of Contents

Part 1

The Aftermath
of Sharon's Death

Mala

A gargantuan void had been left in people's psyches as well as the cosmos after Sharon's passing, especially Mala's. It had taken her a year to fully recover and make some major shifts in her life. Again she changed for herself and knew that looking outwards all the time would never give her a true perception of her inner-self. She began to look deeper at who she was on the inside and found many things about herself that scared the absolute foundation of her real identity.

Mala began to realise that her belief systems were no longer exactly what she had grown up with, considering she had pretty much raised herself – with the help of Sharon and Noor, of course. And now with the resurrection of her mother in her life, something inside her was brewing and she had begun pondering parenthood and what it meant to be a filial child. The latter was something she seemed to have been struggling with lately even though she was sure she had been doing the right things all her life. With the arrivals of her mother and the twins into her life, Mala's whole foundation had taken a massive shift.

The twins were a true miracle; at the risk of sounding cliché, she managed to beat all the odds, and it was clear at some point in her life that Mala had reconciled with the idea that she would be childless. Riddled with endometriosis, the doctors had confirmed that IVF was the only path for her to become a parent.

After Sharon's passing, and the instantaneous proposal from Washington, Mala felt the urge to seek counselling from a doctor who could help her fulfil her dream of having children. With the money bestowed to her from her deceased father, Mala used some of her fortune to invest in creating a family with Washington. The doctor had warned them both that the treatment could take months if not years to work. Nevertheless, true to Mala's nature, she was blessed with the gestation of twins on the doctor's third attempt, and her wish of having one boy and one girl thus came to fruition. There was however, a looming notion of some minor disability of the children because of her age. And, accurate to what the doctor predicted, Michael was born with a few challenges.

At Bazica on a fresh London morning in July, Mala was sitting with Sophia, Alister, and her newly arrived twin offspring Shania and Michael. Bazica had a mummies and babies group every Saturday, and Mala had just finished mingling with the other mums. Sophia and Alister walked in and sat like family at their regular spot, Table Number 8. Bazica, in keeping with its propensity to make everything seem special, made such a fuss about each table that each's number was treated as a title – almost a throne.

The twins, now barely a year old, were Mala's miracles. She had no idea how they had selected her, especially with her aged womb, but the universe had chosen to give them to her and Washington at an extremely mature time in their lives. Something had chosen Mala and Washington because of pure love. Durga, who believed that children choose their parents, was proud of her daughter even though Mala didn't feel it sometimes.

Despite all of the worry and the obstacles posed by Mala's age, the heavens had chosen the Cannelli family to stand out no matter what circumstance was in their way. Mala lived a miraculous life. The Cannelli family had love, understanding and an unbreakable bond. Mala's void had been filled with abundance by her two beautiful children.

"So, Mala, all okay? Have you heard from Noor?" Sophia still held her tender Eurasian accent, even after moving back.

"Actually, yes I have. She says she's coming into London in a few weeks' time, smack bang when my mother is planning her visit."

"Oh wow, are you going to be okay with all that excitement?" Alister interjected.

"I will definitely ask you to babysit Al, if that's okay?" Mala sipped her cappuccino.

"No probs, Mala. Anytime. You know how much I adore your little ones."

Sophia, looking up from her cappuccino, enquired, "So, you sure you're going to be okay with your mum and Noor here at the same time?"

"I have to be, Sophia. What else am I supposed to do?"

"Well just remember to stay calm. Your mother is from a totally different generation and is sort of stuck there. Whatever's going on in your immediate family is amazing. You're doing a great job with your kids. And don't worry about what other people have to say, just be you, Mala."

Mala sighed. "I know, I just have to be me. I get it."

"And don't let yourself get irritated by the small things your mum says. She's actually quite sweet and really doesn't mean what she says."

"Like what?" Mala interrupted. "Like when she said that my womb was a 'dust cupboard' and wondered out loud how two children could even come out of there?"

"Yeah, comments like that." Sophia was giggling. "By the way, what is a 'dust cupboard' anyway?"

"It's a horrible closet where you store all the old cleaning material for dusting things," Mala said with a reluctant chuckle.

"I see," Sophia grinned. "Well, don't get wrapped up with the circumstances and situations your mum and Noor carry around. These, my dear, have absolutely nothing to do with you. Don't carry their baggage around; it's not necessary. You just be your gracious self and trust me, everything will be fine. If you sweat the small stuff, you'll become a dweller."

"Ah yes, a *Dweller* of the *'dust cupboard?'*" Mala asked rolling her eyes.

Both ladies continued their conversation about Mala's mother and Mala managed another small chuckle under her breath despite her annoyance. She knew that her mother wanted the best for her and Mila, but it was just the *way* that Durga approached Mala with situations that made her intuition curl with unease.

Mala was looking forward to her yoga class in the next few hours, while Alister babysat. He promised he would babysit twice a month so she could clear her *chakras*. Mala definitely needed a more permanent babysitter and more time to heal; Sharon's death had given her a very profound outlook on everyday situations and it was a challenge for her to understand how life is the most precious form of energy. She missed Master Kamal and made a mental note to take up a discussion about life and death with him today when she saw him. When time was not on Mala's side for her to visit the yoga studio, she would still listen to the CD Master Kamal had given her, *A Hundred Thousand Angels*, which always led her back to creation – Shania and Michael.

The CD also reminded her of a little old Chinese lady she stumbled upon in Chinatown now years ago, who gave her the meaning of everyone's existence through two numbers: 44, the numerology associated with the Chinese notion that nothing dies and that we are always reborn again in some way. That old lady had reminded Mala that when we die, we actually live.

She thought back to the time when Durga had come to visit her and Washington after Sharon's passing. Durga had seemed to be in awe of Washington. Not complete awe, but there had definitely been something in her look that had vivid enquiry. She would stare at him for long periods of time and then look away. It was not in shame, but rather with a sense of some kind of non-understanding, a kind of 'non' connection.

"*He looks ashy Beti, like Krishna,*" she had remarked one day when they were cooking in the kitchen. Her mother's heavy Hindi accent and tendency to call her daughter *Beti*, Hindi for daughter, was endearing and true to character. It was clear that she had no intention of changing herself for anyone.

"Who, Mama?" Mala asked. Washington was singing to Shania while Michael let out little snores as he lay asleep in the bassinet.

"*Your Vashington. His skin is so dry,*" Durga replied, as she stared more and more intensely.

"I will tell him to put cream on his body, Mama."

"*And you must alvays put oil on my grandchildren, they hawe beautiful Indian skin. Not cream yaa. I want you to rub coconut oil all ower their hair and skin ewweryday.*"

The smell of coconut oil had always made Mala gag. She despised the scent and it gave her the shivers whenever the strong mixture of skin and oil crept vindictively up her nose. Just the thought made her lips curl up in disgust.

"*Vot is the matter Beti? Vhy do you look like that at me?*"

"I just don't like the smell of coconut oil. I think it is very archaic."

"*Old is gold, Mala.*" Durga replied, grinning as she turned away from her daughter, shaking her head from side to side like an old Bollywood actress.

"Old is mold," Mala absentmindedly voiced out aloud, though she had meant to say it only in her head.

"*Vot are you talking about? Do I look like mold?*"

Mala turned away and focused her attention to her two beautiful creations. She was besotted by her young children and was in wonderment everyday of how God had given her such beautiful blessings.

Durga was still staring at Washington while he was busying clearing his instruments which were strewn all over the living room floor again, but this time she pulled her ears. Mala had noticed her doing that more and more often as the days progressed. She actually couldn't wait for her mother to leave for Manchester to go see her sister Mila.

Mala turned to her mother like a hawk and demanded, "Why do you keep pulling your ears when you look at him? What kind of cursing are you doing in that mind of yours?"

Durga's sour face was not so pretty anymore. She looked like she was about to scowl. *"Vhy are you sizing me up Mala? Am I not allowed to hawe any thoughts?"*

Mala knew where this was going. It was so tedious and predictable; she couldn't handle her mother's racist ways. She was just not on the same frequency. She tried not to retaliate.

"It's fine Mama, just drop it."

"No, I vant to know vhy you alvays think I'm picking on you."

"Because you are."

"Says who?"

"Says me."

"Vhy am I picking on you Malsy? Vhy Beti? Vot is it? Just because I pulled my ears?"

"Yes, and I want to know why? Why did you pull your ears?"

Durga sighed, *"I don't know."*

"You don't know what Mama?" Despite her intentions, Mala was getting more and more agitated.

"Vhy do I hawe to tell you vot's in my brain? Huh? Vhy?"

"Okay Mama, like I said, drop it... I've changed my mind, I don't want to know."

"No, but vhy?"

"Why what?" Mala was frustrated and confused. She thought she had just asked her mother to drop the conversation, but Durga was on a different wavelength. Her mind was not conveying formulated thoughts, which in turn were not assisting with articulation. She was trying to be clear and concise in her speech but it just wasn't working. Trying to formulate the words in Hindi, then in Sindhi, then in English, and then back to Hindi, she just couldn't find the right way to say what was at the forefront of her mind. So, she opted for English, hoping it wouldn't be the harsher language and blurted out, the words spilling over, *"Vhy did you have children vith him?"*

Mala was stunned, and stared at her mother. She didn't know what to say or how to react or even respond. There was nothing in her psyche that was helping her comprehend her mother's question.

"What?"

"*I'm sorry Mala, I didn't mean to say that.*"

Mala glared at her mother. "But you did."

Durga looked a bit frightened. Maybe it was because Mala looked a bit like her father at that moment. "*I didn't mean it, Beti.*"

"And what about my children, Mama? Do you pull your ears when you look at them too?" Mala was so hurt and angry all at the same time that she really didn't know what to do with this stuck-in-the-past woman standing next to her.

"*No Beti, I didn't mean that. You asked me vhy I pulled my ears and I told you. There, you asked for my thoughts and I gave them to you.*"

Mala looked at her mother in the living room of their Hammersmith flat and said, "Next time Mama, keep your thoughts to yourself. Especially if they require you to pull your ears!"

The conversation later that evening was curt, unfriendly and full of tension, even when Washington tried to play the divine melody with his instruments.

And so was the beginning of a divide in frequency between Mala's outside world and the longing to believe in herself through her inner manifestations, which were centred around making her family fit into a world sometimes devoid of compassion, friendship and respect. Tradition also seemed to get in her way, and breaking boundaries – and suffering the consequences of doing so – was becoming increasingly normal for her.

Sophia

Sophia was largely content with her new life. The same day as her conversation with Mala about Durga, she left Bazica smiling as stories about Mala's mother and her idiosyncrasies wafted about in her mind. She wished her own mother had personality. At least Mala's was clear, firm, curt, and above all else – bloody hilarious. Sophia actually enjoyed Durga's company and had a good time whenever they were together. She didn't know how it must be to live with her, yet she had a soft spot for the little old Indian lady who she just naturally called aunty. It was the Asian in her. She remembered her mother always requiring Sophia to refer to her friends as *aunty* because they were much older.

On the train home, Sophia pondered about her life in Surrey. She missed some parts of Hong Kong but had no urge or desire to go back anytime soon – not even to check on Uncle Peter's flat. She missed Dave like crazy. He promised he would be in London for the grand opening of the Christian Dior flagship store in South Kensington. It was a strange location to have a flagship store, but South Kensington seemed to always be going through a metamorphosis. She couldn't wait to see him.

She thought about Alister, and how Sharon's death had catapulted him into a different dimension. It was as if her death had acted as an exorcism. Alister had become a different person: he was calmer, almost tender, and had adopted a completely different outlook on life. Upon reflection, Sophia realised that his surge in energy stemmed from a deep loss. Although he was thriving, Sophia knew that Alister needed consistency and rhythm in his life or else he would fail, and end up back where he started. Despite Sophia's worry for her brother, she was, so far, happy with his progress.

Alex, Washington's drummer from La Bella Luna restaurant, was no longer in the picture, and the commitment factor kept becoming her barrier. Once again Sophia got into her own way, this time by not explaining her true feelings about Alex's lack of commitment, his lack of time for her, and just his overall lack of concern for her. So, she had broken up with Alex because he never made any time for her except for when he was working at La Bella Luna and even then, he was never fully engaged. She had carried on with the relationship for about eight months out of sheer loneliness but then decided that hanging on to someone who wasn't committed to her was simply draining. She decided to be alone again.

When she got home to her father's house in Surrey, her two cats, Max and Josie, reminded her about consistency. They were an absolute constant in her life, having been around far longer than she could ever have hoped for. She decided to call Dave.

"How are you, petal?"

"I'm good. I can't wait to see you."

"I'll be there in a few weeks sunshine. How's *Grandmama* feeling being alone again?"

Grandmama. There he was, going off again with his endearing yet all-too-accurate pet name for her. She sighed.

"Okay, I guess." She sighed again. "At least the weather's been good these few months; I don't feel down and cross."

"Wonderful. Don't get cross, you'll get wrinkles. Just watch more *Inspector Morse* and wait for me. I'll be there soon."

They talked more about Hong Kong and Sophia recognised minute by minute that, all things considered, she was content to be where she was that exact moment in time, in Surrey at her father's home.

Noor

Noor was getting ready to leave Paris again and make her way to London. She had decided with her father that she was going to settle down, be a big girl and look after herself. In the process of her decision-making, she had lost fifty pounds and looked like the movie star she was meant to be. Noor was stunning. She had the most flawless skin and with all of the excess weight gone, she once again looked absolutely gorgeous.

Ahmed was no longer in the picture after his bankruptcy had forced him to leave Paris with his tail between his legs. 'The Shark' had drowned, and was forever in Noor's past. She was glad to be rid of him. She knew she needed to be by herself and focus on recreating her true persona.

Sharon's death had sunk her spirit to the depths of guilt, sorrow, and deep loss. She knew that her actions – asking Mala questions about Sharon's death at the funeral for the sake of her own book – had been terrible, but she had been desperate to make a statement, as always. Maybe the funeral had not been an appropriate time and upon reflection, she knew that her actions may have been harsh. Perhaps that was why right now her soul was like a tumultuous river. Her guilt had caught up with her, for no matter how much Annabelle Noor tried to push things away, they always came back to haunt her.

She was tired of feeling so miserable all the time and had agreed to begin yoga with Mala when she got to London. Here, she was in a Pilates class, a boxing class, a spinning class, and a high-power aerobics class. She knew she was on a mission to shine.

Noor was excited to reconnect with her best friend Mala, though she still felt bothered by the memory of the last two instances they had met: once after Sharon's funeral, and the other time when Mala's mother had come to London as well.

After the funeral, Mala and Noor had procured an argument about the true meaning of friendship. Mala was convinced that Noor didn't know how to be a good friend had said so in so many words, and Noor was convinced that Mala was simply over sensitive and had countered accordingly. Their meeting, which would have hopefully helped them connect halfway, had ended with neither of them seeing eye-to-eye on the notion of friendship.

The second time Noor came up to London was when Mala had just delivered her babies. Noor tried her very best to be completely happy for Mala, but was also not so secretly of the same consensus about her womb being a "dust cupboard" as Durga. Noor and Durga took it upon themselves to gossip about poor Mala when she was in labour. While Durga was pulling her ears, Noor had cringed at the thought of how a woman over forty could even think about having children and later proceeded to tell Mala, after she had pushed her twins out, that she was going to be "a hundred-year-old grandma." Mala was furiously unimpressed, leaving both women with the feeling of disconnect yet again.

After a few days of visiting Mala and her twins in the hospital, Noor had returned to Paris to live her very simple and lonely life. She had wondered if she felt a little bit jealous of her friend.

Now it was a few weeks till she would be back in London, and Noor wanted to try one more time to rekindle her friendship with her best friend, *Auntyji* Mala.

She took out her pendulum, which was like her oracle. She used it as a way to ask her subconscious questions to retrieve answers from the unknown, and as she said a prayer for Sharon, Noor remembered the little old man she bought the pendulum from when she was in Boston.

Boston

"This pendulum is like a diamond. You will be able to get vibrations from the earth to find out true answers." The old man in the shop was from Texas and he had a thick American Southern drawl when he spoke.

"What kind of vibrations, I mean… when I ask questions… any questions, I will get the answers?" A 21-year-old Noor exuded intrigue and fascination, which made the old man ever more slyly descriptive about the use of the pendulum.

"You have to have faith young lady, but there is no such thing as blind faith, because that will get you nowhere… you understand, sweet child? This will get you nowhere. You have to believe that whatever questions you are asking are from your true self."

"What does that mean?" Noor asked immaturely, while eyeing the pendulum like a hypnotised child.

"It means, that whenever you ask this pendulum a question, you must be prepared to accept the consequences of your questions, and furthermore, accept what the vibration of the world is giving you at that precise moment…"

Noor interrupted, "…So what you're saying is that I have to listen to the pendulum?"

"That, my sweet child, is up to you, but no matter what path you decide to take, don't ever blame it on the vibrations around you, because we are all moving cells and energy."

Noor caught herself rolling her eyes. "Got it, now how much do I owe you?" Noor knew she was not totally convinced by the little old man. All she wanted was the pendulum and the beautiful fractals of light that surrounded it.

Without hesitation, he replied, "It's 38 dollars."

"What?" Noor was not impressed as she tried to hide her diamond pendant around her neck.

The man was unfazed. "Let's ask the pendulum if it really wants to be with you, shall we?" he said, as he put it up to watch which way it would swing.

Noor didn't want to play his game anymore and blurted out, "Just give it to me please, and I will figure out how to use it myself."

"Okay, if you insist. That will be 38 dollars, please," he said with a smile.

Noor reluctantly paid the man and proceeded to stare at the pendulum's crystal dangling from a very intricate gold chain. As she put it in her purse, the old man interrupted her thoughts and said, "Remember, right is yes and left is no. Don't try and get confused when things are not going your way. It's all about learning the lessons of energy and vibration. Don't abuse your power."

"Great, thanks, and don't worry. There won't be any abusing happening from me," Noor said, slightly irritated as she walked away with – unbeknownst to her at the time – one of the most important objects she would ever own in her life.

Noor then said a soft prayer for Mala, and then one for herself. She was doing what she had set out to do those many years ago, 'to recreate herself anew in the next grandest vision she ever had about herself.'

Chapter 1

Surrey

"I told you already Dave, I want you to stay with me, please. I really don't care what my father is going to say. I mean, I do…, but it will be fine. He knows you're gay."

"Sophia, I want to stay in a hotel. Maybe the Sheraton or something like that. I really don't want to impose at all."

"Well, see how you feel and then let me know okay?" Sophia said with girlish excitement.

"Sure, my sweet petal. It's been so long since I've seen you. I can't believe it's been a year since we last saw each other! You know Sophia, time just seems to escape me the older I get," Dave sighed, looking at his bookshelf which housed his old tattered sketchbooks from the 70s. He managed a half smile as he thought about his younger days at the London School of Fashion.

"Yes, way too long for my liking, and my long distance bill is up the roof!"

"So, why don't you just come back and live here with *moi*, Sophia?"

"Oh God Dave, here we go again. Please don't manifest that for me and tell me that *if God brings you to it he will bring you through it*. I know… I really know what this means, and I don't want to go through that again, especially now since Alister is actually thriving here in Surrey."

"I know, Sophia. Sharon was a Godsend for him. I've never seen anybody transform as much as your brother did after her... passing."

Sophia sighed, "...And they didn't even know each other for long. I really wish she was still with us." Sophia was thinking about how Alister had made a complete turnaround from his drug-dazed days in Hong Kong; it was astonishing.

"Don't dwell in the past Sophia. Remember what I said about the now? We have to live for the moment. It will always set us free. And we never know what's going to happen, so we have to cherish every single second we have been blessed with."

"Indeed Dave, indeed."

Sophia couldn't wait to see her best friend. "Listen, I've got to run a few errands so I've got to go. But I can't wait to see you. Please email me your flight details and I'll be at the airport to pick you up; I've learnt to drive my dad's Jeep!"

"What? Are you serious? No way!" Dave was laughing with delight. "You're not scared, *Grandmama*?"

"Scared of what? All I have to do is get in, switch on the ignition, drive and feel free!"

"I love it, Sophia. I'm so happy you're being adventurous. Your only problem is that you still don't have anyone sitting next to you in the Jeep."

"So what, Dave," she said with determined insolence. "I have myself. And for right now I'm content with that."

"Amazing, petal. Keep that starry attitude going, you'll go far. Maybe one day you'll be famous."

"For what Dave?"

"For being the most adventurous girl that side of Asia." Dave said sarcastically.

Sophia let that one slide. "I have no idea what you're talking about Dave." She was getting ready to check her emails quickly before taking a lazy lunch and running errands.

"What I'm trying to say is that I'm glad you're exploring the big wide world. Someone's got to do it, right petal?"

"Absolutely Dave. I have to go, I await your flight details and can't wait to see you."

"Take care Sophia, and don't go *Jeeping* around too much; you might find you've become a gangster."

"Gangster works for me," she said as she smiled. "See you, bye!"

"Bye."

They both hung up and proceeded to look at their emails. Dave's emails were full of colour chart requests, monthly meetings, feedback on new designs and emails from Craig – Sophia's former fling – that he had been storing for over a year. He didn't want to tell Sophia just yet that they were again in contact with each other.

Craig had contacted Dave three months after he had come back from London. He had had three months of drunken nights, sleazy joints, dancing on bar counters, visiting after-hours pool halls and just simply living in the very murky waters of Hong Kong's expat society. Craig was depleted and Dave knew that Sophia would be the best thing for him – and whether she accepted it or not, him for her. Now it was time for Dave to play matchmaker.

He had been thinking of a plan, but decided to keep it in his heart until he was ready to tell Sophia. He was going to do it with ease, grace and decorum while initiating circumstance between them. He was excited about this new project. In the meantime, he had to stay focused and keep the cat in the bag. He switched his attention back to his now and floated into a Christian Dior abyss of work emails; Dave really loved his job.

Alister had turned into such a gentleman and was a most gracious guest at his father's house. He never felt like the space was actually his as he believed that it would be bequeathed one day to Sophia. It never bothered him that his older sister would be the sole heir of the house. So, for now, he was living in his father's house as a guest.

His room opened up onto the terrace and the field of green, no matter the season, always made him feel so small and ultimately grateful. Occasionally he would get flashbacks from his downtrodden drug days, but would quickly shift his attention to the current moment. He couldn't live in the past, because it haunted him. The physical scars on his arm from needles reminded him every day that his past *must* forever remain dead. Lately, though, he had also stopped living for the future, especially after Sharon had passed. He had sincerely believed that they would have a relationship when he got out of the hospital. But with one quick swipe of universal energy, Sharon's physical form, voice, and stunning green eyes were robbed from him.

He could still hear her voice in his mind reminding him of human truths: *Be brave, precious, and don't be so bloody mopey, it's annoying. Get out, live, be free. Just be free. You are God's amazing creature... use your senses and your capabilities wisely.* Her voice was constantly resonating with these words in his mind. He knew he needed to be free. Absolutely free.

Chapter 2

South East Asia

Craig made an appointment to meet Dave in Hong Kong's Central district, though it was Dave who actually wanted to talk to him. Craig knew that in the last few months he had fallen into a hole, a snake pit, and it was getting dreadfully claustrophobic down there. The day he realised he had to come out of the darkness was when his boss called him to his office and warned him that he was going to lose his job at the bank. Stan, Craig's boss, was unimpressed by his actions of late and the vicious gossip circulating around the city. He had reprimanded him several times, reminding him that he represented the bank and that his actions were not becoming of his stature.

"I can't believe we're still doing this, Craig. How many times am I going to have to call you in? Look at you, you are an absolute mess. You're not the person I hired."

Stan was sitting at his desk, his back to the stunning view of the Hong Kong harbour. The skyline from the bank office was mesmerizing, captivating and resembling something out of a super-hero movie. Stan's big black leather chair looked like a throne.

"Your actions are a terrible representation of what our bank stands for. What kind of antics are you performing out there on the streets? And your sales have gone down! If you keep this up Craig, we'll have to reconsider your position."

Craig was severely hung over from the night before and the flashbacks of his drunken night were slowly beginning to reformat themselves in his brain. He was defensively embarrassed.

"I'm not your slave Stan, I can do whatever I want."

"You are under a contract here Craig, and I advise you to go over the employee handbook so we can be clear of what is and what is not acceptable behaviour."

"What is this, a school ground? You're acting like you own me. No one has ownership of me but me! This is ludicrous… and… extremely embarrassing." Craig was getting squirmy in the seat opposite Stan.

"We have a reputation to uphold, and if you cannot be a good candidate for what our establishment represents, then it's time to think about going somewhere else."

Craig was taken aback. "That's an insult. Think about how much work I've put into this place."

Stan leaned forward a little with concern, "Tell me the truth, Craig, why the sloppy nights, the incessant drinking and the crazy number of women? Why? Have you had your heart broken or something?"

Craig resisted. "My love life has nothing to do with my job…"

Stan interrupted, "Talk to me Craig, man to man, no beating around the bush. Don't be a pansy. What's the real reason? Is it the bird from London? The one you said came to visit you?"

Craig wasn't thinking of the same girl Stan was thinking of. He was not thinking of Jennifer. He was thinking about the other woman in London, Sophia.

"No Stan, not her… not the one you're thinking about. It's someone else."

"Oh, the Bloomberg girl?"

"…yes."

"So, what happened there?"

"I don't know," Craig said, shaking his head as a perplexed frown etched across his brow.

Stan recognised that he and Craig were not the best of friends, but his sudden concern stemmed from an ulterior motive. He was having some problems of his own, and his repeated reprimanding of Craig was more for his own benefit than for anything else. If Stan could be sure that he was going to continue with the bank for another two decades as he had always intended, he would probably have fired Craig on the spot. However, Stan urgently needed Craig to buck up and keep his place at the bank.

Craig, despite the fog in his brain, sensed that something was awry. Stan had never grown personal with him; as a matter of fact, Stan was usually quite distant. Today he looked like he needed something from Craig.

Stan leaned in even closer. "*I don't know* is not an option, Craig… you have to know. You create your own circumstance. It's all about free will, mate. From what I've heard from the office grapevine, it was your decision to let her go."

"I suppose," Craig sighed, thinking about how he yearned for Sophia.

"Just be calm Craig, everything will work out in the end if you exercise focus. There is nothing wimpier than an unfocused man, especially one that is trying to woo a woman. No woman wants to be with a confused man. Pull yourself together and either move on or make a decision to find her. And in the meantime, while you're trying to find yourself and what your true intentions are, please be reminded that the bank does not appreciate out-of-control people… think of your job as a woman you have to impress as well."

Craig looked up from the floor. "I don't understand exactly what you are trying to tell me, but if you want me to hand in my resignation, I can do it today." His defiant attitude was back again.

"As you please, Craig." Stan leaned back into his comfy black leather throne. "If you need anything, I am here. I think reflection and moving in a clear direction would be a good way to start. Maybe some meditation? That really helps the soul and…"

Craig interrupted him gruffly, "Don't worry about me Stan, I'm fine."

He got up abruptly and walked out of Stan's office and into his own office. He slumped on the desk and was irritated by the conversation he just had. Was he that bad? Was it gossip? Hong Kong, with all its people, was a very small place, and gossip was rampant. He wondered if people tried to investigate him when he was out with Dave. Dave always had paparazzi around him. He was annoyed at Dave as well. And then at Sophia. And then at Jennifer. He was just plain annoyed at his sticky web of murky, slimy circumstance. His thoughts shifted to the un-sanitised life he had been dragging his spirit through; he was embarrassed again.

His thoughts erratically switched, and he longed for Sophia again. Swerving again, he thought about calling up some friends to have a beer but stopped in his tracks for all of six seconds. The thought of seeing his mates for a beer and few shots whirled back into his head, vanished and then settled nicely back into his consciousness. He didn't care what Stan had to say or what Hong Kong had to say about him. He really couldn't care less. He was going out tonight and there was no stopping him. Not even his *golden* job at the bank. He picked up the phone and called Tomas.

"Hey mate…"

"What's up? You calling for another round of debauchery?"

"Yeah. Stan's being a twat, threatening me." For a fleeting moment, Craig thought honestly about Stan's demeanour. He was not threatening at all. On the contrary, he had actually been concerned. Craig redirected his attention to the negative aspects of his conversation with Stan.

"Threatening you? How?"

"He had the nerve to say I don't uphold the 'image of the bank!'"

"*Pfff…* what are we? In high school? Tell him to sod off."

"Yeah, I will. Thinking about handing in my resignation soon."

"So what? You're thinking of leaving Asia?"

"Thinking about it mate." Craig was confused, again.

"Right then, that's a reason to celebrate, innit."

"Yes, what time should I meet you at The Fong?" Lan Kwai Fong, Hong Kong's notorious night life party district, was now dubbed 'The Fong' amongst the expat community.

"Meet me there after work mate, let's go wild. Last week you were on fire, swinging your shirt around on top of the bar at *Castles*. My god, you were hilarious."

Tomas was laughing a chesty smoker's laugh which resonated with thick sarcasm in his throat. *Castles* was owned by a very rich Hong Kong entrepreneur. He had married a Filipina woman from Wan Chai, and had made her into his *Pretty Woman*. He thought he was Richard Gere.

Victoria of *Castles* was a true Cinderella story. She was a stunning lady. A kind and generous woman, she deserved the best and Samuel had made it happen for her. His bar *Castles* was named in honour of her because he thought of her as his queen. *Castles* was a sports bar that served the best burgers in town with the best rib eye steaks on this side of China. After dinner, the place became a bar and then a nightclub. People would dance on tables while the DJ played the latest hits, making it a hit with the expat community looking to let off a bit of steam – or, in Craig's case, completely let go.

Craig couldn't even remember what had happened that night. He tried once to rethink and then the second time he shut his eyes tight, hoping the memory would somehow come back. But he still couldn't remember, no matter how much he cajoled his memory; nothing seemed to click. Suddenly he reverted from images to sounds; he remembered the music that was playing that night at *Castles* on the jukebox and a faint image of him unbuttoning his shirt and swinging it above his head started to reformulate in his mind.

He stopped short. Had he really done that? He had probably blacked out after his fifth tequila shot. He put his face in his palms, the memory making him angry as well as rebellious. All of a sudden everything around him was annoying, including thoughts of Sophia, Stan and even the bank. He wanted to run away from it all. "Alright Tomas, we'll meet after work, but not a late one mate."

"Sure… famous last words Craig. See you at 6:30."

"See you." Craig put the receiver down and ran his fingers through his hair, pensively. He knew he was running away. He also knew that he didn't want to do this again, over a woman. First London, to get away from Jennifer, and now this running away from his true feelings about Sophia.

When Sophia had left for London both Dave and Craig realised that the one thing that made Hong Kong joyous for them was on the other side of the planet. The men gravitated to each other because they were connected by Sophia. And Dave, being older, was concerned about Sophia and her wellbeing. He sometimes wondered who she would grow old with and who would be by her side. She had Alister, but he depended on her much more than she did on him; it was obvious.

When Dave met Craig, he knew instantly that Craig was the man for Sophia. He was saddened by their lack of closure when she had left Hong Kong, and the mismatch of timings in their destiny. Yet still, there was something that Dave saw in Craig that would be perfect for his best friend Sophia.

And like a father figure and an older hip friend, Dave embraced Craig like someone he had known for years. A definite kindred spirit, Dave believed they were meant to be friends. Dave loved to rile Craig's spirit with humour, laughter, and of course conversation about Sophia.

Unsure of what to do with himself and his hangover, Craig picked up the phone to dial his friend.

"Hello, Christian Dior, how can I help you?"

"May I please speak to Dave Graham?"

"*Shertainly, hole on.*" A-Wong still had the same voice. Nothing had changed in over a year, and her drawings were still no better. She was the perfect receptionist.

"Hello, Dave Graham, how can I help you?"

"Dave… Craig here."

"Hello…"

Craig interrupted him, "Please don't call me sunshine mate, you know how I hate that. You know I love you, and your lifestyle is none of my business, but please stop flirting with me. You're old enough to be my father!"

"Sorry petal…"

Craig sighed and smiled all at the same time, because no matter how much he asked Dave to stop referring to him by 'pet names', Dave loved the attention, and loved to see Craig get slightly uncomfortable. Maybe this was Dave's way of helping Craig break stereotypes of his idea of homosexuality.

"Are we meeting later this evening?" Craig asked.

"Yes, we need to talk. I'm leaving for London in a few weeks and I think you should come with me."

"What? How?" This was unexpected.

"I can smuggle you in as my Christian Dior love iguana."

"Dave, please." Craig felt violated for a second and was about to insist again that Dave be more aware of how to address him, but decided against it. It was futile, because Dave never listened to Craig regarding his terms of endearment anyway.

Dave loved making fun of Craig, and he could feel him squirming on the other end of the phone. Craig was not Dave's type anyway and would never steal a man from his own girlfriend. "I think you should come for the opening of the flagship store in South Kensington. It will be fun."

Craig paused for minute, and decided to change the subject to the true reason he had called. "Dave, do you think I drink too much?"

"Yep," Dave said without missing a beat, nodding on the other end of the phone.

"What about you Dave? Do you think you drink too much?"

"Yep." Dave nodded again.

"So, you think we both drink too much, right?"

"Yes."

"Can you please stop saying yes? It's annoying the crap out of me," Craig said, sounding frustrated.

"Okay."

"Jesus Christ, mate. Can you give me some full sentences?" Craig's annoyance with the world around him deepened.

Dave put his drawing pad down and began to speak, clearing his throat first for dramatic effect. "Craig, I think you drink too much, you act like a wounded animal when you are out in public, and you give your establishment a trashy name. It is obvious that you are going through a difficult time right now and you need some guidance. You need a big shift because you are drowning in some kind of an abyss. If you decide to move on, you must move on with dignity and grace. The first step would be to stop drinking so much. Everyone in Hong Kong is talking about you."

Craig was stunned. He didn't know what to say.

Dave continued. "I suggest you clean up your act, pull your socks up and get on with it. Make a decision and go with it. You either stay a sloppy old drunkard with the reputation of being a silly *gweilo* in Hong Kong, or you move forward with cleanliness and search for a more fulfilling existence. Hello? Craig? Are you still there?"

"Yes... yes, I am still here." He paused. "I was supposed to meet Tomas, but I am going to cancel my drinks with him now and see you instead." Craig was feeling like a lost schoolboy again, wishy washy and unfocused. No wonder Stan had called him a pansy.

"Good, now shake the devil off your back. It's been many long months of this nonsense. You need a shift, a really big one, or a beating. Whichever one you prefer, my little love iguana."

"Oh, stop it Dave," Craig retorted, trying to keep with the fast pace of the conversation through the fog of his hangover.

"Sorry, sunshine. I will see you later in Central. And we will be having coffee, do you hear? Or a cup of tea. This is the first day of rehab for you."

Craig sighed. "See you later, mate."

Craig put the phone down and felt wounded. His ego had taken a big blast today and he was depleted. Everyone around him was right. Except Tomas. He picked up the phone.

"Tomas, I'm so sorry, I can't make it tonight; I have an urgent meeting with a very old friend. I need to be focused to meet him. Let's catch up next week." Craig was speaking to his voicemail.

He felt better. Step one: change his frequency of people. Step two: stop being a pansy.

Chapter 3

Paris

Noor felt ready for her return to London. She was a transformed woman feeling like a million bucks. She looked at herself in the mirror. She was wearing a blue Karen Millen suit and flat Stella McCartney ballet slip on shoes; thanks to her father's money, she looked gorgeous. She felt a sense of relief, like she was herself again. No more fat, waddling Noor. That part of her life was over. The break up with Ahmed had been so painful that it had jolted her into a dimension where she had no choice but to search for the truth within the depths of her subconscious.

She wondered about her crooked manifestations of love, marriage, and humanity. She cringed at her own thoughts. She was so happy to be her beautiful self again. She picked up the phone to call Mala, hoping that her friend had forgiveness in her heart and would understand that all of Noor's blaming and so many of her broken dreams were totally of her own making. Noor had to stop blaming her family and friends and situations because of her own failures.

The phone at Mala's flat rang and rang and rang. She looked at her watch. It was 6:30 p.m. in London; she must be feeding the twins. Noor decided to call her best friend again later.

As she began to pack all of her belongings, she came across a picture of the three friends. Noor was standing in the middle with a huge smile on her face, and Sharon and Mala were on each side of her. She remembered that day so clearly, like it was yesterday. It had been their last day of university in Boston and they had made a pact that they would all make it to London. They were so young. Noor put the picture closer to her face and looked right into Sharon's deep green eyes. She missed her Irish friend so much. She began to tear-up as she was transported back to that day in 1992.

Boston

"Ay, bungy, so did you tell Noor that we have made a pact?"

"Yes I did Sharon, we're all going to be together in London."

"What, to live?" Noor asked. She had heard tale of a pact, but was unsure of what, exactly, the pact was.

"Yea, if we like it, we stay, and if we don't, we can move back to Boston." Sharon was lighting up a cigarette.

"I think it sounds like a plan," Mala announced.

All three girls were jumping up and down like teenagers – although granted, they weren't far off. They were so excited at the thought of exploring the world after graduation.

"So, you know my dad has a house in London, right? I'm going to ask him if we can stay for a few weeks so we don't have to pay for anything."

"That would be awesome!" Mala didn't know where she was going to get any money to pay for her travels. She did not want to ask her father with whom she had no contact. He paid for her school fees, boarding and lodging, and that was the only communication they had. They never spoke on the phone. Mala also worked three jobs during university and always managed to have enough money, like her rich friends – but travel wasn't cheap.

Sharon said, "My dad is giving my mum a house in England soon. Their divorce is almost finalised and he has a house in Shepard's Bush *that he had bought under my mum's name. So, we might have two places to stay."*

The girls were jumping up and down again like teenagers. Their professor walked past and peered at the three of them, as if sizing up their behaviour. They didn't look like university students at that point; they actually looked like a bunch of screaming middle school girls.

"So, when are we leaving?" Sharon inquired.

"I can leave any time," Mala said confidently. She liked not having to answer to anyone. "I just have to let Mila know and then all is cool aunties... I can't wait!" Mala was so enamoured by her two friends; they were her family. And they always would be, until the end of time.

"I will call Pitaji and let him know we will be arriving soon," Noor said.

"This is going to be the best adventure of our lives," Sharon blurted with excitement, smoke percolating out of her nose like a 1950s Italian gangster.

"Let's take a picture, girls; this is our aunty pact... that we have a contract with each other to travel the world," Noor said as she took out her Pentax camera. She had recently bought the latest one, one with a zoom lens that slid in and out with the control of a small button.

A freshman passed by. "Hey, can you help me take a picture please?" Noor asked.

"Sure," said the young pimply boy. He pointed the camera at the three aunties and said, "Say cheese..."

Noor interrupted and said, "No, girls. Say auntyyyyyy." And with that, the boy snapped the picture, as each lady had the widest grins.

The pact and that photo were the beginning of the fabric of their lives being sewn together.

London

Noor continued packing and switched on some soft jazz. She put the picture in her purse between her passport pages. They honestly did travel the world together, embarking on many adventures. Noor looked at her watch and tried to call Mala again but there was no answer. She thought about calling Sophia, swiftly changing her mind.

She didn't know Sophia very well. Noor considered her to have a very stiff British persona. Noor believed Sophia wasn't the same kind of 'people' as her, Mala and Sharon. She didn't relate to Sophia's humour, and Noor felt like Sophia always looked at her with trepidation. Noor tried to move away from these thoughts and decided to continue packing in silence. She switched off the music that had been playing in the background from her old CD player and packed, lost in her own thoughts, the whole time trying desperately to manifest the good in everything around her.

As soon as she reached London, the first person she planned to call was Mala. Her flight was leaving in the morning and she couldn't wait to squeeze Mala tightly. At 9:45 p.m. Noor tried to call Mala one more time. Still, no answer. She looked at the clock and figured that she must be putting the twins to bed. It couldn't be easy being a 'dairy factory' for two kids. Noor was sure that Mala needed all the emotional support she could get in her life right now.

The next day, as the plane took off, Noor slipped her hand in her purse and placed her palm on top of the picture of the three best friends – Mala, Sharon, and Noor. A void seemed to swell in her, tears naturally descending down her face at the thought of Sharon never being around them for eternity made her shudder. She thought about how she had reacted to her friends in the past and wondered if her cruel nature was the reason she had occasional palpitations reverberating fear. She couldn't bring Sharon back or apologise to her, making her feel strangely regretful. Somewhere deep down inside her somewhat selfish soul she knew and understood that life was precious and time was of the essence for her to grow.

Chapter 4

London

"Washington, please help me babe. Michael won't stop crying. Can you please pick him up?" Mala looked like a racoon today with thick heavy bags under her eyes, dark and deep. She was still breast-feeding the twins and it was proving to be exhausting. Contrary to what others said, the older they got, the needier they seemed to become.

Washington picked up Michael, rocked him ever so gently and sang a lullaby in his ear. In an instant Michael was asleep. It was the way Washington looked at him and cradled him: like a diamond. It was a most beautiful sight of fatherhood. His perfect singing and the sway of his body was heaven for Michael as the rhythm and tone of Washington's voice hushed him into a beautiful slumber; the little baby boy in Washington's arms was asleep in no time. Washington placed him gently in his little blue bassinet and picked Shania up from Mala's lap.

The phone rang and Mala ran to silence the ringer. The babies were asleep and she needed to have some quality time with Washington. La Bella Luna was a memory of the past, as Washington had finally opened up his own music academy. He had borrowed some money from Mala from her inheritance, even though he was a bit sceptical about this endeavour and initially felt uncomfortable about the set up. Still, he managed to sink his male dominated thinking and felt liberated with his financial situation through his wife. Unlike his days as a band member at La Bella Luna, he would now work only occasionally at night, for big parties and events. Since the birth of the twins he was home more often and he made marriage feel real. As he rocked Shania gently to sleep and laid her in her pink bassinet, Washington smiled at Mala. He was content.

They sat on the sofa together and watched TV in silence.

"We have to stop doing this babe, walking on eggshells around the kids. They have to be able to sleep in noise. When I was growing up, I lived in a house with 12 people and there was noise at all hours of the day. I had to learn to block it out and make sure I slept." Washington was making a very true statement. "I feel like we are slaves to their bedtime. What if we wanted to go out and put them in the stroller, do you think they would fall asleep?"

Mala replied uninterestedly, "Sure Washington, we'll do that."

"Are you even listening to me?"

"Yes, of course," Mala said as she closed her eyes. She was just so tired.

"Are you okay princess?"

"Yes, yes, fine… just need some rest." She leaned her head on his shoulder and almost instantly fell into a thick unconscious sleep.

After a while, Washington ushered her slowly into the bedroom, kissed her on the forehead and placed the duvet on top of her. He then went into the study, which was now the twins' room, and kissed both of his beautiful children tenderly on the cheeks. He stared at them for a long time and smiled. A song came up in his mind, reminding him that he wanted his children to study music, to play instruments, and have the power to transport people and themselves into a different dimension filled with musical notes.

He went out into the living room and switched the TV station to watch football. He felt tired too. His mind wondered; he wasn't looking forward to Noor or Durga coming to London. He knew Mala always became depleted when she was around them. They all seemed to suck the energy out of each other, never consistent and always flighty. He didn't want that for his wife. She was much calmer for their babies when she was focused and serene. It was a healthier environment for his whole family.

Washington loved his wife and children entirely. He wondered if they would ever go back home with him – the home of his upbringing, the Caribbean. In actuality, he didn't want to but he knew his family by virtue of culture would expect to see his lineage. Eventually, he switched off the TV and went to bed. He knew Shania, and probably Michael, would be waking up soon. He thanked God for his place in the world and fell into a languid lazy sleep of absolute and divine gratitude.

Noor arrived in London and felt like she was home. She couldn't wait to get to her flat and soak in a hot bubble bath. She had called in advance and asked her house manager, Gloria, to ensure that the flat was in order, all her favourite toiletries were bought and her favourite food stocked. Noor's new diet required her to eat smoked salmon, multi grain rye bread, avocados, and cranberry juice. She would stay with simple foods this week and was eager to find a juicing bar. A liquid diet was currently her menu of choice for a few weeks so she could detox.

She had tried to call Mala again after she landed, but there was no answer; she was getting moderately worried. She had been trying for over twelve hours. Her thoughts went back to Shania and Michael. They must be a handful. She wondered if it was a blessing in disguise that she didn't have children. She paused and the thought was a bit slanted in her mind.

She sighed. *It must feel wonderful to have children*, she thought to herself. She was too old, and *her* 'dust cupboard' was no longer a 'dust cupboard' but rather a 'rubble cupboard.' She giggled inside herself thinking of Durga. The little old Indian lady would have definitely loved that analogy and would probably have pulled her ears.

Noor thought back to when Mala was in the hospital. Albeit slightly jealous, Noor had tried her very best to be supportive, especially during Mala's cries of labour. She also knew that being rude about Mala in front of Aunty Durga did not give Noor a good look; and true to her nature, Noor wanted to paint a very good impression of herself to the outside world, no matter what fake intentions she had. At the end of the day she was highly unimpressed by her friend's decision to have children, yet honed-in on her acting skills to keep her opinions to herself on the day of the twins' birth.

"Ay my poor Beti, I can hear her screaming from here." *Durga began to chant a Hindu prayer.*

"Don't worry auntyji, she will be fine."

"My God how did Lord Shiva do this? She is too old to be doing this."

"Age is just a number, she will be fine. Mala is a very strong woman."

Mala was screaming at the top of her lungs as she groaned and pushed with Washington by her side the whole time. Durga had asked if she could come into the birthing room and both husband and wife had vehemently said no. They didn't want any more ear pulling in their presence, especially with Mala in labour.

"So, tell me Annabelle, vhy did my daughter marry this man? And vhy did she have babies with him? Vot is she really trying to do, create a new race or something?

"Yes, maybe. And there's is nothing wrong with that." *Noor tried to sound as sincere as possible. Working for her father had taught her how to be a good talker... but not such a good listener.*

"Vot do you think my grandkids are going to look like?"

"Absolutely gorgeous," *Noor said as jealousy started to creep up again, because she knew this was the absolute truth and no acting could hide the fact that the twins were going to be stunning, especially with a mother and father like Mala and Washington. Their genetics couldn't lie, not even to Noor.*

Durga smiled; regardless of her apprehensions, she was going to be a grandmother again. She was content for herself. She prayed again for her daughter as she heard screeching cries of pain bounce off the delivery room walls.

Noor's face crunched up as the thought of pushing human beings out percolated in her mind. She shut the image out quickly because it was actually terrifying her, especially with Mala's sound effects digging right into her psyche.

Durga interrupted her thoughts. "In like a banana and out like a pineapple," she said as Mala ripped the hallway with more of her blood curdling screams. Noor was absolutely horrified.

She decided that she didn't want to recall those memories of the sound of labour again and focussed on the present instead. She got into a limousine and made her way to her father's flat, happy to be in London again. Now, all she needed to do was to try to reconnect with Mala again. She heard Sharon's voice in her head.

"Where the *bloody* hell is Mala?" Noor thought to herself.

Chapter 5

South East Asia

Craig checked the clock on his wall. It was already 6:00 p.m. He put on his jacket, straightened his tie, and went to the men's room to wash his face. He looked at himself in the mirror, and realised he had aged much in the last three months. He looked wrinkly, dehydrated, and tired. He washed his face again and patted it dry.

As he walked out of the office, he noticed Stan talking very loudly to one of the Chinese employees. Curious, he asked Kitty what was going on. She looked up from her *Hello Kitty* stationary and said in the squeakiest *baby* adult voice he had ever heard, "Oh, he was caught on camera pissing into a garbage can in Wan Chai this weekend."

Craig was stunned, "What? Are you serious?"

"Yes, Mr Matthews, he is in big trouble. Stan says he's had enough of people making him look like he's lost control."

"When did he say that?"

"All the time sir."

"I see." Craig wondered if this was a sign to change his own ways. He shook his head and proceeded to the lift. He turned around and saw Kitty resume reading a bright pink and white *Hello Kitty* magazine. "Bye Kitty, see you tomorrow."

"Good bye Mr Matthews," she said as she smiled with rotten teeth.

❧

Craig's office was very close to Central, so he walked down the busy road and met Dave at Dolce Vita, Sophia's favourite place.

"How ya doing Dave?" Craig sat next to him at the bar and, without thinking, ordered a draught beer.

Dave eyed him as he received his order, and took a sip of his latte. After a moment, he frowned slightly and said, "Great. You look distracted mate, what's going on?"

"I just saw Stan lecturing another employee about being 'presentable' for the bank."

Dave took another sip of his latte. "Well, he has a point. We do the same at Christian Dior; we don't need tossers at our establishment."

"So, is that what you think of me? A tosser?"

"Craig, mate, don't take everything so personally. I wasn't talking about you specifically."

Craig sighed, and after a moment said, "I feel so low Dave."

"Drink some more, your demons will live in you forever. Drinking is a downer. And too much of it is just down right unhealthy."

"Okay, okay, no lectures, what do you want from me?"

Dave went into rescue mode. "I want you, you little love iguana." He was quite loud, snorting through each thick laugh. Craig did not even crack a smile.

"How many times do I have to tell you Dave, not to call me that?"

"I'm sorry sunshine." Dave was really taking the piss this time.

Craig's shoulder pads of his suit jacket were rising to his ear lobes. He looked slightly embarrassed again. His cheeks flushed red and Dave, the attention seeker, was laughing some more.

"I am going to leave Dave."

"Don't be so dramatic Craig, live a little…"

"I do…"

"How?" Dave said, leaning in closer to Craig.

"I go out…"

Dave interrupted, "Oh yes you do, you LOVE to go out, don't cha," Dave said like a rapper.

"Well, I don't want to do that anymore."

"Do what?"

"Go out anymore."

"Good. So, let's go home right now then." Dave put down his latte.

"Dave, can you please be serious for once in your life mate, please? Life doesn't have to be like a bloody MTV video all the time. This is real life."

Dave looked down at his latte. "I know, Craig. This is real life."

"So, why are you saying we should go home?"

"Because you just said you go out too much, and look at you sitting there like a stiff twit… in your jacket. You look like you're ready to go home already."

Craig stood up, pulled his suit jacket off, and hung it next to the bar. As he sat back down, he ran his fingers through his hair and sighed. "So, what do you want Dave, what did you want to talk to me about?"

"Sophia."

Craig looked up from his beer. "What about her?"

"I think you need to get back together with her."

Craig threw his head back and laughed in disbelief. "How is that ever going to happen, Dave?"

"By you responding to your intuition."

"What does that mean?"

"Crikey Craig, what the hell do you mean, what does that mean," he said imitating Craig as if he was a primary school boy. "It means that you have to use your gut instinct."

"Oh, like when my stomach feels all funny," Craig said sarcastically.

Dave ignored his tone. "Yeah, that's right. When your stomach feels funny."

"I don't have that feeling about Sophia, Dave."

"What? Really?"

"Yes, I don't want to be with her. I don't. I think."

"What do you mean? You either know it or you don't."

"I don't think she wants to be with me…"

Dave was by now exasperated. "Make up your mind. You sound like a bumbling fool. Is it because you don't want to be with *her*, or because you think she doesn't want to be with *you*?"

Craig paused. "I don't know," he said a little confused again, as he took a big swig of his beer. Stan popped back into his mind. *Pansy*.

"One thing you need to do more of, Craig, is to make solid decisions. First, you shouldn't be having that beer that you are drinking now." Dave pushed the beer away. "Second, you should recognise that you are being a tit at the moment. Third, you need a shave, a facial, a haircut, hell, even a severe manicure and pedicure. And finally, when you are feeling and acting like a human with your higher faculties functioning again, only then can you make a decision if you want to be a real man, or a man with no perspective."

Craig looked at himself in the mirror behind Dave. He felt he looked old and silly. He knew he was acting like a high school kid and that he needed to change his attitude. His earlier defiance with Stan had left him.

"So, what do you think I should do first?"

"Detox."

"Okay. I can do that."

"No more late nights."

Craig paused, and looked away. "I can do that."

"Book a haircut and facial, manicure and pedicure at the Mandarin Oriental; you know this always does the trick for me – I feel pampered and dignified at the Mandarin, and you need this right now. Just get on track Craig. Seriously, get on track."

As Craig gazed at his now confiscated pint of beer, Dave's consciousness drifted back to his childhood in East Concord, Australia, and the rough neighbourhood where he lived. He couldn't believe how far he had come in this lifetime.

He felt deep gratitude for his talent, all the while thankful that he was able to step out into the world with meaning and purpose. He had become famous in the late 80s and travelled all around the world opening flagship stores for very reputable name brands across the globe. This greatly contrasted with his childhood, which was rough; some days, he and his four brothers didn't even have a proper hot meal to eat.

Craig excused himself for the restroom as Dave re-connected with the image of him sitting at his second-hand desk, colouring and colouring for hours on end. His brothers would laugh at him as they made nuisances of themselves out on the streets, with his father shouting for them to come in after 7 p.m. Dave was always home with his Ma and would imagine her in different outfits as he played dress up in his mind.

One day his brothers were making fun of his drawings when he received the call that would change his life – an answer to an application he had put in on a whim to the London School of Fashion. He had won a scholarship! His talent had been uncovered by a famous fashion designer in London; it was a matter of applying to the right place at the right time. If Dave had not agreed to accept the scholarship to become an apprentice as well as a designer's muse, his life would have never turned out the way it had.

His mind flashed across his life as he thanked his angels for placing him in the right place at the right time. Reflecting on his own road to success made Dave feel like Craig was being overly sensitive and like a wet blanket.

Dave thought about his father; both patriarch and religion were his nemesis. Dave was never allowed to reveal to his father about his dreams of becoming a fashion designer, nor was he ever brave enough to face up to his father about his sexuality. He shifted his mind to Craig, and imagined "reality" as a person slapping him in the face. As Craig returned to his seat, Dave snapped back to the present, his own reminiscence ready to now further his efforts to save Craig.

"Craig, there is no better day than today to get on track and follow your goals."

"I know. I really need to. I'm not getting anywhere like this; Stan is right," he replied, shifting uneasily in his seat.

Suddenly, the pair became aware that the paparazzi had found their darling news item, Dave. Flashing lights started in their direction, and Craig put his hands up to his face. "Hey, Dave, tell those wankers to stop it please." This was not helping his mood.

"Boys, boys, please, don't be so rude. Let's go on the sidewalk and we can take some graceful pictures." But it was too late, the paparazzi were briskly walking away from the scene like they had hit a gold mine. Dave was smiling; he had gone from a pauper boy to a paparazzi boy – if only his mentor could see him now. A nice title for a book, he thought to himself – *From Pauper to Paparazzi*. He imagined what the cover of the book would look like. Craig interrupted his thoughts.

"Now, look at what they've gone and done. Stan is going to fire me for sure."

Dave tried to hide a grin. "Good."

"What?"

"Good."

"What do you mean, good?"

"It's good, then you might be able to move on in your life without being a slave to yourself."

"How can you be a slave to yourself? That doesn't make any sense."

"Of course you can…"

"How?"

"Look in the mirror, Craig, you are a slave to yourself."

"Anyone can say 'look in the mirror.' That doesn't explain a damn thing, Dave." Craig was getting antsy and wanted to leave Dolce Vita.

Dave turned sharply towards him, looking him right in the eyes. "When you look in the mirror Craig, what do you see? Try to study yourself, your mind, and try to connect it to what your body and your conscious mind are doing to you."

Craig looked for a moment and sighed. "I know Dave, I do have to look deeper at what I want in my life."

"Yes, indeed. You really do. And let me tell you something else, if there is only one thing you take away from tonight it should be that procrastination is your biggest enemy… do you understand?"

"Yes, definitely."

"You should know that. You are a businessman, a banker – an investment banker – and you know that time is valuable and that precision in decision-making either makes you or breaks you. Right?"

"Yes, that's true." Craig said looking at the table behind him.

"So, you need to reassess how you plan to move forward in a positive way." Dave turned back toward the bar and sipped on what was left of his latte.

"Agreed." Craig caught himself staring at the girl behind Dave at another table. Who was she? She looked so familiar. Craig was afraid to catch her eye, just in case he had met her on one of his drunken nights. He returned his gaze to Dave, realising he was right.

"I am in total agreement with you. I will not go out late tonight. I have work, I'm going to realign myself and ensure I use my higher senses to elevate me." To himself, he thought, *No more pansy.*

"That's my boy," Dave said grinning. "You are now, at this precise moment, on the right track. Keep moving."

The two men finished talking and got up to leave Dolce Vita to grab a bite at Post 97; they were starving. Craig glanced again at the girl sitting at the table behind him again. He needed to find out who she was. It was irritating him that he couldn't remember. Dave caught Craig's eye's shifting his focus to the other table.

"Why do you keep looking over at that girl?"

"I can't seem to place her right now but she looks awfully familiar."

Dave walked ahead of Craig and said, "There is no need to remember. Forget about her. If you were meant to know her, you would. Now stop staring like a big-eyed toad, you're making me uncomfortable." Dave wanted to drag Craig away from the present situation and force him to think of his precious petal Sophia only.

The night was young. Dave had time.

Chapter 6

London

Noor got to her flat – well, her dad's flat – in Holland Park. It was always calming to be in her domain, and the clean and pristine facade of the house was nicely nestled within an alcove of green. In the winter when it snowed, the trees looked like a magical snow land. Every season that inevitably changed brought new freshness and rejuvenation to Noor's home.

The five-bedroom flat was a mansion, especially for London. When Sharon and Mala used to visit, they each had their own rooms. Noor had flashbacks of when they used to have movie nights and take turns being the *chef* for the night. Mala always cooked Indian, Noor made steak and grilled vegetables and Sharon, stir-fry. She remembered those days like they were moments ago.

Her mind drifted back to the day after graduation. They had taken a plane from Boston to London for their first adventure.

"Wow, this is so gorgeous Noor," Mala said as she looked around the apartment with awe. She couldn't believe she was in such a beautiful house in London. The molecules in her body were jumping up and down with joy and she was feeling like a princess. Everything in her life seemed so far away. The present moment was gorgeous and she wanted to feel the shivers of ecstasy all through her body as the excitement of freedom engulfed her whole spirit.

Sharon was also in wonderment. "Thank you so much Noor, this is the best graduation present ever. Thank you, thank you, thank you," she gushed.

"You guys are so welcome, my home is your home, and we are all in this together, united, sisters for life. They hugged each other tightly standing in the middle of the living room for what seemed like ages. To an outsider, it would indeed look like they were praying.

Noor snapped back to reality and was greeted by Gloria. She wiped a tear from her eye and said kindly, "Hi Gloria, thank you for receiving me."

"You are welcome, Ms Noor. I have prepared your bath and a light dinner for you. What time would you like to eat?" Gloria was so unassuming and successful in her job as a house manager. She had worked with the Noor family for over a decade. She was loyal, dedicated, and professional.

Noor looked up at the clock; it was only 4:30 p.m., so she thought about Bazica, and calling Mala after her bath to try and meet her there. She looked at Gloria with a smile and replied, "I will dine at around 8:00 p.m., thank you."

Noor walked into her bedroom and the vast land of green in front of her bedroom window elicited a big contented sigh. She looked in the full-length mirror and recognised her true self. As she languorously soaked in the tub, Noor picked up the phone hanging on the mirrored wall and dialled Mala. She answered. Finally.

"Mala, *auntyooooo*, it's me."

"Noor, my *auntyji*! How are you? When did you get in?"

"About an hour ago. How have you been? Is everything okay?"

"Yes, everything is great. I am just very busy with the twins, I feel like I was born to do this."

"That's wonderful Mala. And... how is your journal writing coming along?"

Mala thought about her conversation with Noor about book writing, and instead of revealing too much she humbly replied, "It's actually going really well. I have some big plans coming up."

Mala's dream was to become a writer, and become published with her story of adversity and racism when she was dating Washington. She had started, stopped and then started again a number of times, but his time she had clarity that a book was going to help get her name – and more importantly, her story – recognised in the literary world. Her manuscript had been her little secret for years and she intended to keep it mystical until she was ready for its release. She remembered getting into an argument with Noor after college about "intellectual plagiarism" in case they had equivalent anecdotes; Mala was sure that every writer had unique ideas, and her story was definitely more interesting than Noor's.

"That's great Mala, I am so proud of you. My manuscript is almost done, and I have so much to tell you. Do you think we can meet at Bazica in an hour?"

Mala thought back to the days when she had so much freedom, with Bazica as her constant respite. Nowadays, though, things were different and the twins had proven to be the ultimate centre of her universe, her core and her foundation. She didn't mind meeting Noor for a coffee, but first she had to see if her other babysitter was free – well, really her primary one; Alister came far less frequently. Her babysitter was the soft-spoken Sri-Lankan lady who helped Mala clean up her classroom every day after school when she was still teaching. Kumari was a good lady who loved children and Mala trusted her.

They had been working with each other for years at the Montessori school. When Mala left, Kumari said the new teacher was mean, and expected her to do more than her job description. She told Mala that one day he had asked her to nail some broken desks, and he expected it done! She was getting tired, but needed the money.

Kumari lived close to the school as well, in Hammersmith, and it was convenient to call her after school hours around 4:30 p.m. She never left before that because Mr Mark always left copious amounts of mess wherever he went, much in contrast to Mala's time at the school.

Washington promised her that once his music academy was up and running he would hire her as their full-time nanny. But for now, Kumari was always there for Shania and Michael whenever Mala needed some time out, even though she was grateful for Alister babysitting twice a month as well.

"Sure Noor, I'll meet you at six. Is that okay?"

"Of course, Mala, I can't wait to see you!" Noor sounded somewhat sincere.

"Me too Noor, I've missed you so much."

"Me too."

"I'll see you in a bit."

They both hung up. Noor was enthusiastic to see her best friend. Mala called Kumari and arranged for her to be with the twins from six to eleven. She wanted to go for a drink after Bazica.

Mala sat on the sofa and let the familiar feeling of sadness wash over her again. The void was so strong sometimes, missing Sharon every single day. The three friends had been inseparable, and had each other's backs since the beginning when they met. It was a sisterhood that was always honest, sometimes very raw, but always encased with love, kindness, and magical moments.

Michael was crying so she picked him up, smelled his baby soft skin, and sang Tim Maia in his ear as she rocked him into blissful sleep. The universe always seemed to be comforting Mala these days. She returned to her feeling of balance, more protected by the forces around her. In the past she was jumpy, sometimes unfocused, and overly sensitive. The twins had brought precision, grace, stability, and answers into her life

Noor got out of the steamy water, slipped on her robe and sashayed over to her walk-in closet. She wondered what to wear. On her previous trip, she had given away about two hundred and fifty pieces of clothing. All good stuff. Name brands, but in bigger sizes. Her weight loss allowed her an absolute revamp; she threw out everything old and oversized, and downsized her life in every way, from clothes to food and ultimately, herself. She felt less antsy and less… well, rude. She was feeling good about herself, something that she hadn't felt in such a long time.

She slipped on a black jumpsuit and towel dried her hair. She looked in the mirror; she was beginning to look like her mother. She looked closer and saw her mother's face; she smiled and missed her. She felt sad when her father had been widowed and absolutely heartbroken. He had never fully recovered from Mrs Noor's sudden passing.

She said a small prayer for her mother in her heart and sent her angels to kiss her in heaven. 'Love you mama,' she whispered under her breath.

Mala was looking for something to wear; she was having one of those 'fish days' again. It was so annoying. She could have tried on her whole wardrobe, but in her mind nothing looked nice. She closed her eyes and picked something randomly out of her wardrobe – a rose-pink turtleneck and jeans. She tried them on, decided she looked too sexy and took it off again. She was lucky she hadn't gained much weight with the twins, but her breasts were ginormous. She was sure she looked like a brown Pamela Anderson. She hastily pulled off the turtleneck and settled on a black cardigan and a small string of pearls around her neck.

'There, more decent,' she said to herself in the mirror. Mala was evergreen; never aging, she looked the same every decade.

As both women left their apartments, they sighed and let out a breath, simultaneously at their respective flats, into the crisp London air. Mala looked up at the sky and gave Sharon a flying kiss, and Noor did the same for her mother. Someone, somewhere in the celestial heavens had been looking out for these two women, these two beautiful women whose heritage stemmed from ancient lands. Their spirit guides had always led them back to each other constantly with a promise of renewal. This was the day the fire of friendship would once again be lit, and the fabric of their torn love through harsh words would once again be sewn together by perception and growth.

Or so Mala believed.

Chapter 7

South East Asia

Craig was sitting in his office, with contentment in his heart. He had promised not to stay out late and committed to be at work on time every day this week, something he hadn't done in many months. He shaved and had a haircut. Even so, contrary to Dave's advice, he thought manicures and pedicures were a bit too pansy, and decided he would use his own clippers to handle his own nails.

He thought about his walks home from work every night and the exercise they provided; as the air was getting cooler around the island, Craig was feeling more alive again. He also thought about what Dave said regarding Sophia and quickly made the thought vanish.

He didn't want her anymore. He was sure of it. He didn't want to fall in love so deeply again; he wanted to take it easy. He was also sick of having so many one-night stands, which didn't always end up in his bed; there was always some sloppy kissing and unflattering groping that went hand in hand with his careless drunken nights. He was over it. He was going to change. He picked up the phone to call Dave. A-Wong, Dave's ever-present secretary, answered and very politely transferred the phone to Dave.

"Hello, Dave Graham here, how can I help you?"

"Dave, it's me."

"Oh, hello young man, how are you?"

"Dave, I have something serious to ask you."

"Okay, go ahead mate, what is it?"

"Okay, here it goes," Craig sighed, "I know I don't want Sophia anymore..."

"Okayyyy..." Dave said, interrupting him whilst trying to ignore the fact that Craig was trying to ruin his matchmaking ideas.

"But..." Craig seemed apprehensive.

"Yes..." Dave was beginning to smile.

"There is a part of me that knows that if I don't settle down, I will become the biggest arsehole this side of Asia."

"So, what are you saying Craig, you want to *settle* with Sophia?" Dave's eyebrows were perching on his hairline again.

"No, no, not at all... I mean, she would definitely be my dream girl, but I don't want her anymore."

Dave was extremely confused, and disliked feeling this way. He had no idea what this guy on the other end was talking about and, frankly, had better things to do than waste his time trying to figure it out. "What do you want me to do, Craig? Wave my magic wand and make everything okay? Do you think I'm a fairy godmother or something? I mean... I can admit to the fairy part, but godmother part... um... no, I don't think so."

Craig sighed. "What I'm trying to say, mate, is that if I don't find a girl soon, I'm going to end up being one of those old, fat, beer-belly expat men who settle for some disgruntled fat Asian *mamasan* from Wan Chai who is only in love with money and who fleeces me out of cash every day to run her bordello."

Dave laughed. "You are what you think Craig, that's all I can say to you right now. Thoughts become reality. If that's what you see your future as, then so be it. I can't help you change how you visualise yourself. What I can do is be here as a friend to you, and remind you that you don't have to go down that road."

"I know, I know, Dave. That's what I'm trying to tell you. I really don't want to walk down that path, and I see it happening because..."

Dave interrupted again. "Because you are not taking responsibility for yourself or for your actions."

"Yes, you are right. And I've been good since the day we met at Dolce Vita last week. I have been so good, Dave. Not drinking every night. Going home early, eating salmon and asparagus, and boiled eggs, and exercising every day at lunch time, even walking home from the bank to Happy Valley."

"Wow, I am very impressed." On his end of the line, Dave had a coy look on his face. "I am very proud of you. So, what is the problem then?"

"I want more; I want to feel like I have someone to go home to. I'm tired of all the one-night stands."

Dave cleared his throat and asked, "Have you been tested Craig? I mean, seriously. You know that Wan Chai is not the place to be having unprotected sex. Have you been careful?"

"Of course I have," Craig quickly replied. "I'm not stupid, just the heat of the moment and I was just always… lonely."

"And drunk," Dave interjected. "Well, let me tell you this. I want to say that you are, right now, on the right track. You just have to be consistent. If you are not, you will fall into the snake pit, or to use a cliché, fall off the wagon again, and then it will get messier and inappropriate. I suggest you keep doing what you're doing and when you feel the need to call Sophia, or be on the same vibration as her, then give her a call. If not, don't worry about it. No one is putting a gun to your head. You make your own decisions and ultimately find your outcome."

Craig absorbed his wisdom for a moment. "That is awesome, Dave, I really believe what you are saying. Thanks, mate."

Before hanging up, Dave teased Craig a little more and knew his reverse psychology about Sophia might actually be the first indication of the sparks of his matchmaking tactics for Craig.

As Craig put down the phone, he looked over at Stan's office. He looked very dishevelled today and not in his right mind. He decided to take it upon himself, his new self, to start a conversation with Stan.

He knocked on the door and Stan looked up from his desk.

"Hey, Craig, how are you? Come in, mate. You're looking great."

"Thanks Stan, how are you doing? All okay?"

Stan looked up from his paperwork, put down his pen and said, "Actually Craig, everything isn't okay."

Craig's suspicions were confirmed. "What's wrong Stan?"

Stan motioned for Craig to sit down. "I am thinking about moving on, leaving the city, going back home for a bit."

Stan had been with the bank for almost two decades, a handsome man who made the company shine with pure expatriate delight. Yet now, he looked like a puppet who had sold his soul to the darkness of the corporate world. "I am really sorry to hear that, Stan." He didn't know what else to say except, "Is there anything I can do?"

"Thanks Craig. But no."

Stan shook his head tiredly, then put his head down and continued working. Craig was absolutely lost for words. He walked back to his desk and slumped into his chair. What problems could Stan possibly have? He lived in a massive house that overlooked the ocean in Deep Water Bay, had three cars – a Mercedes, BMW and Mini – three live-in helpers, a gardener, a pool man, and two drivers. What was going on? There had to be more, and Craig was eager to find out. He wondered if all men went through a midlife crisis the same time as women, and as if in one intertwined ball of elasticity, people were snapped away from loved ones. Was it money and greed that got the better of these people? He was confused and annoyed. Again.

He didn't want to think about Stan's situation anymore. He was feeling fit, healthy, and ready to move on to the next chapter of his life. He was going to create something new in his life, he just didn't know what it was yet. He switched off his computer, changed his shoes, took off his jacket and tie, rolled up his sleeves, and got ready for his daily walk back home to Happy Valley.

On the way home, on this crisp evening, he couldn't help but think about Sophia. He wondered what it would have been like if they had ended up together and if she had stayed in Hong Kong with him. They would have been the golden couple, especially with Dave as their paparazzi king. He imagined them walking into Dolce Vita together, with Dave and the flashes of photography streaming past his eyes. The next day he would be in the paper, as one of the bank's top corporate leaders, and in no time he would have received a promotion and lived in a stunning house, on a cliff, overlooking the bay.

As he daydreamed, he walked up the tiny hill to his apartment and felt like a new man; the endorphins released in his brain made him feel energetic and fresh. After his shower Craig sat on the sofa and had a soda water. While it wasn't beer, at least it had some fizz. He looked at the clock and calculated the time difference between London and Hong Kong; he couldn't stop thinking about Sophia again. Craig wished he hadn't talked to Dave before he left work, as he had put something in his head that wouldn't go away. Feeling like Dave had put a spell on him, Craig picked up the phone, then put it back down again, finally getting irritated at himself. He was acting like a silly schoolboy and tried to oppose the feeling.

This is ridiculous, he thought to himself. He wanted a stronger self-image and to avoid thinking about London or Sophia, he switched on the TV and watched *Talk Asia* on CNN. The anchor was stunning. Even so, everywhere he seemed to turn in his mind, the idea of Sophia kept popping up.

He went into the kitchen had another soda water, while making a decision to force himself to stop obsessing about Sophia for the day. He didn't want to think too much about her, because he felt like he was falling into his own trap of fantasy land.

He decided to order some food and contemplate about his future, realising that it was never easy to plan precisely what lay ahead; ordering out helped him resist the temptation of reverting to his usual ways, as temptation and Hong Kong went hand in hand. What he wanted was to feel attached to something tangible; something or someone that would make him feel like a whole man, a companion who would be by his side through all the ups and downs he would face throughout his life.

After a hearty meal ordered from the Italian restaurant down the road, Craig felt somewhat connected and went to sleep. He felt like he was on the right track.

Chapter 8

London

Noor and Mala were at Bazica at Table Number 8 sipping on a latte and a mocha, respectively; seemingly in tandem with the birth of her twins, Mala had developed an affinity for chocolate. She couldn't have too much coffee; otherwise when she was breastfeeding, she felt like the twins were on some kind of a high. It always took them longer to sleep. Eventually, she had started ordering weaker cappuccinos and café mochas. Fatima, their long-time friend, waitress, and daughter of the café's owner, came over and hugged both Mala and Noor at the same time.

"You look so gorgeous Ms Noor. How did you do that?" Fatima was absolutely impressed by Noor's transformation since their last encounter.

"Do what?" Noor asked, coyly, knowing that she wanted another reaction out of Fatima, but this time, she wanted her to use the word 'thin.'

"How did you become so… thin?" Fatima asked with her palms pointed upwards and indicating her thoughts through her hand movements, moving in a vertical manner.

Bingo, Noor thought to herself. "Well, I just got rid of things in my life."

"Like Ahmed." Mala said.

"Yes, like Ahmed. He was someone who wasted my time. So not worth it. It's in the past and, frankly, I don't want to talk about it anymore."

"Wise decision. What is going on in your life now?" Mala's inquiring and inquisitive voice sounded patient yet concerned.

"I'm moving back here, and we'll see where the tide takes me."

"Are you going to be working?"

"I was thinking about opening up a trendy coffee shop in SoHo. Wouldn't that be so cool?" Noor was bright eyed while Mala looked at her suspiciously, wondering if Noor was riding on one of her whimsical ideas in la la land. "Please don't look at me like that, Mala. I'm serious – it's something to do! At least I'm not just sitting around waiting for my father to send me money, right?"

Mala looked deep into her friend's eyes. "That's right, but you have to commit to it, not get bored so easily and find a way to make it your true passion."

Noor looked away. She knew that a coffee shop was not her true passion. What was her true craving? She couldn't quite figure it out. "You're right," Noor relented.

"I know I am; I've known you for so long. Let's see, you've tried to get married about twelve times, you've tried to open a school with us three times, you've tried to open four restaurants; oh yes, and let's not forget the costume slash party shop you tried to franchise. It's all a bit much, Noor. You have to be grounded and find your way. You have to give yourself a chance to find out what it is you want to do long term." Mala realised that her tone was exactly like her mother's; she got a few goose bumps – not enough to send her shivering, but just enough to feel somewhat connected to parts of her mother's spirit locked in her DNA.

Noor sipped on her coffee. "I know, and I look like such a fool floating from one idea to the next and never feeling grounded or secure. I suppose I've always thought travelling would help me clear my mind and think about what I want to do… it made me more confused."

Mala knew exactly what her friend was thinking. Noor always branded her travels as 'clearing her mind,' but everyone around her knew that when the *travel* angel pierced deep within her soul, she was actually 'running away.' Ghastly amounts of business endeavours would never work out and she was always left desolate, obsolete, without a spark of fire and then nothing. Her father was constantly angry at her. Her tears and the fact that she had no mother to guide her was always an excuse for her to ride on her father's coattails again, ensuring she wouldn't ever lose control of her inheritance. Now, she wished she had followed her dreams based on her desires rather than being in bondage because of money.

"I want to do something with my life. Will you help me Mala?"

"Sure Noor, what exactly do you want to invest in?"

"Myself?"

"That's a good start." Mala was happy her friend was making some inner intellectual progress. "And how can we base a business on something that is close to your heart and involves all of you?"

Noor gazed into her latte. She couldn't think of anything. She started to travel into the pockets of imagination in her mind and there was nothing embedded deep enough to excite her. Except her book. Well, her writing had become four notebooks of scribbled ideas and notes – could she actually call that a book? Everything Mala was talking about was true. She was absolutely right. Noor saw herself as a constant runner, a marathon runner who just kept jogging out of the spectrum, running into walls, colliding with fears and sprinting towards some imaginary finish line with an abundance of wealth and luxuries.

What a boring, wasteful life, she thought to herself. Whatever had fulfilled her before was unrecognisable, a sheer reflection of how indecisive and extremely flighty she was in her ways. Maybe she needed to travel very far away and live in a foreign land for ten years. The fleeting thought made her cringe of having to settle anywhere permanently for a whole decade.

Fatima separated Noor's thoughts by interrupting them as she carried the empty latte and mocha cups away. In her true style of exotic Middle Eastern grace and beauty, Fatima turned around to Noor and said, "I am so glad you made the decision to move back to London. I think this is the right way for you. You look great Ms Noor, and I'm happy to have your familiar face here again." With that, she bowed ever so slightly and floated back to the kitchen as her grey eyes twinkled with mystic splendour.

Chapter 9

Surrey

Alister was busy in the garden at his father's house. In fitting with his nature, he was addicted – this time to tending the flowers and he had planted a mini vegetable garden. As well as being captivated by nature, Alister began to use his previously untapped talent for cooking. He had a very passionate personality and anything he got his hands on would be a long-term commitment. Alister could spend hours in the garden and not worry about anything around him. After his rehabilitation, Alister never found work but played in a band twice a week, making a very minimal amount of money. He got a disability stipend from the government every month, which he used to buy supplies for his garden. Uncle Peter's flat was up for sale very soon and the Martin family didn't have to worry about finances for a very long time. The flat was being sold for twenty-five million Hong Kong dollars. Some of the money would go to taxes and a land bond, but the rest of the cash would belong to Sophia and Alister.

As she watched Alister in the garden, sipping on her coffee and contemplating the huge shifts she had made in her life over the past year, Sophia thought long and hard about whether she wanted to sell the flat, but the decision was clear. No Chinese family wanted to rent it, because there had been a death in the house; no Indian family wanted it because it was too small; no Japanese family wanted it because the rental was too expensive. In the end, the only people who would buy it were a very young fashionable French couple who decided to gut the whole flat and turn it into a photography studio. However, the building inspector then made it clear that the structure was for residential purposes only, so they agreed that one of the bedrooms would be their living quarters. Sophia now had to wait for the tax papers to go through and then they were set.

Sophia hadn't found work either and was not convincingly content living like a *Tai Tai* in her father's home, and her friends could see it sometimes in her conversations by the way she presented herself. Still, she joined yoga with Mala when she could make it to London, read a lot and played the stock market for a bit of fun to jolt her left-brain up a notch.

Living the life of luxury was proving to be quite boring for Sophia. She thought about setting up a business with Alister, maybe a nutrition clinic, or somewhere adolescents could go learn about the benefits of healthy food. But, the thought left her very quickly; Sophia knew deep in her heart she needed someone to commit to an idea with her, something that would keep her going so she wouldn't get bored. Mala had her children and was constantly busy. By default, she had the best job in the world, looking after two beautiful children who had chosen her as their mother. That was the most amazing job any woman could have, she thought to herself.

Sophia knew that a fair number of women wouldn't be on the same wave length as her, yet knew that somewhere in her mind the notion of parenthood would have been a fun as well as mesmerizing journey. Sophia pondered a little bit longer, realising she had definitely missed that boat. The prospect of her having children now at her older age made her feel tepid inside and scared at the same time. Although Sophia knew that a part of her would love the challenge of parenthood, at this point in time she didn't feel like she would have ever been a nurturing parent because she blamed her parents for leaving so much baggage around her and Alister. Sophia knew that blame was not the solution and once again shifted her mind and began to drift back momentarily to the past.

She thought about her own parents and how they didn't even talk to each other. There was never any screaming or shouting or any noise in her household when she was growing up because her home was boring, silent, even somewhat stifled and lifeless on most days. Sophia's parents were distant and treated each other like roommates. They never laughed with each other or spoke of travelling together, nor even about a book or a movie they were interested in. They spoke about nothing. The silence and lack of passion was tiresome in the Martin household in Asia.

This was until one day, Margaret left and didn't come back. She said to Daniel in her most mundane lifeless voice, "Please tell the children I love them, and I will see you soon, Daniel. I'm sorry, but it's just not working and it hasn't been for over fifteen years now."

With that, she disappeared from the house, only calling once per week to check up on Sophia and Alister. After six months, she invited both her children to visit her in Indonesia and introduced them to her even more boring boyfriend. Sophia never understood why her mother had no need, or raw desire, for excitement in her relationships.

That's why Alex had been so intriguing and spontaneous; that had really turned Sophia on. However, the monotonous side of her DNA always emerged and the barrier of fun or lack of consistency made her retreat. She needed to find a balance of being consistently true to herself all the time: not too boring, but not over the top like a soap opera.

Balance was key in her life right now. She picked up the phone to speak to Dave, but he was not at the office. Again, she thought about how excited she was to see him in a few days for the opening of the store. She was going to pick him up from the airport. In the meantime, Sophia thought about what she needed to do about her future. Living in the now and the present moment had made her more solid, less of a noodle, more structured and with more faith. But still, she felt lonely. Very lonely.

She thought about Mala and Noor, feeling grateful that she knew some people in London. But they were not her lifelong friends. She didn't have a connection to them like they did with each other. She felt like an outsider at times. Her only friend was Dave and everyone knew that. She felt lonely again and began to feel sorry for herself for no reason. Suddenly she began to cry. Tears began to fall down her face as she thought about how much she hadn't accomplished in her life. In her moment of weakness, she tried to call Alex for some kind of comfort. Even after the break up they had remained friends, but Alex was flighty and had no concept of time or whether it was day or night. Sophia then tried Mala and she answered.

"Hi, Mala, it's me Sophia."

"Hey, how are you? All okay?"

Sophia sighed. "No, not really, I'm feeling so down."

"What's wrong?"

Sophia began to cry again.

Mala wasn't sure what to think; she took the receiver off her ear, looked at it, and frowned. She couldn't understand why Sophia had lost her composure. She felt sorry for her. "Are you okay? Would you like to come over? The twins might cheer you up," Mala said as she smiled at her children sleeping soundly.

"It's far for me to drive, Mala, maybe next time. I just needed to talk. I tried to call Dave but he's not at his desk."

"Tell me Sophia, it's not Alister again is it?"

"No… no… nothing like that. I'm just feeling like I'm not doing anything. Asia was fast paced and there was so much to do – but over here I feel like I'm just getting older by the day."

"But we are getting older by the day, Sophia, that is a part of life. Don't you want to go back to work? Try something new?"

"I do… I want to engage in a business endeavour and do something that excites me."

"You know, I had the same conversation with Noor the other day. I think it's our age. We have to find our passion and not be wishy washy. We are too old to be indecisive."

"I know, Mala," Sophia sighed. "What do you think is a good thing for us to do? As a business?"

Mala thought for a while. She was quite content and in her element to be a full time parent and she didn't need to start anything new. She felt blessed and very complete. Noor popped into her head and she tried to imagine Sophia and Noor in a business together. What would they do? Both were quite similar in the fact that they had money, but did not know what to do with it, or how to use it to make themselves happy. Maybe what they needed was a meeting... to brainstorm and figure out how each woman could help and foster as well as build up the other one. After all, what good is being in a friendship or a family with women if they are not there to enhance each other? Mala wondered what would work for them. She couldn't think of anything at that moment.

"Don't sweat the small stuff, Sophia. It's really not worth it. Just enjoy the freedom you have. So many people in the world don't have that luxury. What are you stressing about?"

Sophia paused. "I'm feeling a bit worthless."

"Why?"

"I have always lived in a fast-paced world where I felt like I meant something, like I gave something back to society and the community, and now I just feel like a lump."

"A very classy and beautiful lump, Sophia. Now come on, try to snap out of it. Dave will be in London soon and it will all be okay."

"Yes, but what about when Dave leaves?" Sophia said in her soft Eurasian accent.

"You have me, and Washington, Alister, Alex, Noor, your dad. What more do you need?"

"A man."

"I see," Mala said, feeling a little bit sorry for Sophia. It must be lonely not having the warmth of a hug or caressing someone, sharing a kiss or feeling close and loved. She was so thankful and grateful for Washington, and so enamoured by the way he loved her. Yet at the same time, Mala wondered why Sophia was crying over not having a man. Her loneliness was proving to be slightly trite. Mala tried not to sound condescending while trying to remain compassionate at the same time.

"Well, the only way to find a man is to go out and look for one." Mala paused, trying to bring some lightness to the conversation, and mused, "Or, you could try one of those dating agencies."

"That is a horrible thought, Mala, can you imagine me at a dating agency? I would be so rude and pedantic that no one would like me."

"That is not true! You have to be yourself…"

Sophia interrupted, "That is the problem… I'm too much of my boring self. I need to do something exciting."

"Like what?" She couldn't imagine Sophia losing control in any way, shape, or form.

"Maybe I need to go out there and just be different, make a difference or make someone notice me."

"You sound like a teenager, Sophia… and desperate. The right person will come around when the time is right, and when he does, you will know it."

Sophia laughed sarcastically. "Been there done that Mala and definitely not going back there again. Every time I think *Mr Right* comes around, I screw it up." Craig trickled into her head like a sticky maple syrup, a thick consistency that wouldn't get out of her thought process. "And I am not going down that road again."

"Maybe you, and the cats, need a dog," Mala said, beginning to giggle.

"I'm serious, Mala, I think I need some help."

"Okay, lets meet at Bazica tomorrow and I will continue to dissect that pretty little Asian mind of yours and see what we come up with."

Sophia sighed. "Sure, sounds good. I'll see you at Bazica at 5:30."

"Done."

"Perfect."

As Mala put the phone down, she wondered how Sophia led such a boring existence. Sophia played everything safe and never took risks. Her idea of adventure would be to get drunk on wine coolers. Sophia needed to relax, have fun, and just let loose. Mala was glad Dave was coming to rock Sophia's paradigm and shake it up a bit. In the meantime, Mala was content to be a parent and live in bliss with Washington before she had to deal on a deeper level with her mother or Noor. She switched off the light and decided to take a nap and nestled on her bed with the children. She dreamt of her parents again, but this time in a tender light and drifted off into a peaceful trance of willowy slumber.

Chapter 10

London

Noor finished her energetic kickboxing class with a very extravagant instructor, who had silver and bejewelled boxing gloves. Boon was from Thailand and was an absolute powerhouse, blessed with a body that showed her strength, rhythm and precision through the art of boxing. Her *Muay Thai* skills were phenomenal and her body was ripped, supple, and mighty.

Noor walked back to her house and was feeling restless and bored again; she sighed and exhaled all at the same time. Thoughts of Café Des Artistes, her father's restaurant in Paris, shuffled around in her brain and how her best friend Mala was right about all of her indecisive ways. How many times had she failed as a business woman? She thought to herself about all of the money she had wasted. A tinge of guilt crept up inside her. She was grateful for her *Pitaji's* patience. Noor thought back to when she wanted to open a school with Mala and Sharon when they had turned thirty, but that didn't work out at all. The licensure for opening up a school was expensive as well as risky. Dealing with children and their health and safety was not appropriate in the hands of Annabelle Noor.

She recalled how many times she wanted to get married, and winced at herself.

Ahmed seeped into her thoughts and she was happy to be rid of him. He was a rat. She thought back to the day she told him she was exiting the relationship and watched him fly into a rage. The only thing that kept her calm was knowing that she would never have to suffer him again by reacting to his spells of anger. She responded by telling him exactly how she felt and the memory of that day made her mind drift back to Paris.

Paris

"*Why? Annabelle? What happened? What did I ever do to you? I don't understand why you want to leave me.*" *Ahmed was arrogantly stunned.*

"*It's not working, Ahmed, it really isn't.*" *She looked at her plump body in the mirror. Letting herself go was not on her life agenda or in the rundown of her existence.* "*I have to move on Ahmed; there is so much that is a hindrance to me here.*"

Ahmed started laughing like a rabid dog at the top of his lungs, looking like a cross between a hyena and a dragon. There was nothing attractive or cute about him anymore. Noor saw right through his games, his arrogance and his sheer rudeness. She deserved better than this.

"*I am a hindrance, Annabelle? You make me laugh.*" *He was piercingly scary with his Vincent Price laughter – straight out of Michael Jackson's famous Thriller music video. He came closer and peered right into her face.* "*I can't believe you. Look at you, you're such a fat lump, a waste of your father's money and space. No one is going to want a fat emotional girl by their side.*" *He quickly shifted his emotional paradigm.* "*As a matter of fact, Annabelle, I am glad this putrid relationship is over.*"

Annabelle did not flinch. She looked at him right in the eyes and said, "*Me too, Ahmed. I am very glad this is over. I would like us to be friends…*"

"*Friends!*" *Ahmed interrupted.* "*Friends don't do this to each other.*"

"*Yes, you are absolutely right, friends need to be good to each other, raise each other's awareness and be on the same page. We, unfortunately, are not.*"

Ahmed glared at her. "You are probably one of the most ungrateful people I know."

"Sure Ahmed, whatever you say. Now, if we can arrange for my belongings to be shipped back to London I will be very grateful."

Ahmed was not cooling off; as a matter of fact, the more steadfast and serene Noor was, the more agitated and nervous Ahmed became.

"Look Ahmed, there is no need to get into a whirlpool of negativity because it will get us nowhere. I want us to end amicably because our fathers are friends." Noor didn't want her father to blame her – again – for not being able to find a man to be her husband and she realised that she was sick and tired of him putting traditional stipulations on her.

"Yes, they are, and I will be sure to tell your father what an ungrateful daughter he has."

"Really?" Annabelle coolly inquired with a half-smile on her face.

"Yes, really. And I'm going to tell him that no matter how much I tried to look after you, you just went against me." He grabbed her by the shoulders and made her look at her body in the mirror. Her clothes were tight and popping out of every woven space of material.

"Look at you! Look at what you have become. Do you think your father is proud of this?" He was peering at her reflection in the mirror. She wanted to cry and cry and sob and wail, but she didn't. She kept her composure and listened to Ahmed rant and rave about how ugly she was. His voice seemed to escape her ears and all she could see now in the reflection was her mother. Her mother was telling her that all would be alright, and that she was a beautiful woman. She saw her teenage self in the mirror and longed for that beauty back.

When Ahmed had finished berating her, Noor came back to the present, looked up at him, kissed him on the cheek, and said, "Goodbye Ahmed. Thank you for everything. Especially all of the advice you gave me today. Thank you, actually, for being a good friend. You have revealed a lot of truth to me today and I thank you sincerely from the bottom of my heart for that."

Her barely concealed sarcasm was sharp and concise, knowing that Ahmed taught her how friends shouldn't behave with each other.

She picked up her handbag and left Ahmed's self-proclaimed mansion, which in reality was little more than a glorified flat. She turned her back and vowed never to walk down that path ever again. On the way out, she took one more look in the mirror and said a very hearty goodbye to her old self. She later took out her pendulum and asked the question, am I walking the right path... right at this moment? And the pendulum swung to the right.

London

Six months later, Noor was feeling like a she had escaped a very scary movie. She was now the director of her life and was on what seemed to be the correct path. Again, the only thing stopping her was boredom. Now home, Noor put her thinking cap on and soaked in the bubble bath and thought long and hard about what she needed to do for excitement in her life. Travelling back and forth and around the world was not going to help her with stability and as these thoughts swirled in her mind, she dipped her head into the delicate rose scented water and let the bubbles tickle her beautiful olive skin.

That night when she went to bed, she dreamt of herself being cast in a film, a real array of moving pictures where she was a famous actress. She woke up the next day with a smile on her face. Maybe her manuscript could be turned into a screenplay.

On the other side of town, Mala was having an off day, dealing with two screaming babies, a messy house, and an overdue pile of laundry. She tried to turn some music on to drown out her tiredness and the sound of crying, but it didn't work. Usually she could handle all the mess and the running back and forth from one child to the other, but today she was not in the mood for any kind of responsibilities. A pondering notion crept into her mind about how the twins would be looked after if she was somehow not around or physically able to care of them. Mala knew it was time to have Kumari with her full time, for her peace of mind as well as respite.

Sophia and Alister were having dinner with their father and the scene was silent. They had nothing to say to each other today. Alister wanted to tell them about a new career endeavour he had been thinking about, but decided to keep it to himself for the time being.

Washington was at the music academy with a very beautiful intern who was half his age; she had come in for an audition to be in the band. The Academy, where Washington was the founder and manager, always had an opening for musicians to play with the orchestras performing live for West End Musicals, and Emilia was looking for a position to be in the band at The Academy, because she wanted to play the piano for *The Phantom of the Opera*. When Washington asked her to play for him, she played the piano like an angel. He, and everyone else in the room, could see that she was transported by the music, which mesmerised Washington, and the audience, by her divine melody.

South East Asia

Craig and Dave were at *Post 97*, having a coffee and planning their trip to London together; Craig had finally agreed to go. Craig felt somewhat contented in his space again, and at the same time pondered whether it was the right thing to do to visit Sophia in London. But, he was using his higher senses to lead him in the right direction using his intuition and that 'funny feeling in his stomach' to help guide him through confusing times. Craig had to admit as well that Dave's cajoling was helping him ignite his instincts.

Part 2

Affairs of the Heart

Chapter 11

South East Asia

Dave and Craig were at the terminal waiting for the airline to announce for passengers to embark on the plane. Craig started to look less like a nervous schoolboy, although over the past few months he had definitely cleaned up his act. He lost some of the weight garnered from alcohol and looked clean. Dave was impressed at how much attention he was taking to revamp himself back into the English hunk he was when he arrived in Hong Kong. Dave was happy to be a part of his journey.

"I'm really nervous, Dave. I mean, she doesn't even know I'm coming. What if she sees me at the airport and runs the other way?" Craig began to rethink why he had agreed to go to London with Dave.

"Then that is a sign, you run the other way too." Dave was laughing.

"Here we go again, making fun of me at inappropriate times." Craig was chewing gum and shaking his right leg with dynamite force.

"You need to stop making yourself look obvious." Dave put his hand gently on Craig's vibrating leg.

"What do you mean?" Craig looked down at Dave's gesture.

"Well, for starters you have got to stop shaking that leg up and down… you are turning me on, sunshine." Dave loved making fun of him.

In an instant Craig stopped chewing and shaking and looked deep into Dave's eyes.

"If people start to think we are gay and in a relationship Dave, I will kill you," he said coldly.

"Good. Now, listen here, you are not listening to me and you are always diverting when I try and tell you something." Craig looked at all the crow's feet around Dave's eyes. "You are so transparent and that is a good thing, don't get me wrong. However, you look like a nervous wreck with all your bodily actions. Be calm… that is the only way. If you make a mockery of yourself through your body and your actions, she will definitely go running a mile. If you are not going to do it for yourself, then do it for Sophia."

Craig sat back in the chair and pushed his hair back off his forehead and sat with his right leg folded on top of his left leg. He noticed himself slouching so he sat up in an erect position, straightened his jacket and tried to gain some composure. "How do I look now?"

"Like a stiff twit. Just relax let the energy flow through you and just be you. Don't think of anything other than what you have to do… you know what you have to do, right?"

Dave felt like a life coach, or a father talking to his son; either way, Dave was concerned and wanted the best for Craig as well as Sophia.

"Yes, I really do," Craig said, now looking like a man instead of a schoolboy.

Two days before his departure Craig was about to hand in his resignation to the bank, and then the unthinkable happened.

Craig knocked on Stan's door and he beckoned for Craig to come in.

"Hey Stan, may I have a seat? There is something I would like to discuss with you."

"Sure… sure, mate…" Stan motioned for Craig to sit down. His face looked puffy. Craig looked closer and could see that Stan hadn't slept in days, even worse than the last time he had visited Stan and offered to help.

"What's wrong, Stan? All okay mate?" Craig was not particularly friendly with Stan, but he could see in his eyes that the man had been going through some rough times.

Stan didn't want to hide his feelings from Craig, because he knew he needed him to take over his position at the bank. Deciding to be completely open and honest and speak from his heart, Stan said, "I am filing for a divorce and I am leaving Asia next month."

"What? What do you mean you are leaving? Who is going to take over your position?"

Stan leaned in closer and said, "You are, Craig."

Craig looked at Stan with utter confusion. "What... what do you mean? I don't understand, I came to see you today to hand in my resignation, Stan. I don't think I want to be in Asia anymore either."

"Well, I put your name forward and the big guys, the powers above us, have had their eye on you for a few months. They think you would be the best candidate to take over my position."

Craig thought back to his walk last week when he had innocently conjured up images of living Stan's life. Who was he going to share his extravagant life with? He had thought long and hard, and he couldn't think of anyone. Then, seemingly naturally, Sophia popped back into his head. Her tenderness was so intriguing, and of late his antics as a sloppy expat in Asia were still wearing him down. Would moving to London give him a sense of relief, or was he just running away? Craig enjoyed Asia; all he needed to do was shift up his thoughts and be strong.

"Are you sure you want to leave? I mean, have you thought about it? How long has this been going on?" Craig was talking to Stan suddenly as if the roles had already been reversed and Craig was the boss.

Stan rubbed his face with his palms. "This has been going on for a very long time, Craig. I didn't ever want to admit, to myself, that my wife was having an affair. It was so obvious and right in front of my face. I couldn't understand what exactly went wrong."

"*Time?*" Craig inquired.

"*Indeed. Time. I never made time for my wife; she was always secondary whilst I tried to build my career. Late nights, business meetings, the throng of Hong Kong life, the bitterness of her receiving me at 3:00 a.m. most nights… it just added up.*"

"*I'm so sorry, Stan. I really am.*"

"*There's nothing to be sorry about. It's my fault just as much as it's hers.*"

"*Is she staying here?*" Craig asked politely as thoughts of Yuki at staff parties at their home circled his mind. They seemed to be a loving couple, exhibiting nuances of stability; nothing seemed amiss. Perception was in the eye of the beholder, as one would never be able to tell that they had any serious problems. As husband and wife, their acting skills were on par with the happiest of couples. Craig wondered if it was the idea of 'face' again, and having to comply to certain habitual behaviours that were not part of the Caucasian tradition. The Asian notion of 'face' was very prevalent all around him, and he understood the concept of shame and humility more so having lived in Asia for some time.

Stan interrupted Craig's thoughts. "*Yes, she is. With her new boyfriend.*" There was more hurt in his eyes.

Stan was in two minds about his divorce because part of him was feeling fortunate that he and Yuki didn't have children, so kids wouldn't have to suffer any heartache from the breakup. The other part of him wondered and yearned about why they didn't have any children; maybe a child, or a few, would have kept them together. He thought about how offspring could either be a hindrance or an absolute Godsend. He would never know. He felt sad and empty again.

"*I am so sorry to hear that. Do you know who her boyfriend is?*" Craig was trying not to pry, but he could see that Stan was in need of some sincere friendship.

"*No, thank God I don't know him. I don't want to know him.*"

"*Yeah, I think that is wise.*" *Craig looked down at his shoes, remembering Jennifer and her antics.*

"*Yes, I don't want to leave in a mess. I want it to be a clean-cut exit… you know what I mean?*"

"*Yes, Stan, I do.*"

After a moment, Stan said, "*So, Craig, what can I do for you?*"

Craig looked at the envelope in his hand. "*I wanted to give you this today.*"

Stan looked at the envelope and tried one more time to speak with absolute sincerity.

"*Are you sure? Will you consider the position, or is it too far-fetched? You mentioned that you might want to leave Asia as well.*"

"*Well… yes…*"

Stan interrupted, "*Will you consider it before you hand in your resignation? Think about your options before you act in haste.*" *Stan had regained some semblance of his usual professionalism.*

Craig did not want to stay in Hong Kong anymore. He thought to himself for a minute. If his life were a movie… or a soap opera… what would he need in order to stay on in Hong Kong? Sophia struck his mind again; she was not even there. He felt muddled again and extremely sorry for Stan.

His insecurity coupled with Stan's pain made Craig put the envelope in his shirt pocket and say, "*I will think about it, Stan. I am going to London for a few weeks for the bank conference, and I wanted to ask for a few extra days so I can clear my head.*" *The thought had sprung up in his head like a Jack in the Box. He actually had no plans to go to London, but the whole drama with Stan had stopped him screeching in his tracks. He felt like the Road Runner from the Warner Brothers Cartoon. All he could hear was undignified screeches in his head.*

Stan recovered further. "*Certainly, take a couple of weeks off, Craig, and we will put your absence down as a sales trip for the conference. I will manage the fort here, but when you come back I want a firm decision from you. Whatever you decide, please know that the bank is very impressed with you, and your changes, and you are next in line."*

"Thanks Stan. I will definitely think about it and get back to you... and if you need anything, just give me a shout."

Craig left Stan's office and was confused all over again. He wanted to scream into the harbour and disintegrate ripples of confusion, regret, and insecurity. He walked to his desk, picked up the phone, and left a message on Dave's answering machine.

"Dave, it's Craig. I'm coming to London with you. Please help me book my flight and I will reimburse you for the charges. Please also book me my own hotel room. I'll call you later. Cheers, mate."

Craig put the phone down and suddenly felt quite content. He liked adventure and the unknown. His renewed spontaneous attitude was conjuring all kinds of fantasies for his life – what he decided was going to be called the 'brand-new normal.'

He couldn't wait to see Sophia again, he decided, with his newly redirected thoughts.

At the airport, Craig snapped back to the present. He was not shaking his leg with fervour, but rather was sitting still and with poise.

"You alright Craig? What happened? Why do you look so still now, like you've seen a ghost?"

"I'm good Dave, I was just contemplating."

"Oh really? Do you need a mirror for that?"

"No, mate, I'm just reflecting as well as projecting here."

Craig had been feeling increasingly and abundantly more indecisive after his move to Hong Kong and wondered if his antics were somewhat over the top – perhaps even melodramatic. Pansy? After realising that his drinking was hindering him, he was a little bit more focused. Realising that reflection of his past was not getting him anywhere, he decided on projecting into the future while crystalizing his thoughts – when he knew which parts to make solid, that is. One thing that he knew for sure was that the past had to remain where it was.

Dave turned his whole body to face Craig. "Wow son, I'm so impressed with you. I feel like you're on a mission." The metaphor of the mirror being a reflection was sinking into Craig's psyche and Dave was utterly impressed.

"I think I'm going to make a decision to be clearer and faster with making things move and happen."

"Like what?" Dave asked like a concerned father.

"Like settling down, Dave."

"Where? In London?"

"No, in Hong Kong."

"What about Sophia?"

"I'm going to ask her to come back with me."

Dave's soul was giggling and jumping up for joy, but he didn't want to show any signs of his feelings; this was meant to be Craig's *personal* journey. He kept composure and asked, "And how do you think that is ever going to happen? Huh?"

Dave was trying some fragments of reverse psychology again. He was going to make it look like Craig's heart was the inertia behind his decisions.

"I'm going to ask her to come back with me."

Dave paused. "Well, good luck, Craig. Seriously, good luck mate." Dave winked at himself and felt a sense of masculine chivalry dissipate from his aura. He was challenging Craig, and Dave was already loving seeing him try to get Sophia back to Asia. It was going to be a glorious time in London and Dave could already feel it.

The agent at the gate counter finally announced that the passengers should board the plane and take their seats. They had business class tickets and sat in comfort all the way to the other side of the planet.

The flight over was calm and both men fell asleep. Craig obviously dreamt of Sophia and both of them living Stan's life minus the affair. He also dreamt that he and Sophia had children. It was as if the dream was from a different lifetime, a place where it seemed comfortable and beautiful. They were in bliss – connected and real. He woke up and wished it were real.

Dave dreamt of yarns and yarns of fabric falling into a platform of bouncy colours, leaping into life size designs. It was so abstract that only someone like Gustav Klimt – symbolist, painter, and artist of *The Kiss* – would have been able to understand what was going on.

They both woke up and got off the flight feeling fresh. They walked towards the departure gate and didn't say much to each other. The only thing Craig was praying for was that Sophia would run into his arms and tell him how much she missed him. He was getting nervous. Dave could feel his vibration.

"Don't get nervous now, mate, she doesn't know you are here and I don't want you to look like a bumbling fool. If you don't exude confidence, she will not be attracted to you. Think back to why she fell in love with you the first time. Do you even remember?"

"Remember why she fell in love with me?"

"Yeah, do you?"

Craig paused. "I think it was the way I spoke."

Dave was smiling. "You're probably right."

"But seriously, I can't think about why she fell in love with me and vice versa." Craig gazed off, and thought for a long while as his mind drifted back to the endless coffees they had in Central week after week.

Craig looked up from the ground. "Actually, I can tell you exactly what it was. It was the soft-spoken, long-winded, beautiful way she articulated words and stories. Her voice was soothing, calm and made me feel peaceful."

Dave paused, thinking that this was the reason Craig had fallen for Sophia, not the other way around, but decided against pointing out that small detail. "Great. Now, all you need to do is hold on to that peaceful notion and go with it. Got it?" He put his hand on Craig's shoulder.

"Yes. Got it," Craig replied like an obedient child.

Heathrow airport was packed as usual, and the passport control line was enormous. Craig started biting his lip.

"Craig, you have got to stop doing that."

"What?"

"Your nervous movements." Dave sighed as he felt constant repetition was necessary for Craig.

Craig had no idea what Dave was on about. "What nervous movements?"

"Look at your lip, it's almost bleeding! And on top of that, you look like a tart. And you say I do silly things… are you actually trying to turn me on or something?"

With absolute composure, Craig said, "Dave. Please stop insinuating that I might remotely have any fancy for you."

"Well, do you?" Dave was making fun of him again, smiling under Craig's fake homophobia.

Craig was a little bit annoyed now. "No, absolutely not."

"Then stop biting your lip, because it looks like you're flirting with me."

Craig rolled his eyes and waited patiently to see Sophia.

Half an hour passed. Finally, at the baggage counter, Craig was feeling extremely nervous again and wished he hadn't made the decision to go to London with such haste. A part of him wanted to sprint back to Hong Kong and stay in his safe haven at Happy Valley and just live the life of an expat man. He pondered why he was so eager to leave his comfort zone just for a girl. He hoped that this time it was going to be alright.

They collected their baggage and made their way out of the terminal.

Sophia had been waiting for what seemed like an eternity. *Come on, Dave. Can't you pull some strings with customs? You've been here enough times*, she thought to herself.

As the terminal doors opened for the seemingly hundredth time since she had been waiting in the arrivals area, Sophia finally caught Dave's eye. She smiled at him and waved as her smile was getting increasingly bigger and bigger. It was almost instantaneous that her gaze caught Craig's. She looked over at him and as fast as her smile had appeared, it disintegrated into a million pieces of regret and anger. She suddenly did not look happy. She wanted to run as far away from the situation as she possibly could.

She was now scowling at Dave. And with the slay of one look, Sophia annihilated Dave with her hawk eyes. She wanted to dig into Dave's friendship and ask him who he thought he was to intrude upon her life with Craig. This was not the kind of surprise she was envisioning, she thought to herself; as a matter of fact, she was angry, and thrown off her feet, not knowing how to react at all. She wished she could deport both men right back to Asia where they both belonged.

Chapter 12

London

Washington was home late again, because after a long day at the music academy he went to La Bella Luna to meet up with his old gang. It was three thirty in the morning when he finally got home and the twins were in his and Mala's bed. Washington, who was not so pleased with the situation, gently moved the twins gracefully and stealthily back to their own room and snuggled up beside Mala. He hugged her tightly knowing that she was his princess always and no matter what obstacles got in his way – especially with his profession – he knew deep in the bedrock of his soul, that Mala was indeed the mother of his children, and his best friend. But for the very first time in his life, something was missing, or more like he was missing her. Before the arrival of the twins they had so much more time together and the spontaneity of their lives was now non-existent. A part of him, he had to admit, felt lonely, especially with Mala's exhaustion and constant need for sleep.

He didn't want to lie to anyone, especially to himself, so in the morning he was going to tell Mala about the intern and about her divine music – even though it surely was just a passing infatuation. Emilia was an exceptional musician who had external beauty, she did everything in her young power to become Washington's star student. She had the voice of a thousand angels singing in harmony as her voice wrapped around his frequency like a bolt of colourful lightening. He stopped thinking about her and hugged Mala even tighter. She stirred and he gently stroked her arm. He didn't want to disturb her, knowing the twins would be up soon. But his movements as he got into bed awoke her.

Mala turned around and looked right into Washington's face. It was as if she had woken up to something new and different as Washington bent down and kissed her passionately with his big strong lips. She was definitely awake now and feeling slightly overwhelmed. He hadn't done this in so long, especially when she was fast asleep.

"Is everything okay, Washington?" Mala inquired through her grogginess.

"Yes, babe everything is great. I missed you today."

"Oh that's lovely Washington. I missed you too."

"Go to sleep Mala, we can talk more tomorrow."

"Yes, for sure babe, I need to talk to you about something too."

He knew it was about Kumari, because he sensed Mala needed help when he was working. Having some extra hands around would give her some more time for them to be together like the good old days. He would not give up his circumstance for the world but he had to admit he missed having Mala all to himself. He also missed having coherent conversations with her – without her falling asleep half way through all the time. They had set aside once a week to go on 'date night,' but that was somehow not enough for him and definitely not like the good old days when they were younger. He tried not to think about anyone else but her.

In the morning when they both woke up, refreshed and ready to tackle the day, Washington looked at Mala and kissed her passionately again. Mala was taken aback as she stood with two bottles of milk in her hand. She was trying to wean the twins off her breast milk so she could be with Washington more, and at that precise moment in time Mala wondered if the universe was working quickly with her wants and desires. She questioned why he was being so overly affectionate.

"Is everything okay Washington?"

"Yes babe, why, what's wrong? I'm not allowed to kiss you how I did before the twins?" Washington looked at her with an heir of sarcasm in his voice. It didn't mean to come out the way he had said it, in a sharp tone with his arms opened up by his side, but he did catch himself when he realised how he came across – a bit rude.

Mala, also slightly taken aback caught herself and interrupted "No... no... nothing like that. I was just wondering why so much affection this morning."

"I just miss you Mala, and I want to be with you more often."

Mala saw her chance. "Solution: let's hire Kumari right away then, everything will be fine." Mala was smiling from ear to ear, her hair in a bun atop her head, which glorified her smile even more.

"Sure babe, but we have to wait…"

"Oh boy, here we go again… wait for what? Money?" Mala walked away from him in a huff; she certainly wasn't feeling affectionate towards her husband at that moment and was so tired of the same conversation with him. She walked away from him and continued to speak with her back towards him.

"Washington, I really don't care who pays for it, whether it's me or you but I am telling you now," Mala turned around sharply after giving the bottles of milk to her children and said, "Kumari will be starting ASAP."

He looked at her and didn't know what to say because his wife was right; why couldn't the housekeeper's position be effective immediately? What was he waiting for again? Money to fall into his lap from the sky? They weren't that bad off.

After a moment he said, "Okay, ask her to start today."

Mala kept her gaze constant at Washington and said, "Okay great, that's the way babe, just let's go for it. We shouldn't linger around waiting for things to happen, because we have to take the initiative to change our own lives and no one is going to do it for us." She paused, and put on a slight grin. "My mother is coming, so we will definitely need Kamari's help."

"Agreed." Washington hugged Mala again, delicately kissed his children, picked up his instruments, and before he left the flat said, "Let's go out for dinner tonight. I have to stop by La Bella Luna to pick up some music. But after that, princess, I am free."

"Sounds great, Washington. Call me right after work and let me know where I should meet you."

Washington left the house, but something didn't sit right with Mala again. The phone rang but she didn't pick it up. She was deep in thought. She noticed that Washington's movements were the same when he picked up his instruments, as he always did before he left. And his hugs were the same tightness when he held her, so what was this feeling brewing inside her? Mala was beginning to resonate like her mother and the one part of her DNA she disliked was feeling suspicious of people. She shrugged her mother out of her system, this time garnering goose bumps all over her back, shoulders and arms. The bumps pimpled up into a sudden frightful jolt and as quickly as they came up, with the movement of her body, they disappeared again. Was she getting sick? The flu? She hadn't slept well in a number of months, feeling she was getting increasingly exhausted as the days wore on. She wondered how Washington's mother had raised an army of children on her own.

She even began to wonder if he would ever take her to the Caribbean to meet his family, wondering if it was the right thing to do. Slowly, she became consciously aware of the incessant ringing of the phone and finally answered it. She was hoping it would be Kumari, confirming her commitment to being Shania and Michael's nanny, but it was Sophia.

"Hello?"

"Mala, hi, it's Sophia here. I'm sorry to call again, but... I am so angry... livid... pissed off... so... extremely angry, I don't know where to begin." Sophia was talking through gritted teeth.

"Whoa, whoa, slow down *chica*, what happened?" Mala instantly forgot her own situation, almost asking Sophia if it was Alister, but this time she caught herself and tried to stop blaming him every time

Sophia was in a bad mood, which seemed to be a lot lately. Maybe she missed Alex or a companion or even a good friend to help her through times like this.

"It's Dave. He is such a dick. I am so pissed! You won't believe what he did."

"Oh, he's here, that's amazing, Sophia." Mala was confused. "But... I don't understand... why are you so mad at him? What did he do?"

"You won't believe who he brought with him to London." She was gritting her teeth even harder this time.

"Who?"

"Craig. Bloody. Craig. Craig bloody Mathews. Why did he bring *him* with him?"

"Who with *what*? With *whom*?" Mala was so confused; what on earth was Sophia going on about? She was fuming like the little pink dragon from a Disney cartoon. For the life of her, she couldn't remember which specific cartoon; there had been so many running on a loop on the TV since the birth of the twins.

Mala had to chuckle inside herself as Sophia's British demeanour flew out the window and her Asian Chinese lady came streaming through the phone with gritted solid teeth. Her words were hard, strong, and venomous.

"Concentrate Mala," she said, "Dave, the silly old man, has brought Craig, Craig Matthews, here with him to London."

"Are they dating?" Mala's face was scrunched up from changing Michael's diaper.

"Mala, my dear, you are really not listening are you? Of course they're not dating!"

"So, what is he doing here then?"

"I don't know. I have no idea why Dave brought him here." Sophia was pacing up and down on her carpeted bedroom floor. She looked out the window and started to bite her nails and began pacing again. "I don't know why he is here; he has no business being here, and what is Dave doing? He didn't even ask me if I wanted to see him. I don't want to get involved with this guy anymore, plus I heard so many nasty things about him from my friends back in Hong Kong... do you know what I heard..."

Mala interrupted, "Hold on Sophia, just calm down and don't get so angry. London is a free place and maybe he wanted to see his parents because he is from here after all. Right?"

"Yes, but I know he didn't come to see his parents; he was with Dave, and I didn't see his parents at the airport..."

"So, then he came for you." Mala said this in a matter-of-fact manner as she picked up Michael and put him on a tiny swing.

"What is that supposed to mean, *he came here for me.* I didn't invite him here."

Mala was unfazed. "Sometimes love doesn't need an invitation, Sophia, it just knocks on your door and you can decide to open it if you want." Mala paused waiting for Sophia to reply, but there was no answer. "So, what is the problem? Sophia... hello? Are you there?"

Sophia sighed and sputtered with her lips. "I just don't want to go down that road again because I've been there, done that, knowing that it isn't going to work anymore. It's finished. I don't have any feelings for him and I definitely don't want to move back to Asia, so what is the point?"

"Maybe he wants to move here back to London, back to his roots."

"I doubt it... do you really think he wants to be here with that crazy Jennifer woman who was such an oddball who threw a spanner in the works and created such a scene in Hong Kong before I left?"

"Sophia, you are going crazy in your own mind and making up a rendition of your own story. Everyone has something to say. Give him a chance – he might surprise you! You never know."

Sophia began to feel some calmness with Mala's soothing voice and advice. "I suppose you're right Mala, argh! I wish I wasn't so stubborn."

"Sophia, don't be your own demon *auntyji*, be wise and serene and clear. Don't fight what the universe has put in front of you. If you don't let the world around you flow, you will be trapped. Now, just relax. Don't be mean to Dave…"

Sophia interrupted as she recalled how horrible she was at the airport. "I was so mean to him. I feel awful."

Sophia was thinking about her body language at the airport, with her arms folded and her frown so deeply entrenched on her forehead and her crooked fake smile, hurting every inch of muscle, nerve, and capillary on her face.

Dave pulled her aside when Craig excused himself to go to the toilet.

"What is wrong with you, sunshine? I have never seen you so angry. What's the problem?" He tried to put his arm on her shoulder as he often did.

"Let go of me, Dave. How dare you bring him here without asking my permission…"

"Excuse me…" Dave interrupted. "Who do you think you are, Sophia Martin? The Queen, and people have to ask for your permission? He came for the store and the opening. Not for you."

"You made him come with you, Dave. Why?"

Dave looked innocently at her. "He wanted a change from Hong Kong. He was getting antsy and abnormal."

"Then why didn't he contact me?" Sophia's eyes were getting smaller and smaller in her face; she was practically squinting.

"I don't know… maybe he was afraid… looking at you now, anyone would be afraid. You look so cross and mean…" Dave moved back; he was not impressed with his young friend.

"Oh, just stop it Dave! You always have something to say about me. Why couldn't you be honest and tell me he was coming with you, huh?"

103

"We wanted to surprise you."

"Well, I'm not happy and I hate surprises; you should know me better than that."

"So why don't you go ahead and leave since we have made you so angry. Craig and I are two big boys who can take a cab from here, or an airport limo..."

Sophia interrupted, "And as soon as he gets back from the toilet, please tell him to get on the next flight back to Hong Kong."

Dave sarcastically added, mimicking Sophia's anger. "Oh yes, and please remind him that the next time he comes into London to not forget to ask, or better yet, request for your permission."

"Dave, I am angry at you. I will call you tomorrow." She turned with her arms still folded got into her own cab and sped down the road.

Dave was somewhat flustered amidst five suitcases as Craig made his way back to the taxi stand.

"Where did she go?" Craig asked, baffled.

Dave quickly said, "She said she had some family obligation; she apologised profusely and said she would be seeing us tomorrow."

"She ran, didn't she mate?" Craig said sighing. "I knew it, she went running."

"Nah, don't think of it that way. She'll be around tomorrow. Don't worry Craig. Stop overthinking everything. Just let it flow."

The two men left Heathrow in silence, and Dave was feeling a bit drained, but he knew in his heart that Sophia would come around sooner or later. Craig was a bit embarrassed and suddenly some kind of wall of terror emerged in his mind, and he began to feel anxious. All he wanted to do was get on the next flight back to Hong Kong. He thought about what he could do to make the situation better. If nothing else, he wanted to be Sophia's friend. They ended so badly the last time with no closure and Jennifer's interruption; it was not a good ending. He promised himself that if he was able to make a new beginning with Sophia, he would definitely make it right.

They checked into the hotel and decided to have a drink in SoHo, which was so different from the SoHo in Hong Kong; Dave referred to SoHo London as the 'real deal.' They hired a chauffeur to travel around some more and decided to have a drink at one of the local bars nestled up a side street. *Harry's* was Dave's favourite pub growing up as a fashionista in London in the 70s, and it was miraculously still in operation. They ordered one beer and a soda water for Craig and sat some more in silence.

Someone caught Dave's eyes. He was looking for some eye candy and saw a beautiful young woman sitting at the bar with a very strong, good-looking man with a thick Barbados accent. She looked much younger than him. They were working on some kind of document. Dave could not get his eyes off this statuesque, mighty man sitting there. He was glorious.

"What are you looking at, mate?" inquired Craig.

"That man is so strong… he looks divine."

"Dave, please…"

"I know, I know, you can't take my gayness sometimes, but I'm just being honest. I have been so suppressed my whole life with society's madness about love that nowadays I don't care what comes out of my mouth."

"You should care, Dave. It could get you in trouble."

Dave sighed. "Yes, I know." He couldn't stop thinking about Sophia. He made a pact to himself that he would call her in the morning if she didn't make the effort first. Dave being the elder of the two knew that his best practice, especially with Sophia, was to exemplify his actions to create more of an impact. She did act like an insolent teenager sometimes, and that was okay; the thought made Dave smile inside his heart. Sophia showed passion even though she tried to brand herself as the boring one; however, today she proved that she had some fire in her. The only thing left to do now was to tame the fire in her heart and show her that stability and grace was all she needed.

Dave took one more look at the couple at the bar as they stood up to leave. He was the sexiest man Dave had seen in such a long time. With his mocha-coloured skin, he was even more gorgeous than his last fling, Sergio. He towered over the girl and very politely opened the door for her first. Dave looked at his watch. It was already five thirty in the afternoon.

"I think we need to head back, Craig. I'm feeling the jetlag beginning to engulf me." Dave's age was creeping up on him.

"I think I might stay here for a bit." Craig was glued to the football on the TV, a welcome distraction from Sophia's abrupt departure from the airport lobby. At least he wasn't perving on any women in the bar.

"Sure?"

"I'm sure mate, I'll be back soon. Maybe we can go grab a bite later."

"Sure." Dave walked over to pay the bill, waved at Craig and left *Harry's*. As he made his way to the other side of the road to hail a cab he saw the burly dark-skinned man on his phone talking ever so sweetly to what might have been a woman on the other end. He was referring to the person on the other end as his princess. He had a huge grin on his face while looking at his watch. Dave overheard him agree to meet this person in one hour. Dave wondered if it was the young girl he was just with.

Dave smiled at him as he got into a taxi and left the scene. Dave became thoughtful; the universe gives us points of contact when we least expect it and the world had become such a small place for Dave that he couldn't believe how much it had transformed since he was in his 30s. Every day he felt like the earth was not so vast and wide anymore and all of humanity were connected through some cosmic force – through space, time, and sound.

Chapter 13

London

"Hi Annabelle, it's *Pitaji*."

"Hi *Pitaji*, how are you?" Annabelle was beginning to dislike her father's unannounced phone calls and his tone always made him sound like a soap opera character. She was getting too old for his antics, praying this time that his phone call was not another offer to help him with his flighty life. She had some inclination that he was calling to ask for a favour. "Is everything alright, Dad?"

"Annabelle, there is something I need you to do for me."

Annabelle sighed; she was already not happy with his request and was beginning to feel settled in London. She was also at the forefront of finding common ground not only with herself, but with the environment and the community around her. She thought about going against her father's request and then suddenly imagined herself with no money. Their relationship was becoming increasingly weighted and heavy as the years wore on.

"I have a property in India that needs some handling, but first I need you to go to Pakistan to pick up some documents and then make your way to Delhi..."

As Mr Noor rambled on about the property in Delhi and a nice family he wanted to introduce her to, she started to feel the urge to puke, but she held herself back. She definitely didn't want to go to India, let alone Pakistan. It was as if he could hear her thoughts.

"Actually, Annabelle, you don't have to go to Pakistan – just go to Delhi and I will have the papers ready for you there, the legal documents for a very small piece of land in Delhi. I also want you to meet the family who have been helping me look after the place for years. They're very kind and have three sons and are very wealthy, Annabelle. Two of their sons are already married and they have their own businesses to look after, so they have asked me to take back all the responsibilities and their focus will be on their own undertakings." Annabelle could imagine her father with his glasses perched on the end of his nose as he was shuffling through papers he had just received in the mail.

"*Pitaji*, I don't think I can go." Annabelle blurted out. She knew exactly what her father was trying to do... he was trying to arrange a marriage for her. No way! was the very first thought that jumped into her head.

"What do you mean you can't go?" He sounded stern and already annoyed.

Annabelle had to think on her feet; she had to sound mature, not whiny, and be very clear with her father. Maturity was of paramount importance from her side right now.

"*Pitaji*, I have another engagement I have committed to while I'm in London... it's a business prospect. And I need to be here for at least six months to a year."

"What business...?" Mr Noor was frowning on the other end of the receiver.

Noor interrupted with haste, because she didn't want to give her father any more time to brood over her own decisions. "I have started a school with my friend Mala. You remember her, right *Pitaji*?"

"Oh yes, she is the lovely Indian girl. Of course I remember her." Mr Noor said with his frown easing up a little on his end of the line.

"Yes, her. She and I are thinking about opening a school together."

Her father quickly retorted, "Thinking or doing, Annabelle, because those are two different concepts, and if you haven't started yet..."

She interrupted again. "Yes Dad, we have started; that's why I am here in London. And I can't abandon her like that."

"Does your friend Mala have money to invest as well? Or is this just a 'Noor' plan again?"

"No… no… this is a joint venture."

"Okay Annabelle, well… I guess I will have to make the trip to Delhi myself then."

Annabelle was relieved. She felt like her angels had swiftly taken a hold of her and helped her drift into a different psyche.

"Thanks *Pitaji*, thank you so much for your understanding."

"No problem Annabelle, just please make sure that you have the right business partners with you this time. Isn't this the second or third time you have tried to open a school?"

"Yes, Dad, it is, but don't worry." Noor thought about how many times she had tried to open a school – it was definitely more than three or four. Thank goodness for her father's bad memory.

She continued, "This time it's different. I am hoping to invest in something more creative, not just an ordinary school, something that everyone can benefit from." Her attention quickly diverted away from an image of Mala breast-feeding her twins, to Washington and his music academy. Bingo! She had her partner, it could be an investment into Washington's school. She was going to speak to Mala in more detail later.

"Just don't be lazy about it, Annabelle. I am here if you need anything. And please spend wisely. I am not getting any younger and when I am gone…"

Noor cut him off; she didn't want to hear about the 'death and inheritance speech' again. "Don't worry Dad, all will be fine. I promise. Please look after yourself."

"I will for sure." He paused, "I want to ask you another thing…"

Noor thought she was home free with the conversation. As a matter of fact, she thought she handled the whole situation very well.

But, it was her *Pitaji* and he knew how to control a conversation, even from afar she could feel the 'marriage' question at the front of his brain, itching to be unleashed into verbal form.

"Have you not thought about marriage lately, Annabelle?" her father asked with definite sincerity.

"No, *Pitaji*, I am certainly not thinking about that at this present time in my life. Please understand, Dad, that when the time is right, things will happen and fall into place."

"I am so sorry about Ahmed." Mr Noor was not happy about their break up and blamed Noor for creating a rift between the two families.

"Me too," she said with freedom and a hint of carelessness.

Her father paused. "Anyway, I'm having dinner with his father tonight. You take care of yourself. I will call you soon."

"Love you, Dad."

"You too."

They both hung up the phone and almost as if the cosmos had interacted with them at the same time, they both shook their heads at each other as they put the receivers down. Now all Noor needed to do was open up a school with… someone. She picked up the phone again and dialled Mala. They agreed in seconds to meet over at Bazica.

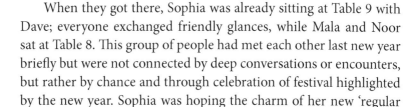

When they got there, Sophia was already sitting at Table 9 with Dave; everyone exchanged friendly glances, while Mala and Noor sat at Table 8. This group of people had met each other last new year briefly but were not connected by deep conversations or encounters, but rather by chance and through celebration of festival highlighted by the new year. Sophia was hoping the charm of her new 'regular haunt' would help smooth-over things between her and Dave. Kumari had finally taken on the job full time, and Mala felt free and was smiling more than usual. She was walking with a sashay of her hips, which ultimately made her curves more appealing. Sophia mouthed to Mala that she and Dave would be over to their table in ten minutes. To be honest, Noor didn't care. She needed Mala's undivided attention.

"You told your father what?" Mala asked, picking up the mocha that the ever-faithful server Fatima just delivered to her.

"I told him that you and I were opening up a school together." Noor smiled.

"Now how in God's name am I going to do that? I just relieved myself for some sanity by hiring a nanny, and then you tell me that we are opening up a school together? Are you insane?" Mala was still sipping on her mocha, unsure of whether to grin at a joke or frown at liberty taken against her. "You are mad, Noor, how can you blatantly lie to your father like that?" Mala decided on the latter; she was not impressed.

Noor sipped on her latte and looked at Mala with her stunning eyes; her eyelashes were like butterflies. "I was hoping we could think of something. I couldn't think of anything to say at that moment – he was forcing me to go to Delhi and then he brought up the notion of marriage again, making me feel sick to my stomach, because I really, really, really don't want to go to India…" Noor had very bad memories of India.

"Why not?" Mala said smirking. "You and I can go back for a few months together. The twins will be with my mother and we can go paint the whole of Delhi red – plus I'll be able to meet your father's idea of what an *ideal husband* is."

Noor put her coffee cup down gracefully and looked deeper into Mala's eyes and sharply said, "No!"

Mala was giggling. "Why not? Let's go back to our roots together, well, half your heritage anyway. You haven't been back in 20 years, so let's go! This time we have money and we don't have to stay in one of those scary hostels or ride the trains that smell like rotten armpit."

Noor's face was scrunched up with disgust as she thought back to the past when the three friends travelled together. Sharon was always a trooper and didn't let any outside situations affect her appetite for fun and adventure. Mala and Noor, on the other hand, were gaging at the crowds and pungent overwhelming smells they had to endure on public transportation in Mumbai. The one thing Mala remembered was that India reminded her of what must be a very colourful acid trip.

Mumbai

The three friends travelled to Mumbai for one of their holidays. The whole city of Mumbai was exploding with life, colour, smells, sounds, and a vibration of merriment, peace, and harmony. The biggest distraction in Mumbai ended up being the ladies themselves. They tried to be 'local,' but with Sharon's fiery red hair captivating everyone's attention it made the three friends almost impossible to be discreet. Travelling around India was one of the best trips the three aunties had taken together. On one particular day they were in the market trying to find a taxi to take them back to the hotel.

"Noor, take your hand off your nose, you silly Billy. You look so rude; everyone is looking at us." Sharon was trying to waft Noor's hand away from her face.

"No Sharon, everyone is looking at you because of your red hair," Noor retaliated. The smell of the sewer on the side of the road was creeping up her nose like stinky fingers.

"Let's walk, you two. What are we doing just standing here?" Mala was trying desperately to lead the 'pack' of two wolves she was trying to tame.

The three friends walked towards the side of the road like true backpackers, their sacks filled with distinct Indian souvenirs and ornaments to take back with them to London. Sharon's backpack towered over her head, making her look more like a dwarf.

"This way, aunties." Mala felt like a traffic warden as she tried to encourage Noor and Sharon to cross the road. At that instant, a baby cow plonked itself in front of Noor and proceeded to take... the biggest dump. She screamed so loud that the local policeman, who was also

the traffic warden, beggar stopper, and probably the district manager, came over to Noor and tried to pacify her. She was not having any of it.

"This is so disgusting; I never want to come back here again. How can they just let animals poop on the side of the road like that? How primitive." Noor was desperately trying to dodge the calf's poop and traffic all at the same time – while holding her nose. Sharon and Mala were on the other side of the road giggling with all their might, holding onto their stomachs and watching their best friend play out all her prissiness on a dusty street in Mumbai. As soon as she got toward her friends Noor was in tears.

"I am never, ever, coming back to this Godforsaken place again."

Sharon wiped the tears of laughter from her eyes. "Oh, come on Noor, lighten up. It's no big deal. This is what the voyage is about. Remember we promised each other, our aunty pact, that no matter what happens we will always embrace our adventures?" Sharon pulled out a cigarette as she tried to calm Noor down.

"I know, but this is scary and unhygienic." Noor's crocodile tears had no effect on Mala or Sharon anymore.

Sharon was giggling even harder. "Come on precious, don't be so dramatic; it's just cow poop."

And with that, Sharon and Mala were once again laughing at their friend on the side of the road in India. To an outsider it indeed looked like this multi-cultural trio of women were connected by a sisterhood. Their connection was solid, strong, and from a distance, to anyone watching, looked like the most beautiful friendship in the world.

London

Mala recalled their trip to India and honed-in on the miniscule details with laughter, giggling into the foam of her mocha.

"…so, no, Mala, I am not going to Delhi. Mumbai twenty years ago was enough for me," Noor said after she listened to Mala recall the whole market scene.

"Well, if you change your mind, I am right here, ready, eager, and waiting."

"Yeah right, Mala! As if… you would never bring the twins with you. You complain about how people can't stop touching their hair down in Chinatown, what are you going to do in India? Walk around with a stick? Anyways, we need to discuss more about opening a school."

It was true; the twins got quite a bit of attention in Chinatown. Their hybrid ethnicity and physique made it hard to avoid. "I don't want to Noor, I'm not ready to work just yet," Mala said with strength. She was not going to let Noor bully her into opening up yet another school to appease her *Pitaji*. And she was somewhat irritated by her comment regarding Shania and Michael in India. Mala knew her mother would protect them no matter the circumstance. Noor was just being her hurtful self again.

Noor leaned in closer to Mala. "How about Sophia, do you think she can handle running a business with me?" Noor was sounding slightly desperate.

"Not sure, maybe you should ask her," Mala answered as she put her cup down, the laughter of her earlier recollection gone.

Noor diverted her attention to Table Number 9. "She looks so busy talking to that old man. Is that her best friend Dave?"

"Yup, that's him and she is not happy with him right now, so I would definitely hold off on talking to her about any business matters now."

"What happened?" Noor inquired like a gossipy *aunty*.

"He brought her ex-boyfriend to London with him."

"Oh…" Noor was confused. "…but I thought he was gay?"

"He is," Mala said smiling.

"So, what is he doing here? With Sophia's ex?" Noor looked even more confused.

"He wanted to surprise her."

"Oh boy!" Noor picked up her latte, raised her eyebrows like an *aunty*, sat back in her seat and sipped her coffee slowly, the whole time wondering how she was going to open a school. While Noor was pondering how to manifest the lie she told her father, Mala's mind drifted back to wondering why Washington was overly persistent about dinner plans. She had Kumari, she had some time with her friends and now she needed a manicure and a haircut. She wanted to look stunning for Washington tonight.

Over at Table 9, Sophia was being profusely apologetic to Dave. Her Asian side of 'face' value was emerging and she felt distasteful for being disrespectful to her best friend as well as someone who was much older than her.

"I am so sorry, Dave. I really am; please forgive me." Sophia's apologetic soft voice made Dave's heart melt.

"It's alright, sunshine. We all do silly things when we get surprised. Well, at least it worked. You definitely were surprised!" Dave was chuckling.

"Yes, I was. Where is Craig now?" Sophia inquired.

"He's at the hotel; I think he's scared to see you." Dave was smiling some more.

"Oh, bless, I don't want him to be scared of me."

"Well, you looked awfully repugnant when you picked us up from the airport. Can you blame him?"

"I know, I must have looked like a real bitch…" Sophia looked down at the table.

"Yes, to say the least," Dave said with concern.

"But you know, Dave, I really don't know what to say to Craig. We had no closure; we didn't even say goodbye to each other. When I got back from Hong Kong my father told me he rang the house. I have just been so mad at him and feeling confused by his actions. Then I hear that over the past year or so he has been drinking and partying with all sorts of different women… to be honest Dave, I am quite disgusted with him."

"I understand. And I apologise for bringing him here." Dave didn't want to dwell too much on the 'why' and thought it was wiser not to grovel or be humorous at this time, so beckoned for Fatima and ordered two double espressos. Fatima looked at him in disbelief. Four shots of espresso would take him on a fabulous highly charged caffeine journey.

"That's a lot of coffee Dave, are you okay?" Sophia asked.

"I am tired, Sophia, and I have so much work to do for the opening in a few days. Will you help me?" Dave's eyes beamed.

"Help you with the store?"

"Yes." Dave was smiling as he imagined dressing her up like a Barbie doll again. He wanted to add a mix into the equation and try to include Craig in there, but he knew he had to be subtle this time and move with caution. No sudden plans or surprises anymore. He didn't want Sophia to run away from Craig again and vice versa.

"What do you need me to do?"

"Dress up for me, my love iguana."

"Oohhh yes, of course I will. I would love to." Sophia was feeling elated. She loved being Dave's fashion muse.

"Great. Can you meet me later on this evening so we can go through some outfits and designs?"

"Sure thing! And again, I want to say I am so sorry for my behaviour." Sophia put her coffee cup down and placed her hand on his. He was like a father to her and she was still feeling the linger of her disrespect.

"Don't think too much. Now Sophia, let me pay for these coffees and go do some shopping, and then I'll meet you at the hotel at around six? Is that good?"

"Perfect. And don't worry about your coffee; we have a tab going here."

"A tab of coffees?" Dave asked with slight humour.

"Yup."

"How did you manage that?"

Sophia pointed to Mala's and Noor's table and said, "Those two."

Dave glanced at the table and saw the two women in stiches of laughter reminiscing more about their childhood again. Table 8 looked like a Broadway production again.

"They look like fun, Sophia. Bring them to the opening at South Kensington."

"I will for sure, Dave. And what about Craig? Please, no more cupid from you."

Dave chuckled, "Well I can't really leave him in the dungeon of the hotel, can I?"

"No, I suppose not, so what are you going to do with him?"

Dave began speaking but made sure his tone was refined and extremely nonchalant. "I think I might ask him to help me play dress up too."

Sophia didn't want to come across as rude, controlling or like the *Queen*. So, she sat back in her seat and said, "Cool."

Dave also sat back in his seat, looked into her eyes and with a very business-like smile said, "Cool."

While Sophia was being a good soul and not imagining Craig in the dungeon of the hotel, he was thinking about Jennifer. He spoke to his parents and informed them he would be seeing them within the week. As for Jenny, he wasn't sure if he should open up that can of worms. They hadn't spoken when she left Hong Kong either. It was as if the city had banished two women from his life just like a light switch. On and then off. He pondered a bit more and decided to hold off on making the phone call to his ex.

Washington Cannelli was with Emilia, finishing off some score writing for a piece of music he had heard her play three weeks ago. She gazed at his strong arms as he scribbled the first semblance of a melody, all the while wondering who his wife was and if he really loved her as much as he said he did. Emilia was intrigued by Washington, enamoured by his sincerity and loyalty.

Across town, as Emilia was staring at Washington, Mala was getting ready for her first proper date night with her husband in months. She was excited as she heard Kumari sing a soft lullaby to her two beautiful children; their skin shining like mocha.

Chapter 14

Surrey

Sophia was looking in the mirror; she knew Craig was going to be there, and wanted to look like a star. The boring side of her DNA had emerged again and she pondered on her last weeks in Hong Kong. She was getting tired of living in the past and needed some kind of manoeuvring with her thoughts, indicating for her to let go. Her constant conversations in her head of 'what ifs' were not assisting in any kind of acceleration; as a matter of fact, they were holding her back and anchoring her so far into the ground.

She took a deep breath and promised herself that she would try again, but in a different manner, more dignified, elegant, and relaxed. And then she exhaled again and again and again. Three times in a row she let her breath release, and at that point in time realised that she was going through the same cycle. She was boring herself and the people around her. She didn't want to turn into her mother, and seriously wondered if she was going through the beginning part of a mid-life crisis.

Sophia heard Alister coming up the stairs to his bedroom and called for him. He knocked on her door and came in. He looked so handsome, like a very young *gweilo* version of Uncle Peter. Alister was the epitome of a chiselled Eurasian boy. He sat on the sofa in Sophia's room and looked out to the view from her veranda. The air was cleansing as well as refreshing and the skyline of autumn fields coupled with the sunset made him feel sincere and creative.

"Al, I have something to ask you," Sophia said as she brushed her long dark brown hair.

"Alright then, what is it?"

"Craig is here…"

"What? Who? Craig, the bloke from Hongkers?"

"Yup, he is here."

"Oh, I didn't know that you were with him."

"I'm not." Sophia turned around to look at her brother. She didn't want him to think of her as loose by any means, and jumping on the relationship wagon as soon as it was available.

"Oh," Alister was confused. It seemed that Sophia was very good at conjuring up confusion amongst her friends and family lately.

"Anyway, he is here with Dave, and it's like a bloody soap opera. He flew all the way from London, with Dave, *my* best friend." Sophia paused as she took a sip of water from a cup, which was lying on her bedside table from the night before. She had begun to sleep with a big cup of water by her bedside, lately wondering if her dry mouth every night was from anxiety or some kind of physiological connection to a mid-life crisis.

She didn't want to sound like she was being demanding or like the queen, and slowed down as she began to speak. "*He* is here with Dave…"

Her brother interrupted, annoyed. "Yes, I know Sophia, who is your best friend… and… you're so long winded, can you hurry up with the story, or at least get your thoughts out quicker… you're boring me." Alister spoke his mind and he was not in the mood for Sophia's typical long drawn out explanations.

Sophia looked back in the mirror while her brother was speaking. She got glimpses of her mother; Sophia's features emanated indications of her. "Do you think I look like mum?"

Still annoyed – his sister had the hardest time staying on topic sometimes – he sighed. "No, not at all, you look so different. Mum is Asian. You look like a *gweimui…* but one thing is for sure: you act like her a lot more now than you used to."

Sophia turned sharply towards her brother and asked in perhaps a more demanding tone than she intended, "Why, because I am boring like her?"

"Oh, don't look so worried. So what, she is your mum after all, of course you will look like her, act like her, speak like her, dress like her…"

"I do not dress like her, look at me now. Mum would never dress like this. She is such a prude." Sophia was looking down at her slim legs and tiny Asian waist.

"I know." Alister was a bit embarrassed and looked away.

Sophia looked back into the mirror and decided to let it go. "So, long story short, Craig is here, and I will be meeting him with Dave."

"That's cool, so what's the big deal?"

"I don't want any drama."

"…So don't create any then." Alister shook his head at his sister and sat down on the sofa; in his mind, he believed she was the one who put herself in dramatic situations – lately more often than not – with her incessant overthinking.

"Oi Alister, are you insinuating I create drama?" Sophia asked as she turned around to sit with her brother on the sofa.

"Sometimes. You make more of something than it really is."

"I see," she said, rolling her eyes. "I don't want to get into any more details of drama, because you could have been the next Bruce Lee and you screwed it up…"

"Anyways Sophia," he interrupted, "we're not talking about me today. I want to know why you asked me to come in here."

She looked around absently. "I guess I just want someone to tell me that I'm doing the right things, and I am on the right track with no fear."

"You have to be the only person to tell yourself that. Not me, not Dad, not Dave."

"I know, but every time, and I'm serious when I say this, every time I'm feeling like I'm on the right path, something or someone gets in the way."

"Yourself." Alister said very matter-of-factly, as he stood and started for the door.

"I beg to differ Al, I really do," Sophia said as she watched him. "I can't keep blaming it on *myself* all the time."

Alister smiled at her with his head half-tilted, just as he used to do when they were growing up together, and left the room.

After a moment, Sophia got up to continue working on her hair in the mirror again. She and her brother, two grown children, living in their elderly father's home. She didn't know if this was right. Sophia's mind drifted to when she and Alister were young children…

South East Asia

Alister would be jumping on her bed in the evening, playing with airplanes and flying around the room, kicking up bed sheets and pillows and making flying sounds with his mouth. He would jump from the chair to the bed, and then to the chair again with his hair in his face. He would wear the same thing every day after school: a white vest and a pair of grey sweatpants.

While her brother was dreaming of becoming a pilot, Sophia would attend to her long brown hair. She loved to plait her hair around her soft Asian face, coupled with her bone structure and her straight brown hair, made her look exotic, different, not from any nationality, because she had the best mix of both her parents: olive skin, a slightly chiselled face and long, dark brown hair.

While the two young children were in their own world, their parents Daniel and Margaret would be in complete silence. It never felt like anyone was living in their flat on Broadcast Drive. It was always dark with only a few side lamps to light the way into their humble home and a small night-light along the staircase going up to the bedrooms. She remembered the smell of the house because it always smelt like jasmine rice on the weekdays and potatoes on Saturday and Sunday, when her father used to cook a roast. On Sundays, the family would seemingly come out of the woodwork and try to socialise with one another. It typically took Daniel two beers to get a conversation going, and then it would fizzle out when there was no response. In true form, he would continue to cook for everyone and switch on all the lights in the flat. It was the only day the Martin family ever spoke to each other, and the only day with light.

Surrey

Alister returned a few minutes later with a soda in his hand; he sensed Sophia still had something on her mind and he owed it to her to be there for her as – he had finally realised – she always was for him.

Sophia was still fixing her hair. "I think we should move out and give Dad back his space. I don't think it's right that two children, of our ages, are here."

"Where would we go? …and personally, I think he would be so lonely if we… I mean… *you* left."

"If both of us left, Alister."

"Yeah, I suppose, but why should we leave?"

"I'm a bit embarrassed to be staying here with him."

"So, move then," Alister said with a tinge of annoyance.

"Where should I go?"

Alister chuckled, looked up at the sky – or rather, ceiling – in true Sharon form and said, "Hong Kong."

Sophia looked annoyed this time and looked at him. "Never, ever, ever, ever, ever."

Alister was laughing now. "Never say never, because you never know what's going to happen."

"Well, I know *one* thing that will never happen." She folded her arms in prayer and looked directly up to the sky. "Never, God, never ever again." She closed her eyes and promised she wouldn't have any morbid thoughts. The only reason she would need to go to Hong Kong would be to see Dave, but never to live there or have any kind of responsibilities there ever again. Right?

"What if Mr Fancy Pants Banker asks for your hand in marriage? What will you do then," Alister asked, half joking but secretly in earnest.

Sophia didn't notice his concern. "I will laugh in his face and anyone who wants to marry me will have to stay right here in England with me."

Alister looked at her calmly. "I see, and what if your prospect is from Italy, or Greece, or better yet from the islands somewhere…"

Sophia smirked. "Then, my little sweet brother, we will have to wait and see when the time comes, because right now I am not going anywhere except to see Dave and let him turn me into a fashion goddess."

"That's great. Now can I go?" Sophia seemed to have regained her composure; his job here was done. He stood up to walk out of his sister's room, slightly bored by now.

"Hey, Al, I just wanted to tell you how proud I am of you," Sophia blurted out.

"Thanks *mum!*" Alister retorted sarcastically as he exited her room.

Chapter 15

London

Mala looked so beautiful. She was poised, relaxed and ready to take on the world and was quite impressed with how little weight she had gained during her pregnancy. She looked in the mirror and knew just what Sharon would have said with her so dolled up. She missed Sharon.

While living in Boston, Mala and her friends used to get dressed up to go out and feel like the universe had given them a good scrubbing. Sharon always reminded her that whatever they were feeling on the inside would indeed show on the outside. Mala pondered back on a conversation she and Sharon had as roommates during their freshman year. Noor had her own tiny flat just off campus – a mere three-minute walk to campus. But, it was her own and she always felt like a grown up. But for Mala and Sharon, their budget as well as lack of communication with their parents made life easier to deal with in the dorm. They didn't worry about any expenses except for a couple of bucks for the movies, some wine on the weekend, and endless packets of gummy bears. It was only when they started to realise that cash got them to New York and travelling that they got up off their lazy wave to find work on campus. As foreigners, it was difficult to find work off campus without proper documentation.

Mala eventually worked at the box office of the university movie theatre and Sharon worked as a cashier at the supermarket. They were not rolling in cash, but they had enough to get by and Noor was always a big spender. Noor loved to spend money on people she adored, and back then it didn't seem like it was a pretentious kind of spending but rather a more loving and giving feeling. Mala's mind drifted back once more to Boston.

Boston

One particular evening, Mala was at the box office working and a fraternity 'guy' insulted her about her accent and the way she looked, wondering if she was from Indonesia. Nineteen-year-old Mala had desperately tried to explain to him where she was actually from, but it was too much for her to explain, and entirely too much for him to understand. In the end, Mala declared that she was from 'the universe.' The frat boy, misinterpreting her innocence, laughed hysterically at Mala and proceeded to heckle like a hyena to his friends about how conceited Mala was in thinking that she was 'Ms Universe.'

In the weeks following that incident, she had become the laughing stock of the box office. Mala didn't want to go to work anymore.

Sharon was, as usual, smoking as she listened to Mala's complaints. Smoking was discouraged in the dorms, but Sharon had decided that the rule must only apply to American citizens. "Listen love, if you sit here the whole time sulking, you will never get anywhere. So what, he called you Ms Universe. What of it? Do you not believe that you could ever be Ms Universe one day? Have some bloody faith in yourself. Act the part, that will shut the silly American idiot up."

"It's not that easy…"

"What the bloody hell… of course it is. Tomorrow when you go to work at the box office, we'll get you a sash that says Ms Universe and we'll go down to the mall, and get you a crown… now you know that if I had the money I would buy you a Swarovski one, but for now just act the part of Ms Universe." Sharon got up and started to catwalk across the dorm room waving her hand like the queen. "See what I'm doing here, Mala, I'm walking like I own this space." She had the cigarette dangling out of her mouth.

126

Mala was giggling. "Should I really do that? Or should I put Ms India, I mean Indonesia, I mean, Indiana, I mean..." She was imitating her silly self, remembering how she had been trying to explain herself to a drunk frat boy, the origins of her mixed nationality and ethnicity which was prevalent from multiple passports she held.

"Don't be so bloody hard on yourself. Just be cool. When tomorrow comes along, you have to play it like an adult." Sharon nodded in agreement with her thoughts.

"What does that mean? Play it like an adult? You sound like a movie director or something."

"Or something is nothing and that's not the way to speak when we are trying to be creative. I want you to think about what I'm saying." Sharon stubbed out her cigarette, put on her PJs and jumped in her bed. The whole room was engulfed with smoke every day. Mala wondered if she would ever die of cancer from being in a second-hand smoke-filled room every day, and opened the window.

Mala sat on the edge of Sharon's bed and listened to her little Irish friend with great intensity.

"Listen love, if you look like crap, you will feel like crap and vice versa. Same as if you hang out with the rich and famous, you're bound to rub off on them and vice versa. You are what you attract."

"So why did I attract such a silly fool that night?"

"Because you were acting like a silly fool yourself."

"How, what was I doing?"

"How do I bloody know, I was checking out bagels at the super-market, I wasn't with you. And it's not even about me or my opinion. What matters is what you think. Not me." Sharon was shaking her head from side to side like an old Indian aunty.

Mala looked into Sharon's deep green eyes. They looked like lost seas from some exotic tropical island. The shimmer in her pupils was alluring and true. "You are right Sharon, as usual. You make a lot of sense and I believe you."

"There you go again, Mala, I am not your guru, precious. You have to believe in you. Get it? Only you..." She was staring at Mala's deep almond eyes.

Mala sighed. "I get it."

That evening at the box office, Mala was dressed in a pair of skin tight jeans, an off-the-shoulder black sweater, with very subtle makeup. She didn't go for her Grace Jones model look, which entailed contoured cheeks and dark, blood red lipstick. Today, she opted to highlight her dark almond eyes and paint her lips with a very soft rose petal pink hue. She looked like a Goddess. Maybe from India, Peru, Spain, the Maldives, Lebanon, Persia, or Greece. She could have been from any-where across the entire universe – fitting of her cause.

Sure enough, as the day turned into night the frat boy showed up again, as if on cue, cackling like a jackal as he walked up the hill towards the box office. Mala sat poised, thought of Ms Universe, crossed her legs and sat up with dignity. As the boy walked closer, his face changed. He wasn't heckling anymore, instead looking at Mala in confusion, as if he was trapped in a sensual dream and she had appeared right in front of him.

"Yes, can I help you?" Mala inquired.

"Um..."

"Cat got your tongue?" Mala said innocently in her best British Indian voice.

"Are you..."

"...the same girl you see every Friday? Yes, it's me... now, you are a cheese ball, and this conversation is very corny. So, hurry up and be on your way."

"Yeah... sure... um... same seats."

As Mala tore out the tickets she looked up at him and said, "You are so predictable and boring, frat boy. You need to change your perception."

He looked at her in awe. "Yes, yes... whatever that means..." He looked down at his four tickets and beckoned for his eerily quiet friends to follow him into the theatre. The three boys followed like puppies *behind their master who had been forcibly turned into a gentleman by Mala Amani that day.*

⨎

London

She snapped back to the present. She was looking radiant on the outside, but something did not sit right with her on the inside. Something about Washington's overly romantic behaviour made her feel insecure once again. She tried to think back to the box office incident, so many years ago during her innocence, and chuckled. She knew she had to feel good inside as well as on the outside, but today, something was adrift.

Mala kissed her twins, gave Kumari a few instructions and left the flat. On her way to town in the cab, she thought about her mother again. She wondered if she was like her, accepting of so many mundane things in her relationship with Washington. She stared out of the window and London looked so beautiful that she couldn't imagine living anywhere else.

The mini cab driver turned the final corner and Mala saw Washington waiting. He had made reservations at their favourite Italian restaurant on the Marylebone High Street. *Pedros* was their date place for special occasions. Her instincts were leading her to believe he had something to tell her, perhaps another music gig on a tropical island. She paid for the ride and walked gracefully to meet Washington. He kissed her passionately again, put his arm around her waist and escorted his princess to the restaurant.

"I'm so happy we finally have time to do this. Was Kumari okay with the children today?"

"Yes, everything is good. And things seem to be working out well, Washington." She looked at him deeply. Her eyes mirrored a depth of silence and fear. She could feel her spirit reminding her that although the gesture was beautiful, the uneasy feeling still remained inside her. As they walked, in silence, Mala wondered if they were drifting apart. It couldn't have been about the children, because the twins definitely brought them closer. She didn't know if it was boredom or habit that was making her feel insecure. Washington knew Mala well and asked, "Are you alright? Why are you so quiet?"

"I'm fine, Washington." She smiled at him, and tried to push her thoughts away. She actually wanted to flush those negative feelings away and remove herself from that train of thought. She imagined a wave of negative words leaving her mind and trying to invite positivity. They sat down at dinner and spoke about Michael and Shania for a while, until their meals arrived.

Mala's favourite pasta arrived; she ordered the same one every time, a very spicy penne arrabbiata with extra cherry tomatoes. The steam from the pasta and the sauce filtered the silence between her and Washington. As the fragrant steam of tomato wafted past them, she began to speak.

"Washington, I have something to say to you. And I don't know how to say it, because when we were younger and every time I felt remotely insecure you would always tell me I was being over sensitive."

Washington was beginning to feel a bit uncomfortable. He wondered if Mala knew about Emilia and if he did have some feelings for her. He couldn't lie to Mala because all he wanted to do was make sure that the mother of his children was happy and safe.

After a moment, Mala decided to go straight to the point. "Is there someone else Washington, because you have been distracted lately and overly affectionate and we don't really talk about important things anymore."

Washington tried to divert her attention away from the hurt she was feeling stemming from her instincts; he could absolutely feel her insecurity and tried to softly manipulate her attention.

"We do talk, princess. The other day you told me how you were going to have so much trouble with Shania's hair when she grows up and how we would have to find an appropriate hairdresser for her. We also talked about the family reunion we will plan soon one day with your mother, and we also made a decision about hiring Kumari... we do talk..."

"Not about feelings…" She looked down at her meal and didn't feel like eating it anymore. "If there is someone else Washington, you have to tell me, I promise I won't be mad, I just want to know how I can make it better, because I don't ever want us to… get divorced…"

Washington jolted at the thought of the 'd word,' divorce; his family would be livid if he ever committed such an act. "It really isn't someone else Mala, it's just work." He tried to redirect his attention away from the beauty of his apprentice Emilia. How would he ever explain her to Mala. She was a half Italian and half English girl who just finished her education at the Cambridge school of music; Emilia was completely different from his wife. He was enamoured by her divine melody and her ability to create such beautiful music and that was it. He hoped.

Mala interrupted his thoughts again, deciding to be bold and tell her husband what was told to her. "Washington, Kumari saw you at the park the other day with a very young lady. Is she your student, or your affair? Or both?" Mala felt the pangs of tears well up on the side of her eyelids.

"Neither…" Washington began to stumble. "I mean… she is neither my affair nor my student. She is an apprentice. She came over to The Academy about a month ago and asked me to look at a piece of music she had written. She wanted a part in a musical on the West End, and asked if I could train her."

"I see." Mala said softly as she looked down at her pasta, which now looked limp and unappetizing.

Washington could feel the sadness in his wife, and trying to make the situation better said, "I know you are feeling a bit trapped with the children."

"Trapped? Washington? Really? Trapped? Is that why you are a parent? To feel trapped?" Mala's voice was getting a bit louder. "If *you* are feeling trapped, then that is a whole different story. Don't put that on me and my beautiful children. They chose us and now it is our duty to look after them in the best possible way."

Washington was getting nervous again. Mala had this propensity to lecture when she was mad, which made Washington always feel small, unknowing, and uneducated.

"Come on Mala, I didn't mean it like that at all… you know me."

"Do I?"

"Yes! Now please listen to me, this girl is nothing but an intern who asked for some help. Her music is beautiful and mesmerizing, and that's it…"

"For now."

Washington was beginning to get a bit agitated as well. "Listen Mala, I would never do anything to hurt you or the children. I don't want you to feel sad, or riled up. She is just an intern."

"What is her name Washington?"

"Does it matter?" he asked, squirming in his seat.

"Yes."

"Why?" he asked like a child.

"So when people see you, I know what you are doing and with whom."

"What is that supposed to mean?"

"I don't want people gossiping about us and me not having the right information." Mala started to eat her pasta slowly. "What colour hair does she have?"

"Brown… who cares?" Washington's eyes looked a bit droopy. He didn't feel like answering any more questions.

"What colour are her eyes?" Mala asked not even looking up from her food.

"Brown."

"I see," she said, lifting up her beautiful almond shaped eyes at her husband. Her gaze penetrated his faltering eyes, and she could feel that he was trembling a bit.

"I don't want to talk about her, this is not a…" Washington tried to stay as still as possible as his heart began pounding a little bit harder.

Mala interrupted, "What is her name, Washington?"

"Her name is Emilia," he said. This time it was his turn to look down at his lamb chop.

For the rest of the meal, which took place in 45 minutes, both husband and wife ate in complete silence. All the while, intuition was playing a very integral part of their relationship.

On the way home, Mala didn't want to feel insecure. Her mother was coming to visit soon and after that calm but hurtful conversation, she didn't want her to get any inclination that there was a gap in her heart. Mala tried to ask herself so many times during dinner why she was feeling this way, and why she felt a void just from the *idea* of Emilia. Washington was quite normal and spoke exactly the same, but when she reflected from the inside, she realised that what she couldn't put her finger on was like a phantom, wafting in the air, lingering and waiting to settle the nerves tangled up in her mind. More serenity was something she needed in her life right now. She felt like going away on holiday somewhere. Alone. She missed Sharon again, as she and Washington sat in the taxi, with his arms tightly around her, in silence. She drifted back to Boston.

Boston

"I'm going away for a few days," Noor had said.

"Again?"

"Yes."

"Why? What's the problem now?" Sharon was dragging hard on her cigarette as she spoke to Noor. Noor was planning another getaway and had asked Sharon and Mala to stay in her apartment while she was away. They had just finished Thanksgiving holidays and Noor had had enough. Once again.

"Why do you keep running?"

"I'm not. I want to spend some time in New York with my cousin. I'm bored."

Sharon looked over at Mala and raised her eyebrows. "We bore you?"

Mala glanced up. "No love, she bores herself." Sharon blew her smoke in Mala's direction and said, "If we keep running away all the time, we will never find what we're looking for. Stay here with us, it will be fun! No one will be here, and we can just hang out, the three of us."

"No thanks." *Noor turned to pack some more clothes in her suitcase.*

Sharon looked somewhat surprised. "That's so rude. What do you mean, no thanks? We're not McDonald's, you know."

"Why don't you come with me then?" *Noor turned around and looked at her friends.*

Sharon grinned. "Shall we?"

"Yeah, lets travel."

Mala was getting excited. "Not New York again; let Noor go alone. Sharon and I will go on an adventure," she said, half to herself.

"Okay. Where? Let's go to California."

"Yeah." *Mala was so happy.*

"Disneyland."

"Done."

"Done."

∽

London

Mala returned to the present and smiled. When they got back into their flat, Mala walked into the study to look for the book Sharon had given her before she passed. She turned to the picture of both of them standing outside the entrance of Disneyland. They had such a good time that day, and in the evening they had gone to a bar with their Mickey Mouse hats still on. She remembered they didn't get home until 2 a.m.

Mala needed to get out of London; it was her turn. But, her mother was coming and she didn't know what to do. She chuckled at herself and at her thoughts. She wondered what would happen if she left Washington alone with her mother. She giggled out loud, and Washington felt her spark of humour. She needed to alleviate stress after that conversation at the Italian restaurant and she didn't want the twins to feel any negative vibrations around her or Washington. Master Kamal had mentioned that vibrations through thoughts and feelings could definitely be transmitted into the cosmos and affect others. She couldn't wait for her yoga class in the morning. Her *chakras* after their so-called date night needed some definite clearing. Mala didn't want jealousy, hatred, or regret to block any of the light inside her.

"What's up?" he asked as he pulled his shirt over his head. He always walked around the house without a t-shirt on. Kumari walked out of the room and scuttled back inside. Mala smiled some more. Kumari was a true reflection of what her mother would have done at that moment; maybe she even pulled her ears. Washington's strong back and arms made Mala's thoughts melt. She didn't want to be upset with him, it was obvious she was hurt and definitely didn't want to see, or talk to, Emilia... ever.

"I was just wondering what you would do if I left you here with my mother and the children while I went away for a while."

Washington looked rather astonished. "Really?"

"Yeah, what do you think?" *That would be a slight punishment for him*, she thought, considering the topic of his new "intern."

"Um... I think... no..."

"Why not?" Mala was enjoying this.

"One of us would kill the other."

"Kumari can be the mediator." She smirked.

"Is that why you hired her? So you can leave me here with your mother?" Washington's sarcastic laugh penetrated the entire flat. He wasn't so amused.

"Shhh. You'll wake up the kids," she said, returning to reality. She reverted back to the uncomfortable conversation, and wasn't so giddy anymore. She suspiciously looked at him and said, "And put your shirt back on. Kumari needs to leave."

He ignored her, walked into their bedroom, and shut the door.

Chapter 16

London

Sophia asked Noor and Mala to come to the opening of the store in South Kensington. Noor was flattered and happy she was going to be getting dressed up tonight. She wondered if there would be any paparazzi. Noor would prove to look absolutely stunning that night.

Mala was trying to negotiate a time with Kumari and with Noor, to make sure she wouldn't be late for the opening. She wanted to have enough time to help bathe the children and then be on her way. Washington said he would meet her there later because he was finishing up a music score. She knew this could take time and swiftly decided to have an *aunty* night with her best friend, Noor.

The beautiful and graceful Sophia Martin was still trying on her outfit for the launch. She was trying to find something perfect to wear, something enticing yet elegant, flowy and graceful. She found the perfect ensemble after trying on fourteen different outfits.

On the other side of the world, in Asia at the very same time, someone was scheming, filtering information for a later date and pondering how to get some kind of peace back in life. It was unclear,

137

at this moment in time, how to be convinced of the deserved goal. For now, waiting in Asia was the most dignified option.

Back in London, Sophia escorted Dave to the opening of the event. They went early to set up and get organised for the fashion house's fans, while Noor and Mala were having a quick bite to eat and a glass of champagne before their grand entrance. Sophia had asked both girls to make a bit of a drama when they arrived, as the press were always hungry for some kind of action. Noor agreed to kiss Dave on both cheeks while Mala decided that she would stay in the background and if she was caught on camera, then well and good, and if she was not, then no big deal.

She wasn't keen on public attention. She got enough stares from the community already, especially with her two beautiful children. She remembered going down to Chinatown to buy a silk dress for a theme party and for whatever reason she had brought the twins with her. It seemed like people were gawking at her, proceeding to touch Michael's ethnically diverse hair every time she went into a store. It was condescending and extremely demeaning. She had thus decided that she much preferred to keep her life on the down low.

"Do I look okay, Mala?" Noor looked absolutely glamourous. She was wearing a nude colour Versace dress draped with a thick gold ribbon in an empire waist style, which made her waist look even smaller than it now was. Mother of pearl earrings brought back from Japan by her father on one of his Silk Road trips sat majestically on each ear lobe. Her hair was put up in a tight French twist and she smelt divine as the scent of Narcisso Rodriguez's *For Her* perfume wafted romantically behind her with every step she took. She looked so different from six months ago: more confident and vibrant – every day looking ten years younger.

Equally beautiful was Mala who sat beside her in a purple chiffon pantsuit ensemble, coupled with a white pashmina scarf draped across her delicate shoulders. They both mirrored the glamour of Hollywood.

"You look fantastic, Noor. This is so exciting; I am so glad we are doing this tonight."

"Me too. And I am really impressed with your bravery, Mala."

"Why? What did I do?"

"I am so impressed that you left the kids alone with Kumari."

Mala felt momentarily concerned, although she didn't have any reason to feel this way. Why did Noor even mention that? She trusted Kumari, but something inside her, in her gut, began to shake. Her yellow *chakra* was beginning to twist. She tried to move away from those sensations, but something kept instigating her thoughts.

"What do you mean, Noor? Do you think she is a bad person?"

Noor chuckled. "You always do this, Mala, it's always black and white for you; never anything in between. I was merely making a statement about your bravery, not about whether I think Kumari's a good person…"

Mala tried to interrupt. "But…"

"Mala, you have to stop reading into everything people are saying and use your instincts. I learnt this from a very old, wise man in Boston one day."

"I am! I mean, I do use my instinct all the time." Her stomach started to twist again, as she thought about the conversation at *Pedro's* with Washington the other night. She hated this feeling, and thought about rushing to the bathroom. Mala was always very good at releasing.

"I'm sure you are using your instincts; all I merely did was enquire about your bravery. Is that okay? And if you think Kumari is a great person and helps you while giving you some space and freedom, then you have to believe that." Noor looked over at her friend and caught her holding on to her stomach. "Is it something I said, Mala?"

"No… no…"

"Then why do you look so nervous, and why are you holding on to your tummy, or your yellow *chakra*?" Noor asked with a tinge of sarcasm.

"Maybe it is something you said…"

"About Kumari?"

"Yes." Mala knew she was revealing half the truth. She didn't want Noor to use any of her pain for gossip, or material for her so-called journal writing.

"So, do you trust her?"

"Of course I do, otherwise I wouldn't have left the children with her."

"What's the problem then? Do you not trust your own bravery?"

"I suppose, and now that I am feeling this way and it is manifesting itself into my body, I want to go home." Mala was certainly not feeling so brave at that moment. She wondered what life would be like without Washington.

"What?" Noor was shocked.

"I don't know why I agreed to come out. You are absolutely right, the children are young… and I know Kumari… I mean, I know her from school, but not well."

"But you trust her, right?" Noor inquired.

"Yes, I do."

"Then don't worry about it, it must be something else in your mind that is making you feel nervous. Is everything else okay in your life?"

"Of course Noor, everything is really good. Maybe I just ate something bad today." Mala was still feeling a little bit queasy in her stomach. She didn't think it was about Kumari now. She knew it was her heart trying to tell her something else.

After dinner, the women made their way to South Kensington and waited for Sophia's arrival with Dave. Sophia was going to be in the newspapers in London, Hong Kong, Japan, Paris and most likely Shanghai. She was so excited. Dave was her jewel, and her igniter. His frequency was always vibrant, real and most of all truthful... he had the sincerity of a miracle and the blessings of a humorous sage. His advancing age never stopped him from being who he wanted to be. Dave was always clear, calm, and never overbearing. Of course, his humour was the soul of his and Sophia's relationship. She loved his easy explanations of life and his sincere love for everything he had in his world, including friends and family.

"You look so beautiful, petal."

"Thank you so much, Dave." Sophia was taking one last look at herself in the mirror. She knew that as soon as they stepped out of the marque, where their dressing room was located, she would have to smile at the flashing lights penetrating her eyes. She wondered how Dave managed to remain so humble. Sophia recalled one of Dave's stories of poverty when he was a child; she smiled knowing how far her friend had made it in this world.

"Are you ready?" Dave looked like a movie star again. His fashion sense was immaculate and always a hit.

"Ready." Dave put his blue sunglasses atop his head, sprayed some more perfume all over his suit and stood straight.

They walked out of the marquee. Sophia was shining, her beauty radiated like the glimmer of the Eastern sun, magical and burning with passion and desire. Her inner glow burst out of her as she walked like a graceful maiden on the arms of her best friend. Dave was chivalrous and elegant in his poise, walking to the red carpet with dignity. The lights flashed as they both smiled. Sophia felt like a movie star.

Mala and Noor were waiting at the exact position Dave's PR manager had asked them to stand. Her job was to make sure the press got the most poignant and important pictures. Sandra was a bulldog. She never let any ugly pictures get through, or any incriminating scenes. She protected Dave with all her heart. As soon as Dave and Sophia promenaded out of the marquee, the flashes of photography showered them as Sophia glided like a beautiful swan across the red carpet towards the front of the store.

Sandra was on her radio with other staff as she beckoned softly for Mala and Noor to standby for the grand entrance. Noor was so excited, she felt like squealing – she was in her absolute element. This was the world for her, and she radiated decorum and sensuality. Noor was glowing like stardust. Everyone was looking at her as she approached Dave and Sophia on the red carpet. Dave turned and kissed Noor, and did the same to Mala as they stood outside the boutique. Dave, Sophia, Mala, and Noor were all radiating a union of universal force. The lights were flashing with fervour, grace and ease. It was like Hollywood. For a moment, Mala felt like her spirit was flying into another realm, and her smile mirrored her inner beauty. Noor pouted into the camera while also engaging her seductive eyes. Dave was serene, happy and fluid while Sophia shone like an iridescent shimmer of twilight again.

The scene was from a movie, a movie of their lives. Three women from different corners of the globe, and a man from the southern hemisphere. All four of them connected by love, friendship, and a sense of family and familiarity. A soul connection, belonging together in harmony for that one magical moment. Just like when Sharon and Mala went to Disneyland.

As the lights flashed incessantly into Mala's eyes, she was transported back to Disneyland with Sharon.

California

It was the end of the night, and they'd had a few beers. They were slightly tipsy and giggling about the difference between Donald Duck and Mickey Mouse, when Mala took the conversation one step further and reflected back on the observation, she was petrified at the direction of her mind and its perversion at that moment.

"So, you think Donald has a small one?"

Mala was giggling. *"That's gross, I don't want to think about it. What happens when we have kids and they're playing with Donald… ewwwww, I'll never be able to look at Donald in the same way again."*

"I definitely think Donald's is smaller." Sharon was giggling.

"This is so getting out of hand, we can't keep talking about this. You are making me petrified – I mean horrified, and I feel a lump coming up in my throat."

"Bloody hell Mala, you are such a drama queen. Have some fun, love." Sharon was laughing some more.

They settled down and Sharon and Mala sat in front of the fountain at Disneyland and talked for what seemed like hours.

"So, what are we going to do after graduation? We can't stay here." Mala's statement was clear and concise.

"We're going to travel the world. All three of us."

"Yeah right, before we know it Noor will be married with kids, and tamed, and so bloody boring. Do you think she will ever leave her father? She is such a wimp. Just watch – she will be the first one to get married."

"And you?"

"I don't have any plans. I know I'm not going to be in Boston my whole life and I don't want to start anything here."

"Yeah, but how can you stop life?"

"You can't Sharon, you just have to keep moving and going forward."

"So, here you go again, contradicting yourself again."

"What do you mean?" Mala looked confused.

"You said you don't want to start anything here, in Boston, but you just have to keep moving forward and forward. That is a bloody contradiction."

"Why?"

"Because if you find the love of your life here, how can you say you won't 'start anything?' It's because you are scared. You can't

143

make up your mind. Look at you. It's so obvious how you wait for circumstance to dictate your life."

"What do you mean, Sharon?" Mala was feeling a bit uneasy.

"If you fell in love with someone here, you would pretend you didn't because you don't want to be here for long. And you are scared of what might happen without genuinely following your heart."

"But my heart is not here."

"Fair enough, but what I'm saying is that if you fell in love, and chose to be with someone for the rest of your life, would you change locations to follow your heart? Or would you be stubborn and say you don't want to live in America..."

"I would have to wait and see when the time comes."

"See Mala, contradiction. Waiting until the time comes doesn't make stipulations on whether you might meet someone in Boston, or China, or London. Do you know why?"

"Why?"

"Because you cannot put circumstance on love. One day you will meet someone and he will sweep you off your feet, and it doesn't matter where it happens. Just don't blame the situation for the way it should be. Go with the flow."

cõ

London

Returning to reality, Mala felt a tear emerge in her eye. She didn't know if it was the flashing lights, or if it was her emotions getting the better of her. She paused and smiled again. They walked away and Mala excused herself to the powder room.

"That was brilliant, thank you ladies, you look remarkable, dazzling... like goddesses; I couldn't have asked for anything more." Dave was beaming as he hugged Sophia and Noor.

Craig had been standing on the sidelines the whole time, gawking at Sophia. He couldn't believe his eyes. He couldn't believe that standing right in front of him was the most beautiful girl he had ever let go. He smiled at her and she smiled warmly and graciously back at him. Craig had butterflies in his stomach – it was the loveliest sensation and he felt giddy like a schoolboy again. Sophia was the only person who made him feel this way. He walked over to her and put his hands on her shoulders as she turned around.

"Craig." Almost instantaneously, Sophia turned around to awkwardly hug him. She promised Dave she would be dignified and try her best to erase the airport incident from everyone's minds. The only way to that, according to Dave's advice, was to be super nice when she saw him and make sure that her rudeness was not his fault, but a sheer lapse of her better judgement. "How are you? You look great," she said, beginning to dissolve the tension between them, or more like, the tension she had created between them.

"So do you, Sophia. I am so honoured to be here with you... and Dave..."

Sophia was blushing, "Thanks Craig. How long are you here for?" She was looking into his eyes as he spoke her spirit began to glow with delight. She wanted to rewind time to when they were in Hong Kong. She stopped her thoughts, took a step back and said, "We should really have a coffee or maybe even some lunch tomorrow. I think we both owe each other an apology."

Craig smiled, "I *am* sorry, Sophia."

She looked down on the ground and smiled. "I'm sorry too Craig, I was just so..."

He interrupted as he lifted her hands up to his and cupped them softly around his heart *chakra*. "Don't worry, Sophia, I don't want to talk about it in detail tonight. It is in the past, and tonight is a celebration. Look at the sea of people here, looking at you and Dave. It's astonishing. I'm having so much fun tonight being around you."

Sophia blushed. She wanted to freeze this moment in time. She felt like part of a fairy tale, but knowing that every time she wanted to create a tableau of her life, she was doomed for failure because of her rigid, boring DNA. She let go of her airy and romantic thoughts and introduced Craig to Mala and Noor. He was polite and Mala looked at him approvingly while speaking to him with intellect and humour. Mala knew she had the propensity to be like her own mother sometimes and tried not to look at Craig up and down like a true Indian aunty. She used humour to diffuse any disapproving thoughts of Craig – from Sophia's perspective of course, when she was worried about his partying nights in Hong Kong. Mala had never been to Hong Kong and thought about maybe visiting one day.

Noor was not paying too much attention to Sophia, because she wanted the limelight. She had an ulterior motive, because she wanted everyone in her mind including exes, past flings, family, her father, and of course Ahmed to see her glowing and in her own divine element.

As the night progressed, the friends meandered down the road to a tiny local pub behind the muses at Gloucester Terrace. *Eddie's* was a great place to schmooze with socialites, as well as have a beer while mingling with press people, top fashion designers, marketing managers, CEOs of modelling and apparel companies, and occasionally a movie director would be lurking, ready to become the agent of a circumstance filled with fame, fortune and abundance. Noor was hoping she would meet someone like that tonight.

Ten years ago, a French director had asked Noor to write a story for him based loosely on her life. She was so excited and thought she was going to make a million US dollars from her endeavour. In the end, he offered her ten thousand dollars and all the rights of her stories. She was so mad, she stormed out of *Eddie's* and cursed the director all the way home. She felt like a laughing stock, refusing to visit the pub for years.

Today, she was on a roll and was going to find the best connection to make her story into a movie. A light bulb clicked on in her brain. She wasn't going to open a boring old school with Mala, she was going to try and write a screenplay as well as direct. She was beaming as her thoughts zapped her into another dimension of freedom and fantasy. It could all come true, if only Noor had consistency and direction. Her lack of awareness would cause her to stumble again. Nevertheless, tonight she was on a mission and she had a story to tell. The Annabelle Noor story...

Mala was on her way home, and surprisingly she hadn't heard from Washington. She had to admit she was a bit annoyed at him for not showing up. He would have made a great impression at the opening, but he didn't make it. Mala felt disappointed again.

She was shocked to see him fast asleep and in a deep slumber when she got home. Stumbling upon the time, she realised it was already two in the morning.

Mala had to stop creating scenarios in her mind about Washington, because the lack of trust was beginning to eat her up inside. A part of her wanted to put the thought of Emilia so far away from her, but the other part of her wanted to actually see what this new character in her life's story actually looked like. She took off her party clothes, washed the makeup off her face, put her hair on top of her head in a bun, went out to the living room where her desk was, switched on her computer, and started to type.

I asked him her name, and asked if she made him tremble. What was the reason for him telling me about this new woman in his life?

Questions bounced around in her mind as she tried to put the pieces of his new friendship with this woman together. She looked at the clock one more time and it showed 4:40 a.m.

She switched off the computer, hoping she didn't manifest more than what really was to come.

Chapter 17

Surrey

Alister was in the garden tending to his tomatoes and orchids; he had built a tiny greenhouse next to his room and the orchids bloomed with absolute magnificence, budding with energy. He tended to them as if the plants were his own children.

His dream now was to go to Hawaii one day to study the intricate, beautiful, and rejuvenating flowers. The orchid reminded him of Asia and his life there with his band mates. It was ironic that the orchids reminded him of the pulse of Asia. It made him think about Asia and the business that was not present or prevalent in his life in England. When he was in his greenhouse, waves of life in Hong Kong would flash through his mind. He couldn't recognise himself every time he had those flashbacks, because they were murky, unclear and so distant from his true self. He had so much to give and with Sharon's passing he didn't know who to share his love with anymore. He wanted to share it with someone who was on the same wavelength as him. Maybe what he needed to seek was someone who didn't know anything about his past. Someone who had absolutely no idea of his Asian life and what he had been through. He had side-tracked his life, realising that Asia was somewhere he had learned about himself. He often wondered if he had any inclination of why Asia had become his burden and his sacrifice and why he had to let it go completely for him to live an adult life.

Sophia was beaming from the night before and Alister had noticed that his sister was much more centred in London. It was also strange how they always happened to live in the same house throughout their lives. He wondered if it had something to do with the *yogi* he was seeing on and off. She had told him that people were always connected by some kind of cosmic force, and occasionally answers about how and why they had to come together would be revealed. He was always with his sister and no matter what place they were in their lives, his sister was always there for him.

She walked with a bounce in her step today. It was very subtle, but Alister knew his sister well, and even a slight glide in her walk would give him an inclination of her inner well-being. It was Sunday morning and after leaving the garden, Alister was lingering in the kitchen, thinking about what to eat. She was there, smiling and snuggling up to an aged Josie.

"Hey," Alister said as he walked past his sister to the fridge and pulled out a very big jar of cranberry juice.

"Hey." Sophia moved to the kettle to make her own tea. She had just discovered the *Indian Provisions Store* recommended by Mala. And Moti, the store owner, had some *masala chai* tea bags which he sold to foreigners who didn't have the wit or the patience to brew real *masala chai*. The authentic tea, made in India, was brewed with twelve different spices and made with precision for subtle perfection. The teabag format was for the expatriate community who needed a quick fix.

"How was last night? Did you have fun?"

Sophia was beaming "Yes!"

Alister looked at his sister as a woman for that one split second and could see the reflection of love and contentment in her eyes. "You look happy."

"I am Al, so happy."

"You look like Cinderella this morning; what happened? You obviously didn't turn into a pumpkin."

"No, as a matter of fact, I didn't."

"So... how was it?"

"Magical." Sophia blew on the smoke wafting from her tea.

"How so?"

"It was amazing – the lights, the people, the attention – but not over the top; it was totally a dream come true."

"That's great." Alister was happy for her; she needed some positivity in her life. "And how is Dave?"

"He is wonderful. You know what Al? He is truly my best friend. Someone I can count on, he's always there for me. No matter what, he is my saviour. Do you have anyone like that?"

Alister didn't have to think so hard about what he saw in his mind. His only best friend in the whole world was his sister. There was no one else who loved him unconditionally like she did. It was a hard act to follow for any girl to be around him and his sister, because she was the epitome of all woman in his eyes.

He tried to avoid the question. "That's amazing. I know how you feel. It's so amazing to have someone like that in your life, someone you can count on and tell all of your secrets to, vent with... I know, Sophia... it's an amazing feeling."

Sophia wondered who her brother was referring to. She pondered if it was a new love interest he was thinking about, but kept it to herself.

"Yes, and that feeling of someone caring for you, and being with you, and knowing every part of you."

"Shame he's gay, Soph."

"Yes." Sophia was not only thinking about Dave, she was also thinking about Craig and how he made her feel like a princess last night. He was chivalrous, kind, sincere and most of all she felt a friendship with him, a kindred spirit who gave her some kind of home. She just didn't want her mother's DNA and influence to get in her way this time.

He interrupted her thoughts. "So, what are you doing today?"

"I'm meeting Craig."

Alister perked up, "Oh yeah? How come?"

"He was quite a gentleman last night, I appreciate his patience and presence."

Alister rolled his eyes and said, "Here we go again."

"Oi, what do you mean?"

"It's the same old love story again. He broke your heart, or you broke his, and then he came to find you, you were not there, then he came to find you again and now you are here." Alister thought this part of his sister's life was flighty and predictable. "It's a soap opera, Sophia."

"You make it sound so simple and boring. It's more than that, I promise."

"So… are you back together, you and Craig?"

"Al, I only know one thing, I'm not getting younger, I don't have too much going on in my life, and maybe Dave being here, with Craig, gave me some excitement… and maybe brought up some old feelings."

Alister looked at his sister and didn't know whether to be happy for her or to be blunt and just give her a man's perspective, contemplating before he spoke. The only word that he could manage to eject from his mouth was, "*Draaaamaaaaa*." He knew this statement, or what he thought was fact, did not make his sister happy.

"Alister, are you disregarding my feelings? Why? It's not *drama*; it's exactly the way I feel."

"And how is that? Giddy and happy and silly? You look exactly how you did when you met Craig for the first time in Hong Kong, like something swept you away."

"No, it's different."

"Really?" Alister perched his eyes up like an old owl, "You could have fooled me."

"What do you mean by that?"

"I mean that you look like a school girl, like how you did in Hong Kong over a year ago when you met Craig."

Sophia's mind momentarily shifted back to Hong Kong when she first met Craig.

Hong Kong

It had been two weeks after their meeting at the Kee Club when Sophia realised she was totally in love with Craig; there was something about him that made her feel like melting whenever she was around him. His handsome demeanour and very caring ways gave way to a sense of freedom, like she could be herself. The perception he had of her was incredible, obvious due to the way he treated her. Sophia's mother once told her that people either gave you energy or sucked it away from you like a vampire. Margaret always believed that Daniel was the emotional vampire in the relationship, because he never had anything to say to her.

In Sophia's case, she and Craig had a lot to talk about and there was never any feeling of emptiness in their relationship, because the conversation was always kind and warm hearted.

Surrey

Sophia's thoughts returned to the present as the steam from the *masala chai* crept up her nose and settled nicely in the back of her throat. She closed her eyes as the mist reached her face and she remembered how Craig kissed her so passionately and tenderly last night after the launch party. He promised to call her and meet with her for dinner. He wanted to tell her about his resignation from the bank. A massive smile crept onto Sophia's face as the thought of her and Craig living in London melted her heart even more. She didn't even ask about Jennifer, who, unbeknownst to anyone involved, had mysteriously and rather psychotically made herself apparent on the other side of the world, harassing Stan about Craig's whereabouts.

❦

Hong Kong

Jennifer was waiting in the lobby area of the bank, hoping to see Craig – again. She had no idea how she mustered enough courage to fly all the way from London to Hong Kong, especially after her last attempt. Craig never wanted to see her again, but she just couldn't let go, there were so many unspoken words between them. She felt like crying again and wondered if she had enough time to say all the things she wanted to say to Craig. The thought of all the Asian women around him made her angry and she felt her neck tense up. Jealously at its worst always made Jennifer sick.

She waited for an hour and there was still no sign of Craig; she wondered if he was at home or if he had gone in early. She definitely didn't want to go back to his house in Happy Valley after what happened the last time. He had practically kicked her out of his home, the district, and Asia. She recognised Stan from one of the Skype interviews Craig had with him over a year ago. She wondered if it was a good idea to speak to him, or wait a little longer to see if Craig would turn up.

She waited for almost three hours, and all the while the security guard was wondering who this lady was pacing back and forth. He finally asked to help her and all she could do was bite her nails and scurry off onto the bustling road. She walked around as tall skyscrapers seemed to look down on her, reflecting a very intimidating view of the city. She walked faster towards the Star Ferry and sat on a boat all the way to Discovery Bay where her hotel was located. She didn't know what to do. When she got back to the hotel, she tried calling Craig but there was no answer. Her thoughts diverted to Happy Valley, but then decided very quickly that the idea was not conducive to her plans. She went to bed and tried to conjure up another plot.

Craig had given her some money before she left and they had a joint bank account together, from which he told her to take everything. When he informed her about the money she was content to have what was hers. Occasionally her mind would submerge into fits of jealous rage and she would begin to feel like Craig had treated her like a prostitute, paying her to exit from his life. Jennifer knew the money was for something, the reason for her longing for answers, which caused her arrival back into the Asian city.

Chapter 18

London

Noor was feeling brave after the launch. She had the most engaging experience with a Chinese man who was an architect; he said he was born in Michigan and had moved to the Bay Area to continue his studies. She had casually asked for his number and thought, *what a gentleman.* His tranquil character was something Noor needed in her life right now. A smile seemed to emerge from her heart, as she thought of what her father would do if he knew she was seeing a Chinese man. She imagined the discerning look on his face, coupled with absolute disapproval. Noor started to slowly lose care for her father's thoughts, recalling the conversation she had with Christopher.

"Is your real name Christopher?"

"Yes, I didn't grow up in Asia, so my family were very westernised; we are as western as it gets. My mom is a very stereotypical Asian mom though…"

"Like my dad." Noor interrupted. "How long have you been in London?"

"I've been here about 15 years, travelling back and forth though, from here to the Bay Area. Right now, I'm here because I am helping a big chain of hotels revamp their rooms."

"Wow, that's amazing!"

"Yes, I love my work. I can't do things I don't like; I get antsy and upset if I'm not doing what I love. What about you? What is your line of business?"

Noor had to think long and hard because she didn't know quite what to say to Christopher, but needed to put on a strong showing. "Well… I have run a few businesses in my life, part of my family's business. It's all quite boring. To be honest, I have never really felt passionate about any of the work I have done in my life. She thought back to her 'journal writing' and the desire to write her own story one day; once again in typical Noor fashion, she had quit… quit on her own story and just floated onto something else, and then something else, and the cycle was omnipresent.

Noor tried not to let her failures get in the way, and said, "I'm actually looking for a business partner at the moment to maybe invest in a school, or something. Maybe even a coffee shop."

"Ahh, that sounds interesting, the coffee shop part. I'm not sure about opening a school. There is so much red tape and bureaucracy here in London. And on top of that, all of the health and safety rules and regulations owners have to be aware of all the time. Opening a school already puts loads of responsibility on you. You are looking after other people's children and that is a huge liability."

Noor quivered at the thought of all the responsibilities involved in opening a school. She wondered if Christopher could ignite her imagination and brainstorm with her on how she could invest her money. She needed a plan quick so her father wouldn't be on her case and she wanted to see Christopher again. Something about him made her feel a sense of familiarity and his calmness made her feel in control. Her old self popped back into her head, and how she looked when she was with Ahmed, never wanting to cross paths with him again. That night, Christopher walked Noor home through the fresh crisp air. He thought Noor had one of the most beautiful faces he had ever seen. He wanted to paint her.

"Annabelle, may I paint a portrait of you one day? I think you have an amazing face structure and those eyes… I would really love to paint you."

Noor was amazed. No one had ever asked her to do something like that. She felt honoured and humbled all at the same time.

"Really? You would like to paint me?"

"Yes. Did I say something wrong?" Christopher's smile was so gentle and effective.

"No... not at all. I mean, I have had many propositions in my life but no one has ever asked me to be a model for a painting."

"Not just a model Annabelle, a piece of art. I want to paint your face like a piece of art."

Noor was blushing. "I really don't know what else to say, but, thank you."

"You are welcome," he beamed.

As they got to Noor's door, she said, "Let's meet up sometime next week for a coffee, or a glass of wine. I would love to pick that artist brain of yours."

"Sure, but we don't have to wait until next week, maybe we can meet tomorrow evening?"

Noor didn't want to rush into anything new and get hurt all over again. She did have the tendency to fall in love easily and quickly. So, she replied with dignity, grace, and a tiny notion of caution, "That would be wonderful, Christopher, but I need to check if there is something I have going on; as you know I work for my father and occasionally I am summoned." She smiled.

"Let me know, Annabelle, and we can arrange something." He leaned in to kiss her cheek. "Have a great evening."

And just like that, the artist from the Bay Area had made a deep impression on Noor. His silhouette on the pavement as he walked away from her reminded her of a painting by... who was it again? She couldn't remember for the life of her. However, the image always struck a chord with her about rebirth. She inhaled the fresh cool breeze and with a very sustained sense of happiness in her cells, she walked into her home and imagined what life would be like with an artist...

The next morning when Noor woke up, she decided to wait on calling Christopher. She wanted to ask for Mala's advice concerning her new-found love interest. She thought about his prospects. He was eleven years older than her, which made him nurturing and more aware; he had money, which meant that he would never depend on her for anything; he had a good family background and was a seasoned traveller, which meant that he would be willing to journey with her whenever she needed to run for her *Pitaji*. He seemed to have all the right qualities she was looking for. She made a mental note in her mind that he had covered the criteria she was looking for. She ticked the boxes in her imagination.

She retrieved her pendulum for the first time in a while and began to ask if Christopher was the right match for her. She then redirected the question and asked if she was the right match for Christopher and the universe kept indicating 'no.' She wondered what that meant; did that mean that she was not good enough for him? Once again, Noor harrumphed at the universe and pondered on how she could use her cosmic force to make her utterly connected to Christopher. There was something else holding her back. She couldn't put her finger on it. She called Mala.

"*Aunty*! How are the kids, are they okay? Did you give them a big slobbery kiss from *aunty* Noor?"

"Hey Noor, how are you?" Mala had just finished weaning the twins and she was sitting down to feed Shania from the bottle. She was good, but Michael was still fussing and making the separation anxiety worse for himself and quite unpleasant, with his screeches, for anyone in the house. He had actually lost a few pounds in the last few weeks of *Training Day* away from the breast.

"I'm good, Mala, did you have fun last night?"

"Yes, it was fun! And I worried for nothing; everything was great when I got home." Mala was lying.

"Are you okay? You sound a little bit frustrated."

"I'm good." Mala sighed

"No, you're not, what is it, what is going on?"

Mala hesitated. "Well, I got home last night and…"

"Washington wasn't there?" Noor said in a dramatic tone waiting for some juicy soap opera story.

"No, he was fast asleep," Mala replied cooliy.

"So?" Noor sounded disappointed at the direction of the story. It was going to be a boring one, she could feel it already.

"He was just there, asleep, and when I tried to wake him, he didn't even flinch. Can you believe that?"

"So what? He must have been tired."

"He's never like that."

Noor rolled her eyes, "You know he is a little over 50, right? And people get tired, right? Maybe he was just exhausted."

"I suppose you're right." Mala sighed again.

"I don't understand you, Mala. It seems like you're looking for some spectacle or something, I mean, if he didn't come home, then that would have been a different story, right?"

"Yes, of course, then I would definitely know that he was with someone else."

"Yeah, so what's the problem, he came home to you and the twins last night and fell asleep. So what…"

"He's never done that before; he always waits up for me."

"Well, there's a first time for everything… and stop manifesting these ridiculous things; otherwise they will really happen. Sharon used to remind us of that all the time. *You are what you think, bloody hell*," she said, imitating her sweet friend.

Mala smiled and again missed Sharon so much.

"Do you ever think of her, Noor?"

"All the time, Mala. I can't stop thinking about the way it ended and how I didn't even get to say goodbye to her. I have felt so guilty all the time. Not a day goes by that I don't miss that crazy spit fire."

Both ladies smiled. "I know, she really did bring us back down to reality so many times."

As a memory flooded her mind, Mala began to giggle uncontrollably. "Do you remember the time when she had that half Korean and half American boyfriend?"

"Yeah, she would always make him follow her around and then get irritated when he was around her... what was his name again?"

"Shuno."

"Yes, ha! And do you remember, every time she would want him to go away, she would say, *shoo, no?*" Mala and Noor were in hysterics.

Mala was imitating Sharon getting rid of Shuno by waving her hands and telling him to *shoo*.

"Why did we let her get away with being so sarcastic all the time? She is so lucky she didn't get into trouble." Noor was still smiling at Sharon's brash demeanour.

Mala looked down at the floor on her end of the line. "Do you think, if we had told her to stop smoking, she would have been with us longer?"

"You know what Mala, there is no such thing as counting the days of your lives. One day you could be here and the next you're buried, or in your case, burnt to ashes... we can't live everyday like we're afraid. We never know what's in store for us."

Mala's eyebrows moved a few millimetres above their normal position; she imagined staring, through the receiver, at Noor and sarcastically said, "Really now, Noor, since when did you become so philosophical?"

"Don't make fun of me, Mala. I was merely stating that if we don't live for the now, we will never be able to ever live in the moment and if we can't match our behaviour with our thoughts, then we might as well be dead."

Mala felt confused again. "What do you mean?"

"It's not rocket science, *bungy*, seriously, it really isn't. If you are not consistent with your thoughts and behaviour, then there is no use. We have to live in consistency every day and be the person we want to be by acting it out."

Mala couldn't resist replying, "I see, so lie to yourself and everyone around you every day?"

Noor was wondering why her friend wasn't comprehending her very civilised explanation of the power of now. She looked up to the sky and said, "You have to live for right now, because if you don't, no one else will do it for you. And if you keep counting every second that hasn't even happened yet, you will be forced to live in the past."

Mala was getting even more confused; her head had started to ache. "Noor, what are you reading?"

"What do you mean, *bungy*?"

Mala knew her friend very well. "Every time you read a new spiritual book, you become a preacher…"

Noor interrupted, "No I don't."

"You do."

"How?"

"You get all intricate about the universe and the power of now, and then you try to apply it to our lives so that you can help mend people with the art of what you read."

Noor rolled her eyes. "You, my dear, are not making any sense. What I was merely saying is that we have to live for the moment. And while we are living for that moment to swim, eat, fly, give birth, or whatever it is, we should make sure that we are wholeheartedly doing whatever it is we set out to do."

"I see, Noor." Mala was not buying any of this, because Noor could switch on and off like a light bulb when it came to consistency. She had no idea what she was talking about; she was merely being a parrot. "So, what book are you reading?"

"I'm reading a few."

"Okay, so let me rephrase my question, which book keeps you up at night?"

"*Friendship with God* by Neale Donald Walsh."

"I see," Mala said, imagining her friend like a lost child. "You need to finish the whole book, Noor. You have read this a few times and never finished. You should really get to the end; you will feel enlightened, empowered, loved and your vibration will be on a totally different level."

Noor spoke to Mala like a strict school teacher, "And I suppose you've read the whole book already?"

"Oh, yes I have," Mala smirked to herself, "four times front to back, right after Sharon passed away. The book was my only healer, my only prayer, and I felt like God was listening to me through the book."

"Wow."

"Yes."

"That's what I call the power of vibration, Noor. It was the most amazing feeling. And yes, I do totally understand what you are stating about the power of now, because this is the only time we have. We have to seize the day and make it happen."

"Yes."

"Yes."

Both women allowed a silence on the line, and coincidentally, if coincidence exists, Sharon was percolating in both of their minds. The celestial heavens through Mr Walsh opened-up in their subconsciousness and gave them some interesting insight into the power of friendship... with themselves... with each other... with family... with strangers... and ultimately with God.

Noor interrupted both of their thoughts. "That was a great conversation *Malsy*... I'm feeling better." She changed the subject. "So, when is your *mamaji* coming?"

Mala was looking forward to her mother visiting, because she knew Durga loved her grandchildren with all her heart; she had six and another one on the way. Mila was pregnant with her fifth child. Durga had requested that they have a family reunion soon because she wanted to introduce her daughters to Steve, her 'new' husband whom the sisters had never met.

Afterward, Noor thought about why she called Mala, and forgot that the reason she rang was to tell her about Christopher. Noor wondered if she should call her back, and then thought, that would be a whole new conversation. She wondered how he slipped her mind so easily. Maybe it was a blessing in disguise that she didn't mention him to Mala yet. She dialled his number and after a quick but warm conversation, agreed to meet him next week; at least she wasn't rushing, advice or otherwise.

Mala had Michael on top of her breast; he had been crying the whole night, and she had ultimately given in to him. She felt so sorry for her little baby and that night he snuggled up much closer to her. She gently moved him off her chest and snuggled up to his warm, soft body, his head rested right on her heart. She knew Michael was going to be a musician one day.

Shania was sound asleep in her basinet with a glow in her cheeks. She was the bigger twin and Mala knew that her baby daughter would be just as independent as she was: strong, focused, concise, and utilising all of her higher faculties to obtain what she desired. As Mala put her head down to sleep, she heard Washington come in; he was quite late again. He walked softly and gently into the bedroom and kissed Mala on her forehead. He smiled at his son.

"What happened, princess? He couldn't be away from you?" Washington was stroking Mala's jet-black hair.

"No babe, he just cried too much. I couldn't see him like that."

"You are a fantastic mother, babe. Now, go to sleep. I will be in soon." Washington kissed Mala on the lips and walked out of the bedroom. He went into the twin's room and kissed Shania a little bit harder than how he kissed Michael. She stirred, snored a little from her cute pug-shaped nose and turned over with a smile still on her face. Her cheeks were so rosy. Washington smiled at all of his blessings under one roof.

He opened his bag and placed his current piece of music on the dining table. He knew it was late, but he wanted to finish the composition soon so he could see Emilia play it for him one more time on the piano. He made himself a mocha with the new automatic coffee machine he had recently bought; having his own business allowed him such luxuries. The smell of chocolate percolated in the air. Washington's sweet tooth was getting the better of him every night, especially with creamy coffee drinks laced with sugar.

There was one note, though, that kept going off key. He couldn't quite place his ear on it, and it was taking him a long time to find the right sound. When Emilia had played today, the tone of the note was off, not centred – it needed some kind of melodic accompaniment. Emilia had suddenly become part of an intriguing melody that was driving Washington a little bit off course, although perhaps he was not willing to admit the temptation of this young beautiful intern.

Mala, on the other hand, began to feel content with her family and while the man of her dreams was making melodies with numbers and signs, she fell into a grateful and connected sleep. She dreamt of her twins and how they chose her. She smiled as Michael instinctively moved closer to his mother.

Chapter 19

Hong Kong

After her previous failure, Jennifer decided on a new approach. She took the ferry over to the island, and made an appointment with Stan. He remembered her from their last encounter, and was not amused with her rough demeanour; she seemed to switch from overly vulnerable to fanatical. This time she was crass when she spoke on the phone and apparently rather unaccustomed to the ways of city life and etiquette, especially Asian politeness. She was not in tune with the sophistication of protocol associated with the bank and the values they held as an upstanding establishment that dealt with people who mirrored sincerity and grace. Sadly, Jennifer was a poor representation of those tenets, and she definitely did not highlight Craig in a good light.

Stan agreed to meet her outside for lunch, but Jennifer insisted she come up to the office to speak to him in private again. She didn't believe that Craig was not in the office. Stan's current situation with his ex-wife and the emotional turmoil he was going through made him give in, because he didn't want to play any more games with this silly woman. He asked her to come up to his office after lunch to assure her that Craig was not in the office, and she could come and see for herself that he was not lying. He imagined her to be like a bulldozer and prepared himself for their meeting at 2:00 p.m. *Let's just get this over with*, he thought to himself.

In the meantime, Jennifer walked around Central and the Wan Chai area of the city on the island side of Hong Kong. She was horrified at the location because she could see massive signs advertising prostitution. Establishments called "Sticky Fingers" and "Midnight Galore" with offensive images jumped out at her. She quickly decided not to go deeper down that road and aimlessly walked back past Admiralty and then back into Central; she really had no idea where she was going. She gave up and stopped off at a McDonald's and waited patiently for 2:00 p.m. She looked at her watch. It was already 1:30.

Stan made a decision to stay in the office and asked Kitty to order him some noodles from the local Chinese restaurant. He wanted thick *ho fun* noodles with chicken and *choi sum*. He was going to miss all this wonderful food and the magic of Asia. He knew he couldn't stay any longer and couldn't wait for Craig's arrival back into Hong Kong. Stan was praying every day that Craig would take the offer and relieve him of his CEO position.

After he finished his noodles, Stan walked over to the mirror in his en suite office and washed his face. He asked Kitty to buzz him before Jennifer was allowed to enter his office. He also wanted a short rundown of her demeanour. Stan could always count on Kitty to find out information about people as well as suss them out. She was a great performer too, especially with her façade of Hello Kitty paraphernalia all over her desk, stationary, and life.

The buzzer rang and Stan put the phone on speaker.

"Yes, Kitty?"

"Yes, Mr Shtan, she is a vely clazy lady lah…"

"Okay Kitty, let's please be more professional, shall we?"

Kitty cleared her throat and put on her best British accent. Whenever she was excited or had 'juicy' information she would tend to speak in her *Chinglish* accent, which would irritate Stan. She began fanning herself with her Hello Kitty fan.

"She is a little bit scruffy Mr Stan… she looks like she has not slept

lah... in maybe five days lah... wahhhh, I low when a woman hasn't slept... she looks quite rough lah..."

Stan interrupted her. "Okay, okay... and was she rude?"

"Oh yes." Kitty was fanning harder.

"How? What did she do?" Stan asked, wondering if she was over exaggerating.

"She asked me where Mr Craig's desk is and then she just walked over to the desk and sat down in his chair and was looking around for some things. *Wahhh... so rude lah!*"

"Oh boy," Stan said, putting his face in his palms, wondering why he had agreed to see Jennifer and why he was getting himself into more trouble. He wanted to leave Hong Kong today.

"That's not all Mr Stan, I asked her to politely stay away from his desk, because there might be some private banking information in there, *lah*, and she turned around to me and told me to piss off."

"Oh boy, well, let's not fuel this meeting with anymore drama. Politely tell her to come into my office. Please just give me five minutes, Kitty. And whatever you do, don't make her mad, because I don't want to have to call security; that would be a blemish for Craig and we can't have any of that during these fragile times. Do you hear, Kitty?" Stan felt like he was Charlie talking to one of his angels from *Charlie's Angels*.

Kitty was desperately trying to keep up with what Stan was saying, because he had the propensity to speak faster and punctuate his native accent more when he was nervous. He was also very intelligent when he spoke, never speaking to any of his Asian employees in a manner that he thought that they couldn't understand. He spoke to everyone the same way, and never in a dumbed-down version. Befitting of his intelligence, he also spoke five languages, Mandarin being one of them. He would speak to some of his Chinese staff in Mandarin when he didn't want any of the other foreigners to under-stand what he was saying. He used the language as his buffer between the expat and local community. He wondered if he was going to have to dumb himself down to connect with Jennifer. He certainly didn't want to waste too much time with her.

As Kitty switched off the intercom, she looked at her watch. Hello Kitty's arms, on her fuchsia pink watch, would indicate to her when five minutes would be up so she could politely, with all of her *Asianess* and 'face,' tell Jennifer to kindly follow her into Stan's office. The countdown started and Kitty, like a pink CIA agent, peered through her pink cat carnage fan to execute Jennifer's delivery to Stan in a very dignified manner.

The hand struck on the fifth line right on the number three; five minutes had passed, Kitty got up from her desk and with her most famous smile, asked Jennifer to gently follow her into Stan's office.

Annoyed but not in the least bit perturbed, Jennifer followed with her bag in front of her, across her body, and her arms folded over her bag. She was a bit hunched and tried to stop biting her nails. She took her un-manicured hands out of her mouth straightened her hair and walked casually into Stan's office. His 850 square foot office overlooked the whole skyline of Kowloon Bay, with a spectacular view. The harbour in the distance glimmered with hope and sincerity. Stan motioned for Jennifer to sit down on the sofa, which was beside the meeting table. There were too many papers on the boardroom table, so instead he motioned for her to sit in a more comfortable part of his office. He motioned for Kitty to leave them alone and she closed the big oak door behind her, grinning as she left.

Jennifer sat down with her bag still in front of her body. She looked so uncomfortable, unfeminine and uneasy.

"Would you like some water, Ms…" Stan didn't even know her last name.

"Just Jennifer is fine, mate. Listen, I don't want to stay too long. I just want to know where Craig is." Jennifer was curt.

"I'm so sorry, I can't give out that information, as it is confidential and he has asked everyone here at the bank to keep his whereabouts…"

"A secret?" Jennifer's voice was beginning to get very loud.

"No… no, dear…" Stan sat down beside her on the sofa.

"Don't call me *dear*, mate. I just want to know where my *ex fiancé* is?"

Stan looked a little confused; he never knew that Craig had asked Jennifer for her hand in marriage."

"Fiancé?" Stan inquired.

"Yes, we were supposed to get married, Stan… and he didn't even come back to ask for my hand in marriage. He said he needed a break and some space and time to think, and he would come back to London and we would live together and start a family…" She was rambling, still clutching her bag.

Stan wanted to put his hands in his face again, but he resisted and combed his hair with his fingers. "Well, I don't know what to say Jennifer, he is not here at the moment, and I don't know what went on between you, and I am so sorry I can't be of any more help."

"Did you know her? Did you Stan? The little Chinese girl he was with? Do you know how it makes me feel to know that he had me waiting around in London? Do you?" Jennifer leaned closer to Stan; she was sitting on the edge of the sofa and her eyes started to look like marbles; glassy-like tears were stuck around the rims of her eyes.

"Like I said Jennifer, I wish I could help you, but I don't know what to say or do. What I can tell you is that I never saw Craig with a little Chinese girl." Stan knew Jennifer was referring to the Bloomberg girl. And he had to admit after that break up, he did see Craig with *a lot of little Asian girls.*

She started to cry. "You know Stan, it has been very difficult for me. Have you ever felt the sting of rejection right in your heart? Do you know what that feels like?"

"Yes… I do Jennifer, I really do…" Stan thought about his own divorce from Yuki. Or, more accurately, Yuki's divorce from him.

Jennifer wiped her tears. "You see, it's this side of the planet, mister; there is something here that makes me feel insecure… it's not like back home. There are too many foreigners here. It's like a constant cocktail party."

"Jennifer, you cannot blame race, culture, gender, Asian, white, economy… all of this doesn't add up. You really cannot put the blame on people. You have to reflect on yourself. You can't go around blaming everyone for your feelings. You chose to react this way. Who in their right mind would fly half-way across the planet to see someone who told them never to come back to this city?" He got up from the sofa and looked out the window. "Do yourself a favour, Jennifer. Move on. Don't dwell on what could have been, or what should I do now, or why didn't I do or say this before. All that stuff doesn't work. The *shoulds*, the *coulds*, and the *woulds* will never help you follow through. Do you see where I am coming from?" Stan turned back around to her as he noticed his tone was a bit on the 'banker' side.

Jennifer was getting sadder and sadder by the minute. She didn't know what to do anymore. She felt defeated again, resonating someone who kept lurking in danger, never understanding the consequences of her frightfully dark personality similar to an intense brew of coffee – a potent cup of espresso that had been warmed up too many times.

"I understand. I really do." She had nowhere to go, and she felt like she didn't belong anywhere. Not in Hong Kong, not in London, not anywhere, maybe not even in this world. She stood up slowly like a zombie and caught Stan's eyes. The reflection of her eyes shocked him because all he could see was a hollow, terrified, insecure woman looking right back at him.

He wondered what happened in Jennifer's childhood to have made her this way. But that was not where his mind wanted to go; her eyes revealed a very painful upbringing of abandonment and stress, topped with a very severe inferiority complex. Stan's heart felt a twinge, like his mind was trying to tell him something. His heart was trying to convey something to his intellect, that if he let Jennifer out of his office without seeing her again, she might do the unthinkable and then no one would ever see her again. The movie of that tragedy flashed in his mind like a horror story. He could already see the headlines:

> Jennifer Ball committed suicide in Hong Kong last night. After speaking to the CEO of a very reputable bank in Hong Kong, she walked to the top of the 60-storey building and jumped off with her white cloth bag still attached to her body. Inside the bag were articles of clothing and a picture of a man identified as Craig Matthews, who is also an employee at the bank.

Stan drifted back to reality and dragged his imagination out of the made-up news headline. He looked sincerely at Jennifer and said, "Let's meet for a coffee after work. You don't have to go anywhere Jennifer; if you would like to sit here and wait until I finish it won't take any longer than three hours. We can go have a chat in a more relaxed environment away from the office." Stan was speaking more out of fear than concern. He didn't need any distractions from his plan of leaving Asia and pacifying Jennifer at this moment in time was the best thing to do to ensure his strategy did not falter for Craig's promotion at the bank.

Jennifer looked even more deeply with her lost eyes into Stan's and an extremely faint glitter seemed to catch Stan's attention. She seemed to calm down a bit.

"So, what do you say? Coffee? After work?" Stan was beginning to sound like a negotiator; he definitely didn't want anything to happen to this woman, neither did he need his reputation or the bank's status on the line. It was quite a fine line to walk.

"Sure, Mr Stan." Jennifer looked slightly better seemingly, sitting up a little bit straighter.

"You can call me Stan, just Stan. Do you want to sit and wait here?"

A small grin flashed across her face. "No, I'll go have a walkabout, and meet you later."

"Okay, there is a very cute coffee shop up in the SoHo area, it's called *Meetings*… you can't miss it, it looks like a converted library.

We can have a nice chat over there and they have very good brewed coffee from all over the world. If you feel like it, they have this amazing vanilla cake made with apple crumble sauce." Stan managed a weak smile. He missed Yuki. Or was it just a female presence?

"Sure, Stan." A very small crease on the side of her lips assembled onto her face.

"Okay, so shall we meet at around six?" He looked at his watch, just a few more hours. "Would you like Kitty, my assistant, to take you around?"

Jennifer was taken aback; she couldn't quite figure out why Stan was being so kind to her. "That would be lovely, I hope she doesn't mind." Jennifer felt his kindness warm her up, ever so slightly, because she didn't feel like there had been much kindness in her own life of late.

She thought back to the first time she met Craig, his sophistication and soft demeanour was the exact opposite of her personality. In her mind, they lived a very simple life in London, until he got the job at the bank and then moved to Asia to be an expatriate. The break up between them, before he left for Hong Kong, was tumultuous and abrupt. She thought back to their breakup, which was still fresh in her mind.

∽

London

"Why do you have to leave? Jennifer was slightly tipsy. Again.

"I am going to test the waters Jen, see if we can both move to Asia, maybe we will have a better life."

"I told you, I don't want to go!" She was getting louder. She didn't want to leave the comfort of London.

"Why? You have never left Europe, it will be a nice... different experience."

"I still don't want to go, and if you're serious about marrying me one day, I want a confirmation as your fiancé."

"*Fiancé?*"

"*Yes,*" *Jennifer said boldly.* "*Why do you not have the balls to do that Craig? I always knew you were a bit of a pussy boy.*"

Craig was annoyed, and he wondered if marriage would ever be a fruitful endeavour between them. They had been arguing a lot lately and Jennifer's bottles of Malbec four times a week was not helping him make a clear decision to be with this woman. "*Well, Jennifer, we will have to wait and see.*"

"*I am going to tell everyone you are my fiancé.*"

"*What?*" *Craig was confused.*

"*Yes.*" *Jennifer looked smug, with her eyes slightly glazed over from the wine.*

"*Why?*"

"*Because I am right?*"

Craig didn't know what to say; he knew that when Jennifer was angry she would get into a rage, and this would lead to days of silence and make them extremely uncomfortable around each other.

"*Sure Jen, whatever you say.*" *He didn't want to talk to her anymore.*

"*Okay great, now that we are on the same page, I want you to leave me some money before you go, so I can make a few arrangements.*"

"*Like what?*" *Craig was feeling even more confused. What did she need money for?*

"*To make some arrangements, maybe for a new house and to come and visit you when you're there… in Asia.*"

Craig was insecure about the direction of the conversation and felt like Jennifer was blackmailing him for some reason. He didn't want any more arguments and gently pushed the idea away and said, "*When it's time for you to come and see me Jen, you can rest assured that I will pay for all of your expenses.*"

This statement, based on her tipsy perception, had gotten Craig in trouble later, when Jennifer demanded a semi pre-nuptial, even before they were engaged.

Jennifer snapped back to the present and heard Stan clarifying her question regarding babysitting from Kitty.

"No… no… not at all, I can tell her to take you to a few of the shopping centres around here, we even have a massive Marks and Spencer here for all of us folks who get homesick sometimes." Stan was trying to make connections to London and wondered if that was a good idea.

"That's nice." Jennifer was insipid, which was certainly out of character.

"So, I will just ask Kitty to get organised and I will see you at *Meetings*. She will drop you there at six. Okay?" Stan felt much better knowing that Jennifer was not going to be alone for the few hours he was not available to counsel this lost soul. He picked up the buzzer and spoke to Kitty in very eloquent Mandarin, about how she had an extra job today, and she would be in charge of looking after Jennifer for a few hours and drop her off at Meetings. Kitty obliged like a good pink angel and agreed to make Jennifer laugh and show her a very bright side of Asian culture. With the plan underway, Jennifer being in safe and secure hands, looked at Stan and said, "Thank you."

"My pleasure Ms Jennifer. I will see you later."

As the two women left the office, Stan felt like a father who had just rescued his daughter. He sighed, shut his office door and wondered where he had gone wrong in his own marriage. Stan knew his path had moved somewhere else and maybe meeting Jennifer today taught him about being instinctive and sincere with his relationships. Especially around women.

Chapter 20

London

Two weeks had gone by since the launch and Dave was still in London with Craig; there was so much work to do and Craig was in love with Sophia all over again. It was like a dance, like the tango but with a sense of British flair. Sexy and slow, yet conservative and fluid. Sophia yearned for Craig not to leave, and neither did she want her best friend to leave again. She wished both of them would stay in London with her forever.

Craig finally told Sophia all about his plans to leave the bank, and he revealed everything about Jennifer. Sophia didn't have a very good image of her and quickly realised Jennifer was not on her level. Craig admitted that he was scared to move back to London because he didn't know how volatile Jennifer would be, and how she would take the news. Sophia was a little bit taken back at why he hadn't even called her yet. She wondered if he just didn't want to have anything to do with that crazy woman, but she cautioned him about giving up his great career at the bank. One never knows what the future will bring after all.

Dave was getting ready to pack up and prepare for his next opening in Paris in six weeks. He had asked Sophia to please meet him there, and of course he wanted Craig to be there as well. One afternoon before he left, the three of them were sitting at Bazica, waiting for their coffees. Dave was gleaming like cupid; he had achieved what he planned. He had finally helped Sophia realise what it felt like to be in love wholeheartedly.

Craig and Sophia were holding hands under the table as Sophia beamed with delight. She was happy again and Dave had stopped calling her *grandma-ma*.

"So, when the both of you are back in Asia, are you going back to your evil ways?" Sophia was looking right at Craig.

"Not at all, for me now, it's working out how I can come back here. I have my speech for Stan all planned out," Craig said confidently.

Fatima delivered the coffees gracefully and elegantly to Sophia, Dave, and Craig.

"Thank you so much Fatima," Sophia said as she looked gently at the stunning Middle Eastern beauty.

"You are so welcome; I am here to serve you if you need anything else." She bowed slightly and walked away as her father summoned for her to deliver food and juice to Table Number 2 at the front.

"She is so lovely, that girl, what a delicate woman." Craig was impressed and sincerely felt like Fatima's presence made him feel serene and calm.

"I just had an idea," Dave said as he blew on his freshly brewed coffee made with African coffee beans. He closed his eyes as the aroma of the dark, steamy drink transported him home. His creative mind began to conjure up images of Fatima walking down the runway at the next show in Paris for the Christian Dior show. He closed his eyes and imagined a screen as the opening, and a still picture of Fatima's eyes encased by her silvery grey *burka*. He closed his eyes and then imagined her coming out in a couture dress still with the silvery grey *burka* on her head.

"What? What idea, Dave? You look so lost in thought," Sophia said.

Dave blew on his coffee again. "I am going to ask Fatima to be one of my models for the show in Paris."

"Really?" Sophia asked sarcastically, while laughing out loud.

"Do you think her father will ever let her out of this coffee shop?"

"It's an opportunity petal, and someone should help me talk to her about it."

"And who is that someone, Dave? Me?"

"Yes."

"Why me, Dave? Why?"

"Oh Sophia, don't be so downtrodden again. Think about the potential this girl has to change the world through self-image and perception. Can you see it now? Just close your eyes and imagine her walking down the catwalk with a couture dress on, her *burka* still on her delicate face and smoke – dry ice – coming up from behind as you see this stunning Muslim girl take the stage like a boss, like a woman of substance who is modern yet grounded in her ancient traditions, beautiful and magical and a fusion of the east and the west. Wow… imagine it." Dave was so excited; he could see every detail in his mind clearly, like it was already happening.

A moment passed before anyone said anything. Craig was first to say, "Wow." His imagination was floating on the same wave as Dave's. The image was universal, and had a clear image of people being on the same plane.

"That would be so amazing, Dave." Sophia was now also entranced by Dave's vivid description of using Fatima's beauty and culture as a symbol of art and respect for tradition.

"Sophia, are you going to help me talk to her now?" Dave asked with a little bit of cockiness in his voice.

"Yes, absolutely. I have a plan. I am going to tell her father that she will be accompanying me. And I'll see if Mala and Noor can come along as well. I know Noor has a house over there, so she is set, and Craig and I can stay together and Mala and Fatima can be together. It will work out. Benjamin, Fatima's dad, loves Mala. When do you need a confirmation?"

"I like your style, petal. I need to know ASAP, because I want to base my whole concept on multiculturalism and how we can all come together as one force to help each other, breaking down stereotypes. This is going to be such an amazing show. I would like your friend Noor to consider doing something for me at the Paris opening as well."

Sophia's mind was going into different places; it was so much fun helping Dave plan out his life. She wondered if being his personal assistant would be something that he could create for her, just so she wouldn't be so bored. She was jobless and needed some kind of mind stimulation. She was going to ask him right now, today actually, and find out what he would say. So, she blurted it all out at once.

"Wait Dave, you know I have been wondering, if I could possibly… maybe as an international liaison… like someone who could help you on this side of the world… and…"

Dave interrupted her and took the words right out of her mouth, "…and be my personal assistant for Europe and America?"

"Yes." Sophia looked like a little girl, beaming as if Dave truly understood her. "Would you consider it? Would you let me be your personal assistant?"

Dave looked into his coffee and said, "No, petal, I would never do that to you. It's not easy working with me."

Sophia sat back in her chair, disappointed. "Are you serious, Dave, what do you mean? You are one of the most consistent people I know. Why won't you let me have the job, do you think I don't have the wits to do it? I suggest you try me, and if I don't work out…"

Craig interrupted, "Fire her."

"Oi, Craig!" Sophia was getting slightly agitated, and wondered why Dave said no so quickly.

"Trust me Sophia, being with me as my muse is much better than working for me."

"I don't want to work *for* you, I want to work *with* you."

"Let me think about it." Dave finished his last sip of coffee and motioned for Fatima to give him the bill.

Sophia was sitting with her arms crossed. "I told you, you don't have to do that. We have a tab here."

"I know you do petal, but I just want to see this girl's gorgeous face one more time, and let's see if you can start negotiating with her about the beauty of breaking free and finding art in her culture and true self."

"You sound like a human trafficker." Sophia was sulking.

Craig started laughing. "You two really remind me of an old married couple."

"Listen to him, doesn't he sound like a scary creature, asking about her?"

"Actually, Sophia, not at all," Dave interjected. "It's not me being a scary creature. I'm thinking about it on your level. I see opportunity for this beautiful young lady. Opportunity for her to become a universal agent of change. Someone who can adjust the world."

"Profound Dave, I like it mate." Craig was nodding in approval.

Fatima came over to the table and Dave was once again lost in her silvery grey eyes.

"Thank you, Fatima, that *is* your name?"

"Yes sir…"

"Oh, please don't call me sir." Dave was looking down at the table.

"I am so sorry, I didn't mean to offend you, but this is the way I address all the male customers here at Bazica. My family and I wouldn't have it any other way… calling you sir was in no means a way to offend, but rather to show hospitality and manners."

Dave was looking up at her again, lost in her eyes. He looked like he was being hypnotised. She nodded slightly at him, and picked up the cups. "Your bill is there, sir…?"

Sophia answered on his behalf. "David."

"Thank you, Ms Sophia. I will remember the next time you are in here to have a coffee. Nice to meet you." And with that Fatima walked away.

"Wow," was all Craig managed to say again.

"She is absolutely stunning. She has to be in my art show." Dave looked over at Sophia. "Okay petal, if you can get her to Paris, and I can make my whole campaign about being people of the universe, then I will consider giving you the job as my European and American Liaison. How does that sound?"

"Fantastic," Craig responded on behalf of Sophia.

"Done. If I get this beauty to you in Paris, you can't *consider* the job. I want you to give it to me without hesitation."

"Fine. Now let's see if you can use all of your higher faculties including focus to help me with this campaign. And if you can think of anyone who would fit into this opening, showcasing different nationalities, religions, race, language, culture, whatever that makes us different… those are the kind of people I want."

Sophia interrupted his thoughts; she was thinking of her network of multicultural friends – Mala, Washington, Noor, even her own brother. She had this in the bag, she just didn't want to tell Dave just yet that all of her friends would fit in perfectly… she wanted him to stew a little bit. "I have a network of friends I know who would benefit from this amazing campaign."

"Good, now get to work. Craig and I leave in three days; Craig needs to get back to Hong Kong, and you and I have to start planning for the Paris show."

Sophia's mind was in full force. She was going to call Noor tomorrow to set up a meeting with her about the Paris show. This was going to be so much fun.

Chapter 21

London

Noor was sitting at a very posh Chinese restaurant with Christopher. The conversation was light, and full of humour. The previous night she posed as his model while he painted the structure of her face and shoulders. When he was painting, his eyes were glued to the canvas like a lion. He never let go of his goal, which was to find the exact beauty on Noor's face highlighted by time, lighting, and a flawless face of mixed beauty.

"The painting turned out so beautiful... I want you to see it after I have framed it."

"You are going to frame me?"

"Yes, and sell you." Christopher picked up a piece of vegetable with his chopstick and looked into Noor's eyes.

She didn't know whether to feel enamoured or insulted.

"Sell me?"

"Yes, sell you as a beautiful piece of art."

Her heart was definitely encased with admiration for Christopher and his ways. She tried to catch herself not going into the same direction she always did, which was one of struggle and over-bearing love and insecurity. She took a deep breath and made a decision to leave the old Noor behind; she unquestionably didn't want to make any more relationship mistakes.

"What is the matter? You look tense. Was it something I said?" Christopher put his chopsticks down and was genuinely concerned.

"No, it was not something you said, don't worry, it's just my thoughts getting the better of *me.*"

"What thoughts… you can tell me."

"Really?" Noor said, smiling coyly at him.

"Yes, of course, we are both artists here, and sometimes we can feel more than others, not to say that we are more superior, but our senses lead us, guide us, and then we create."

"I love how you use words to paint such a beautiful picture of life."

"Thank you. Now, what is bothering you?" Christopher sounded and looked like a humble sage, trying to encourage his apprentice.

Noor let out a huge sigh, like the ones she did when she was alone, a blowing sound and pursing her lips together to sound like a horn. Christopher started to giggle.

"What a cute sound. You definitely look frustrated, especially with those duck sounds."

Noor was giggling too.

"What do you say we hurry up with our dinner, and go have a glass of champagne around here somewhere?"

"That sounds like a plan."

"And you can reveal all of those sounds from your mouth into real words, and turn your sighs into sentences when we can speak over a drink. Doesn't that sound good?"

Noor was in love… already. "That sounds amazing, Christopher."

They paid the bill, left, and went down to *Eddie's* to have a glass of champagne.

Chapter 22

Hong Kong

Weeks had passed since his trip to London, and Dave was feeling very powerful that he had received confirmation for his model, Fatima, to help create a human-centred story for his catwalk. Dave was ecstatic. Work became a fury of globalisation, ideas flowing from country to country, with an array and fusion of colours flashing across his drawing pad. Colours and images on paper were always the beginning of his artistic gestation, and Dave knew his fashion sense for this show was going to blow the roof off Paris Fashion Week. While exhausting work – he couldn't remember being so tired – he was electrifying the fashion world with ideas of multiculturalism.

Weeks had passed since *his* trip to London, too, and Craig was feeling very giddy. He was jubilant that he was going to be with Sophia in London, or anywhere really. He couldn't wait to find a way to live with her and have a home with her. Craig couldn't wait for the changes around him to flourish. He was so impressed with Sophia's organisation for the Paris show, and how she used her charm to find all the appropriate people for Dave's presentation, including Fatima.

He was mesmerised by her authenticity and sincerity. She never used people for her advantage and always made everyone feel important. No wonder Bloomberg didn't want her to leave. She was an absolute asset and a people person who always managed to bring life and comfort into any situation.

Craig found out about Jennifer and wasn't surprised by her interaction with Stan. It didn't seem to phase him at all, because he had newfound strength and power that he never felt before. And he was always smiling. Everyone noticed, and Dave was always the first person to acknowledge his giddy schoolboy behaviour.

Craig and Dave were down at Dolce Vita again.

"You told Stan, and now everything is okay? And we have a deal that you are going to be my second muse in Paris, right?"

Craig was feeling a little bit uncomfortable again and his shoulders were near his ears above his head. He didn't know if he could make it to Paris for the show. He didn't want to live with Daniel Martin and neither did he want to go back and live in his parents' home. He was going to use the time to find a little apartment for him and Sophia. Perhaps adding to his discomfort above all, he had yet to give his resignation speech to Stan, who was getting antsy for an answer.

"Um… well…"

"Well what? What is the problem, your little love iguana is going to be there, and she will need your support. Look for a love pad, or a love shack later. After Paris."

"But where are we going to live?"

"The noble thing for you to do, Craig, is to ask for her hand in marriage and then ask her father, and then delicately take her out of her father's home into a love pad, but it won't actually be a love pad, it will be a home. A proper one with a husband and a wife."

Craig was feeling more uncomfortable. His shoulders were so high, his shoulder pads from his suit looked like wings above his head.

"Look at you Craig, your body language is telling me something again."

"What? What now, mate? Why are you always trying to analyse me… and Sophia… and people?"

"Because that's what I do, and it looks like you are about to lift off, take off into the atmosphere with your shoulder pads kissing your cheeks. Now, just relax. I know what the problem is."

"What? What is the problem, I have no problem whatsoever." Craig was shifting around in his seat, trying to look for a comfortable position.

"Yes, you do have a problem. And the problem is marriage. You have no sense of commitment and you want to live with Sophia first, test her out and then make the decision, right?"

"No." Craig was still feeling a bit uncomfortable.

"Of course you do. You can't commit to something you think is an absolute fantasy right now."

"Yes I can."

"Then marry her."

Craig still couldn't find a comfortable position; he was moving as well as shaking his leg. He tried to divert the conversation again, by looking behind Dave.

"Stop looking behind me, and focus on what I'm trying to tell you."

"I am focused, and no I am not scared of marriage, but yes you are somewhat right about me wanting to test things out first."

"But why?"

"Because I've been hurt and burnt and played all over the place, mate. I'm such a silly sod, I fall in love so easily. The last time I thought I was supposed to get married, I ended up running away because Jennifer turned out to be a crazy person."

Dave interrupted. "Upppp, upppp, uppp… let's not be rude to the needy, shall we? We need to help those who don't exercise higher faculties, and being mean and horrible to Jennifer is not the solution. We're not talking about her and she is a different circumstance from the past. C'mon, Craig, please focus… we are talking about Sophia here. She is not a Jennifer, or a Fatima, or a Mala, or a Noor; she is her own person, someone who has so much humility, dignity, and a person who takes pride in everything she does. Imagine for one moment Craig, just close your eyes for one moment and imagine her as your wife."

Craig closed his eyes and he saw the perfect picture in his mind… exactly like those cheesy American advertisements shamelessly trying to sell milk, or cheese, or bread, or even instant chocolate cake, where the wife is a homebody, yet sexy and flirty. In his mind, the vision of this woman had a very exotic flair.

"Okay, that's enough Craig, now open your eyes. I know the image in your head is so kitsch and cliché, that I can sense how corny you are being in your sub conscious right now."

Craig opened his eyes and sighed with a smile on his face. "I know, and I am certain I'm not ready for marriage." He sipped the last bit of his beer, got up and said, "I'm off Dave, I'm going running tomorrow, for the bank's annual marathon. This will be the last time I participate and I want to make it worthwhile." That's what he was telling himself, anyway.

Now it was Dave's turn to have a very unenlightened vision of Craig in his mind. He sipped the last of his beer, stood up, put his jacket on, and said, "Alright Rocky! Go get 'em." Both men parted and went on their ways.

As Dave walked towards the Peak Tram, he thought about his journey in Asia, and he felt a stinging pain in his heart, like someone had taken nail polish remover and wiped the front of his heart with a moist cotton bud of acetone. He had nothing in Hong Kong, except his work. With no play, Dave was becoming a very increasingly antsy man. He thought about moving to another part of Asia or maybe even somewhere in South America. The thought of London slipped through his mind, but he threw it away like an old train ticket floating in the wind. London was definitely not on the cards for him.

As Craig walked back to Happy Valley all the way from Central, the thought of marriage popped in and out of his brain in milliseconds. He was not pondering deeply about marriage at all. He wanted to live in a little cottage with Sophia with no strings attached, just pure love. He wondered what she would say. A few more weeks and he would be back in her arms in London.

On the other side of town, Stan was on a Skype call with Jennifer. He had no idea she would be so high maintenance and draining. He was desperate to get off the phone with her all the time, but something was pulling him back, something was making him feel like he had to rescue this poor woman. He was tired of living in two frequencies and wondered if he should tell Craig that he was beginning to feel harassed. The conversation had ended about Craig and now Stan felt like he was caught in Jennifer's web of entrapment, guilt, temperament, and a very rocky outlook... was it love? This is exactly what he didn't need. Jennifer was scheming to make Sophia's life miserable, along with the ghastly details she was revealing to Stan. The lengths at which she would go to rid Sophia – a woman she had never even met – of Craig's life was beginning to frighten Stan. Her jealousy was overpowering with a disillusioned idea of relationships.

After he finally got off the Skype call with her, he poured himself a whisky. It burnt the back of his throat; he squinted in pain, and tried to call his ex-wife. There was no answer. She had cut him off in every form.

Stan was in between two very venomous women, each looking for revenge. He scratched his head, and sighed. With nowhere to go he sat on the terrace of his beachfront home and pretended to pray. That night he began to understand how prayer was something he should have used a long time ago. He began to talk out loud and feel the pulse of himself reverberating to the universe his thoughts, feelings, and actions. Three whisky shots later, Stan was on the terrace staring at the night sky with tears in his eyes. The power of nature and all the energy and molecules it had to offer, resonated in his soul that night. He reflected and reassessed his life. He wondered what Craig's decision would be; Stan definitely needed to change everyone in his periphery, right away.

Chapter 23

Surrey

Alister was thinking about Sharon as he tended to his orchids. Some days he missed her so much, but talking to Mala made him feel less anxious about death. She was the only one who knew how to pacify him when he was feeling low. Not even Sophia could help him manage the pain of his loss. They had promised to be together when she got out of the hospital and be in a relationship for years and years. She was so real, and raw, and so humbling to be around. Her hard sense of reality always made him feel like he had structure; he had fallen in love with Sharon and she had left a massive void in his heart.

He went inside and called up Mala.

As usual, she was soft in her tone and comforted him, and she told him stories about their friend that made Alister happier.

"There was this other time that we went to this bistro in New York and she was lecturing someone, and you know Sharon, she always finds a victim, someone who needed a spiritual washing and cleansing with words, and the victim happened to be a body builder from some wrestling foundation. She proceeded to tell him that he was fake, and all his moves were acting.

Mala's mind moved to the scene that day.

New York

"So, you're telling me mate, that your big burly body jumps on top of people and you don't kill them?"

"Yeah, it's technique."

"What bloody technique? Go on, tell us, what is it that makes you so bloody special?" Sharon was barely past the man's knee. He was a gargantuan man with thick strong arms. He could crush Sharon with his bare hands if he desired. But in true Sharon style, she never gave in and was always up for a challenge.

The man, named Bandit Bob, was dressed like a cowboy and a pirate – it was bizarre. He showed a lot of skin, but he looked like a cross between someone from the high seas and the mid-Western prairies.

"Bob, right? That's your name, right mate?"

"Yep," he grumbled at the tiny redhead.

"So, Bob, tell us, with your big ghastly body, how come you don't manage to kill anyone, you just look like one of those bouncy toys, bouncing up and down like a dodo?"

Bob, annoyed, leaned in closer to Sharon, and his shadow seemed to engulf the whole space, like a shade-giving tree. She was not phased one bit.

"Don't call me a dodo, and no it's not an act, I am not an actor, I am a fighter."

"I see," Sharon said pulling a cigarette out of her bag.

At that moment Bob was irritated and grabbed the cigarette out of her hand, "This will kill you one day little lady, if I don't."

Sharon coughed. "Are you bloody threatening me, Bob? Did you just say you wanted to kill me?"

Mala leaned in to her friend and whispered, "I think it's time to go, Sharon, we don't need to get into the nitty gritty of how anyone is going to die today."

Sharon nudged her arm away and scowled, "I'd like to see this big lump try and wrestle with me."

Bob was in hysterics, "You should be careful what you wish for little lady. Some force might punch you where it hurts and you won't even know what hit you."

Sharon was getting more and more agitated; she was not going to let the wrestler get the last word.

"I see, so why don't we go on a date then, an ass kicking date where I come here, and you show everyone how you are going to punch me where the universe don't shine? Huh?"

Bob was in hysterics.

"What is so funny?"

"You are hilarious. How about a coffee sometime, that would be easier than us going into the ring together?"

"Who do you think you are, you big beast of an actor? I refuse to go out with you anywhere, until you admit that all that malarkey you do in the ring is fake."

"Why would I do that?" Bob looked over at Mala and said, "This one's a real spit fire you know... what are you going to do with her?" He was chuckling even more.

Mala managed a very weak smile. "I think we should go now." She pulled Sharon towards her and smiled timidly at Bob.

"Right, I have a great idea Bob, why don't we go on a date in the ring. I want you to pretend that I am a contestant and you pretend to kill me." Sharon was still instigating the situation.

"Great idea, red head." Bob picked her up with one hand and cradled her like a puppy in his arms. The whole time Sharon was smoking; it really looked like something out of a comedy sketch. Mala had her palms on her face but continued to stare at the scene through her interspersed fingers, which were supposed to be covering her eyes.

Bob was using Sharon as a dumbbell as he lifted her up and down like an object. She was giggling the whole time, still with a cigarette hanging out of her mouth.

That night, after Bob had promised to introduce Sharon as his 'playmate' on stage, they both managed to have a drink after the match. Fighter lifestyle and his need to treat Sharon like a dumbbell became unappealing and tiresome for her after a while, and after a month of travelling around the US to be his side kick, Sharon got bored and came back to Boston. She was done, but no worse for the wear; she liked a good fling.

✍

Surrey

Mala told Alister the story over the phone, as he imagined Sharon as a popular wrestler for a month. When Alister laughed, it was definitely from his heart. When he got off the phone with Mala, he was feeling lighter and more in control of his feelings.

Mala, on the other hand, was feeling like someone had stolen her divine melody. The aching in her heart was making her feel very insecure, and her longing for Sharon to be alive was beginning to consume her more frequently. She thought about writing down her feelings, but never had time anymore. The days she would write made her feel better; it allowed her to release something inside her that needed to be unleashed.

Mala remembered back to her days in Boston, when one night she was so angry, she took a big red marker and wrote in her notebook, "Blood is blood son," a meaningless statement representative of her frustration. And just that one statement made her feel a little bit lighter and a bit more connected to something she thought was family. Mala thought about why her heart was so heavy, and tried to erase the image from her mind. On her way to *Moti's* one day, she stopped at the park and saw Washington sitting on a bench looking at his music score, with a very young girl. Again not wanting jealousy to get the better of her, she began wondering why he was sitting with another girl so openly in the park for everyone to see. Jealousy was not a good emotion and whenever she became bitter, a very ugly side of her character would emerge. She didn't want to keep going over and over in her mind about the young girl sitting next to Washington.

When he got home that night, he was absolutely normal, very happy, loving and wanted to spend time with Mala. Nothing seemed off kilter. Emilia was his student after all and they were probably discussing the technical aspect of his music in a clean and refreshing environment. She had to give him the benefit of the doubt because he was home and she didn't want to make a big deal about something so small. Or so she thought.

She took a deep breath and continued with her chores. She looked at Michael and realised that his petite frame and his minor disability still made him the cutest little black boy ever. Whether or not she admitted it, he was Mala's favourite child in the whole world and nothing more than a cute saliva-infested smile from him would make her heart melt into a million pieces. When he was born Michael had a shorter right leg, and this meant that this leg would be stunted for the rest of his life. He probably would not be able to walk the same time as Shania, the doctor announced when he was born. Mala's feisty tigress and the stinging pain of her mother's words regarding disability made her believe that her little boy would indeed run one day and would be an excellent sportsman. Only time would tell, and with the strength of love and healing, Michael would grow up to be an amazing man.

As the months wore on, she and Washington started to drift slowly apart, and Mala could see that age was creeping up on everyone around her. She looked at Washington and realised that he was already 50 something, and when her mother came into her head, she felt like time had been wasted between them. The lines on her face grew deeper and her supple skin was beginning to lose its elasticity and strength; her tiredness was apparent and obvious around her eyes. The thought of Mala losing anyone else in her life made her core resonate with fear. She knew that death was a way to birth and that through death indeed life would emerge, however, she believed that strength, patience, perseverance and ultimately love were the pillars and the foundations of life holding the pieces of our fragile minds together.

Paris

The Paris opening and show finally arrived. They were marvellous and heralded in a feeling of new beginnings and a new life for Fatima. She was the talk of the town, as was Noor. It was spectacular, and Mala was thankful that Washington had supported her choice to go for three days. Dave's dramatic and theatrical layout of the whole production was pristine and thought provoking, while leading to some very interesting stares and grumbles from the older generation – Dave's generation, in fact. Mala found it fascinating that after some of the older sponsors found out how old actually Dave was, they nodded with approval, and didn't brand his show as kid-like, high strung, millennial and cliché. They actually thought the theme of universality gave way to a more spiritual air for fashion week. Dave was extremely pleased, and after this show, he was going to take a very long hiatus and go to Greece for a few months. He needed the rest, and some relaxation after working so hard, as it was starting to show; Sophia, his only true confidant, had noticed, and as the Paris events came to a close, she gently insinuated as much – he wasn't eighteen anymore, after all. They both knew that if he hoped to stay healthy at his age, giving 110% nonstop wasn't an option.

Noor was very much with Christopher, and they were flying all over the world for his art projects. She was in her element, and her connection with her father was limited to his various travel-related requests. She was feeling more comfortable in her new skin and feeling very enamoured by her Oriental hunk. They were glamourous when they walked into the room together and people would stare and smile. They both looked clean, pristine, wholesome and most of all, very sincere. Christopher had proven to be exactly what Noor needed. Mala and Sophia were, as usual, somewhat worried about the speed of her connection with him, as well as her label of him as her "boyfriend" after only a few weeks. However, Mala, knowing her friend and her antics, could sense, again, that there was something not quite right between the two. Christopher was much more genuine and confident than Noor and she felt like Noor's conniving and sly nature would emerge somehow in the not so distant future...

Jennifer was still back and forth from Hong Kong to London, wasting all of the money Craig had given her. This time she was caught in a web with Stan and his ex-wife. The relationship between these three people was getting sticky, heavy and was going to cause an unavoidable crash in the cosmic force. No one understood how these three landed up together, but there is a belief that whatever you ask for will come to you. All three people, Stan, Jennifer and Yuki, had one plan, whether they knew it or not: to destroy each other.

Time moved on at its unavoidable pace, stopping for no one, and the interwoven fabric of everyone's lives was bound to experience unexpected ripples. No matter where they were in the world, there was something pulling at the very threads of life... for better or for worse.

Part 3

The Poetry of Time

Chapter 24

Somewhere in the Universe

Ten years passed in seemingly an instant, and everyone's lives seemed to be moving in clear and concise directions, with few issues and no drama; everyone was working towards perfect harmony and balance in their lives, which undoubtedly made it feel like they were all on the right course.

Sophia and Craig got married in the summer in London and moved back to Hong Kong, where Craig had eventually agreed to take over Stan's position. After much discussion and planning for the future, Sophia and Craig finally decided that the most feasible place for them to live together, with an abundance of money, was to go back to Asia. It was a bit difficult for Sophia, once again, to change her thinking – even eating her staunch words of refusal to ever return to Hong Kong – but this time she eased into her new life with no complaints; instead, she did so with the maturity of a married woman. Craig realised that it wasn't his location of residence that had given him so much turmoil, but rather the company he kept; when all was said and done, he was glad not to have rejected Stan's offer.

Stan left Hong Kong and became entrapped by Jennifer. She had somehow managed to use her manipulative charm to marry Stan, and his overflowing stash of money was helping her create more havoc between people and their relationships. She managed to fight against Yuki in a gruesome court battle over Stan's finances, creating a quick process of aging for the poor man. Jennifer, with her shrewd nature and brash style, was very precise in her actions, her hidden agenda being to utilise Stan's money for revenge against Craig… somehow.

Craig was bemused by the turn of events and had warned Stan about Jennifer and her very volatile ways. Something about Jennifer aroused Stan's dark side, and it had become difficult to communicate with both Jennifer and Yuki; Craig had given up.

Alister's path to recovery eventually led him to move out and get an apartment of his own near his father, and Daniel Martin was once again all alone again in his peaceful Surrey house. He missed Sophia and her presence but in his heart, he knew that his daughter had to move on.

Mala and Washington and the twins grew together as a family everyday as *friends*, and although Washington tried to include Emilia in a few of their family gatherings, Mala's decision to oust Emilia from her life was steadfast with rock solid clarity. She felt betrayed by the *musical witch*, and didn't want to see her if it wasn't necessary. As long as she and Washington remained friends and looked after their children with respect, gratitude and humility, Mala was okay with that. She never thought that the two of them would ever live apart, and the love she felt for him was like no other.

However, as time wore on, fascinations changed. Washington realised he couldn't talk to Mala like a twenty-one-year-old anymore, and the passion he had for her as his 'little girl,' began to die. It was Mala who eventually demanded the separation and thought it was the best for them at the moment. The word divorce came up twice in the decade they had been separated, but both decided it was the best option to remain married, yet live separately with integrity. Mala had to admit that maybe somewhere in her heart, she would rediscover her soft spot that would make her melt when Washington looked at her, but for now, her heart had hardened like rock, almost impenetrable. She didn't ever want to be betrayed again, and Emilia was Washington's biggest betrayal as well as mistake. Mala realised she was not put on earth to judge anyone, because she wanted to love, teach and heal, and that is exactly how Mala was going to spend her days with her two amazing children.

And like the stars had planned for her, and as the universe listened to her, Michael was walking with a half limp and with one leg brace instead of two. She hoped Michael would be able to play on the basketball team by the time he was fifteen. He took his first step at four, and from then on Mala was on the case to make sure he was constantly moving forward. Shania helped her brother every step of the way, and proved to be a very intellectual person. Her mother hoped she would use books as well as writing to help her with the power of change.

Noor and Christopher were still travelling the world, yet something was amiss. The pair had been across and around the globe, increasingly trotting around for Noor's father rather than for Christopher's art. The notion of completely settling down was still not in the cards for Noor.

Dave was back in Hong Kong after his long holiday. Instead of a couple of months, he took eight off, and visited London again in the summer for Sophia's and Craig's wedding. After the fashion show, Fatima was an international superstar for one moment in her life, but was swiftly dragged back to her old frequency as a waitress. If Dave had the energy he would have done more PR for her, but he was simply too tired, and Mala couldn't act on Fatima's behalf alone. Everyone was happy, free, and living and as they do… as everyone does, doing their best to avoid any bumps in the road along the way.

At Bazica one fine morning, Noor, Mala, 11-year-old Michael and Shania, and "Uncle Al" were sitting at Table Number 8 wondering where life had taken them. Over a decade had passed by since Sharon's passing, and although some things had shifted like growth, acceptance and metamorphosis, inevitable episodes of age were proving to cause some pain. Durga was almost eighty, and Dave was already in his early seventies – although he naturally would never admit it. And while all these individuals were contemplating how much they had moved on in their lives, the stinging realisation that not every-thing is constant gave them a sense of sadness as well as acceptance. Nothing lasts forever and this was a time of pure reflection.

The madness of their lives had caught up with some of them while the internal conversations of each person revealed a script that no one would ever know. Independently, they had each decided to write down something in their lives that mirrored impact. Some of them would state the obvious and some would be raw and real, while others would hide behind a façade of guilt and shame. And on the anniversary of Sharon's death, the friends were going to meet up and reveal their own personal scripts. It was a memorial between them, meant to give each person the stability, control and demeanour to move on through life with the idea of change and new-found perception. They needed some healing before the next stage of their lives, and they knew that they would all count on each other, as the curtain and lights would begin to fade on some of their connections and relationships.

Chapter 25

London

They agreed to meet… to commemorate… 30 years of friendship for some of them, and tonight was the night they all had something rather meaningful to say, deciding to congregate at Mala's. She was still in Hammersmith, but had upgraded to a much bigger apartment, because the twins needed space. She bought the old flat from the owner and used it to collect rent from Emilia and Washington. She also gave up her flat in California for rent, allowing her a comfortable life as a landlady.

"Mum!! Mum!!!" Michael was screaming down the hallway for some soap.

"Yes! What is it?"

"Soap, Mum, soap!!!"

Mala was already a bit agitated at Michael; he never checked anything and would depend on others to help him with simple tasks too much. Mala disliked his disorganisation and sighed.

"Next time, please check what you need before you get into the shower. I am having everyone over tonight and Kumari and I are busy in the kitchen." Ten years on, Kumari was now as much a part of the family as anyone, and Mala often reflected on the blessing of finding her.

"Ya ya, sorry Mum."

Michael's beautiful face and thick Central London accent was going to melt a lot of hearts. Mala smiled at her handsome son. His skin was glowing like a rich café mocha. Shania was studying, rolling her eyes. The feisty one of the two, Shania decided that she was going to go down to the local library to study while Mala and her friends pretended to be Celtic witches. Shania giggled at her own thoughts.

The three family members were getting ready to have their own fun on a Friday night, whether it was being a nerd at the library, or playing video games at a friend's house, or commemorating a passing of a friend, each one was content to be in their own zone. Washington, on the other hand, was feeling irritated, again, that he couldn't find the right note in a score he had written. He and Emilia tried so hard to find the perfect sound and melody to introduce the chorus into a song he was composing for a new musical on the West End. He missed his children and didn't want to be apart from them, but this was the life he had chosen, and temptation is a very devilish concept. Emilia was like Eve and had enticed him for so many years, so why couldn't she help him with the divine melody now? What was her problem? She was losing sight of poor Washington, and her still young flirtatious and very bouncy character was beginning to make the old man from Barbados very, very tired.

"Mum, what time are your friends coming over?" Shania was asking in a sweet tender voice. She knew her mother wouldn't let her be out too late, and she hated the 'Indian Mum' in her... she didn't actually hate it, she just never got used to it, and always took refuge with her father when Mala was getting all *auntyji* in her face. Washington believed in freedom and allowing his children to explore the big wide world. On the other hand, Mala was more conservative and exceedingly protective over her children. She wondered if she was turning into Durga junior. She sometimes felt the urge to pull her ears, and quickly caught herself and stopped. Mala shook her head. She was not going to indulge in ear pulling no matter what circumstance was thrown her way.

"My friends will be here in about an hour, so I have time to drop you to the library..."

Shania, feeling all together antsy and irritated, retorted by saying, "You know Mum, I am almost a teenager, and the library is just down the street, why can't you just let me go? Huh? It's like 35 steps away."

"That's great, so next time you can walk, but today I will drop you."

"But Mum…"

"Please Shania, just don't worry me. One day you will know how I feel."

Shania grumbled and mumbled something under her breath while realising she had absolutely no idea what her mother was talking about. All that was going through her mind was how dramatic her mother was being. Again.

Mala finished up in the kitchen getting ready for her friends' arrivals. She had written her script last week, then changed it twice, and then wrote it again forty-five minutes before everyone's entrance. She hoped it would be okay, and prayed that no one would get offended. She invited Washington as well since has was the same soul family and once again Mala made it very clear that Emilia was not welcome to this very personal event. Emilia was definitely not in their soul family, and Mala wondered how she had been able to penetrate into their little cluster of love. It was beyond Mala how the universe had allowed her to make her way into the Cannelli household. Maybe it was Mala's fault, maybe she didn't give Washington enough attention, or hadn't any energy for him at the end of the day. Nevertheless, he was the father of her children, and on Sharon's memorial passing, he had to be present. Mala lit the candles, lit the love and light corners of her house, lit some vanilla and patchouli incense, listened to her *Hundred Thousand Angels* CD and waited for her friends… it was almost time.

Chapter 26

South East Asia

While Mala was getting ready for her friends and reconstructing her thoughts, Sophia and Craig were in their Deep Water Bay house overlooking the ocean. Craig's high position at the bank allowed him the salary to afford a house on a hill, overlooking the bay – something few in Hong Kong could dream of affording. He had his arms wrapped tenderly around her waist, standing behind her, as her scent caressed and tickled his nose. He looked at the stunning view and couldn't believe how the cosmos had brought them back together.

She was living like an elegant *Tai Tai*, on Craig's arm. She was also committed to looking after Dave and making sure that his now 'part time' position at Christian Dior was truly *part time*. She had finally convinced him that it was time to cut back on his ridiculous work hours, especially considering his condition and his advancing years. Sophia was his muse through and through, and no matter what happened, the universe had always brought her and Dave back together; with him by her side, Sophia knew she was always safe.

Sophia looked out to the view with Max and Josie by her feet; they weren't as spry as they used to be, and no longer moved with ease, but her best feline friends still served as a constant in her life. As she enjoyed the view, she realised pressure on herself, to always make a sharp steer from sheer stubbornness, was always her fault. She stopped fighting with the forces of nature and embraced her life wholeheartedly in Asia as her destiny. She hugged Craig tighter and committed to stop worrying about Jennifer, Stan, and Yuki.

Those three had been harassers over the decade and lived in a cesspool of hate, destruction, and pure greed. Yuki's plan was to destroy Stan and make sure he would bestow his fortune to her, and Jennifer's evil force was jealousy. She got Stan wrapped around her suicidal finger and had coaxed him to move back to London to live with her. Yuki was in Hong Kong with a part of Stan's fortune – as Craig and Sophia's neighbour. Yuki was the epitome of a Japanese *Tai Tai*. She feigned decorum, grace, and used her Samurai intuition and skill to execute her plan with Stan. Jennifer, in Yuki's eyes, was like a deflated ninja warrior with no ammunition. Her Asian prowess and her selfish desires pushed Stan and Jennifer back to the colder side of the world.

Sophia didn't want to think about those three anymore; she visualised them as bandits caught up in a very unappealing movie. Their theme was centred and based around abuse of the human spirit, and abuse of each other.

The soft Hong Kong breeze languidly stretched across Sophia's shoulders. She looked up at Craig and spoke.

"Love, do you know that I actually don't miss Surrey at all, and I can't believe how time has flown right past us. There are so many memories… obstacles… heartaches… failures… and it's all worth it in the end, because you can say that you tried very hard to reach the summit, and you did."

Craig smiled at her long-winded explanation of 'comfort.' "I know what you mean love, it is a blessed feeling to just feel content and happy where you are." Somehow, Craig had managed to do what Stan could not – maintain a healthy work/life balance, and enjoy the fruits of his labour.

"Agreed, and no matter where we are, we have to feel like we are doing the right thing."

"Yes."

"Yes."

They hugged each other tighter and smiled into the atmosphere as Max and Josie purred at their feet.

Sophia knew a short decade had passed since she met Sharon, Noor, and Mala. She remembered that today was the day of her passing. She closed her eyes even tighter and prayed for Sharon's soul to forever live in everyone's hearts. And in silent prayer, she asked for the safety of her brother; she would call him in a few days, and wondered what he was doing today.

✑

Somewhere in the Universe

The years had flown by into an abyss and the same melodies and movies for some of the women were on auto rewind, or just stuck on play and looping. It seems to be a philosophical constant, that with the end of something indeed brings beginnings. After over ten years of the same movie, boredom and dissatisfaction were rearing their heads for another life shift, although perspective for some of the friends was very hard to see. Age brought beauty and renewal as well as a newfound outlook on birth, but it also brought the beginning of drastic change, a movement that required reflection and understanding all over again. As time passed, it was clear that beginnings and endings were not that dissimilar to one another. Somehow subconsciously, this wisdom encouraged them to engage again in a direction of speed, growth, and hopefully fulfilment.

And while some embrace change, the rest of the world resists what is a God given creation, until it's time to evolve and change again. And again. And again...

Chapter 27

London

The day before Sharon's memorial, Noor was with Christopher in her flat. He was painting again as she sashayed around her apartment in a stunning light blue silk kimono with a yellow dragon embroidered across the back. It was her favourite attire when she got out of bed, and right before she got into bed.

"Chris, you know my father is coming again…"

Christopher interrupted, a little bit agitated. "Yes, so…"

"Well, he has asked if we can go to Russia for him on another trip."

Christopher put his paintbrush down, unbuttoned his raw silk shirt, and looked at Annabelle. He was tired of the same conversation, and finally decided to be bold and direct about his opinions. "You know what my dear, I think I'm tired of being your father's pet. I am also so tired of living here in this house with you, like your possession, and I have made a decision that I'm not going to do any more dirty work for your father. It's…" he couldn't bring himself to say the words, but he blurted it out once and for all today, and he made sure that Noor was paying attention… "Money laundering, Annabelle." He looked around to make sure, there were no visions of ears sprouting out of the walls, and continued quietly. "Your father uses you to launder his fortune all over the world."

Annabelle was shocked by Christopher's outburst. They had had a similar conversation over and over again, although he had never been so blunt. She didn't know how to pacify him. In her mind, carrying $85,000 in her luggage and pocket was not money laundering. She explained to Christopher a countless number of times, that her *Pitajee* was giving her pocket money.

On one occasion when the topic came up about Noor's pocket money, Christopher listened to her pathetic explanation and cover up. He laughed in her face, and abruptly left the apartment with his linen shirt unbuttoned from sweating over Noor's ridiculousness. Noor just didn't get it.

"It is not money laundering, and we are doing ourselves a favour. The money is ultimately for us; we are just merely helping him store it."

"Well… I don't want to have anything more to do with this… absolutely nothing, and if you want me to be around, you will have to tell your father to start respecting me as a man first, and then as an artist, and then as an equal… he has to stop referring to me as 'China man.' He thinks it's funny, but I don't like it."

Noor grinned. "He is old…"

"And very foolish." Christopher continued, "I am not doing his dirty work for him anymore. It's been ten long years of this nonsense… and I feel…" Christopher looked down at his paintbrush. He wanted to paint a different picture, like the cartoon from *Ah Ha's, Take on Me* music video and run into another dimension, an animated space full of freedom and adventure. He didn't sign up for this kind of voyage, following Annabelle Noor around the world like a puppy, being introduced to her family and friends as the "Chinese Artist." He was getting increasingly more annoyed, and the more he tried to fight how he was feeling, the deeper he entangled himself into a web of entrapment and habit.

"What is the matter Chris? Why are you getting all heated and angry again?" Noor sashayed back to him in her powder blue silk gown. Her body somehow looked better and better every day, even after all these years. She never stopped working out and the muscles on her fifty-year-old body were strong, enhanced, sexy and full of playful delight. Noor had the most amazing sex appeal, she was giving, but also courageous and enticing in bed. She knew how to use her red *chakra* for perfection and balance in the physical world. In the past, she would have sulked and ate copious amounts of chocolate, but nowadays, she was more simple, less uptight, and didn't feel the need to overly protect herself. Noor knew in her heart that if she and Christopher were not meant to be, even after ten years, she was okay with the outcome of the consequence.

"I am just not happy with this life anymore."

Noor felt bad. Did she know that it was coming, because she manifested this for herself?

Christopher picked up his paintbrush and waved it in Noor's direction, as if the tool was part of his speech and symphony for renewal. This was the most riled up Noor had ever seen Christopher. His voice was exactly the same level that he spoke all the time, however, this time she could feel the trembling of his heart, the nervousness of his actions, and the pain of all his lack of decision-making.

He gracefully pointed the brush at her, like a symphony conductor, and said, "I have to leave Annabelle. I am so sorry I'm doing this to you, but I really have to be on my way. I have to make a move and just find myself. I'm going back to the Bay Area. When my mother passed away she left me an apartment there, and I need some space and time… to think… and paint…"

Noor thought back to the first day she saw Christopher paint, when he painted her face ten years ago. She knew he was an ancient dignified soul. "I understand, Christopher. I really do. And if you need me, you know that I will be here in London, or maybe Paris, or New York…"

He interjected again. "Or Russia, or Pakistan, or India, or Japan, or Thailand… the list of where you might be goes on and on. London is just your headquarters for you to scheme and plan, to envision how you can hoard your father's money. You don't have a business. Your business is about being sneaky."

Noor was beginning to feel extremely hurt and a bit angry; she could feel the heat rise to her head, as she thought of the ten years they had been together. Why was he talking to her like this, in this manner of rudeness?

"Sneaky? Who do you think you are, speaking to me like this? We have travelled all over the world doing things and exploring the world together, just like how we discussed when we started to 'consciously couple'... whatever the hell that means." Noor was getting distressed as her thyroid started to wobble in her neck, that was a sign of extreme self-protection. She wanted to grab a candy bar, but instead walked away and took five deep breaths. She didn't want this to end in an ugly manner and neither did she want to lose Christopher as a friend. A decade is short, but when you live with someone, time seems endless, carefree, steadfast, knowing that the person will always be there. But like one swoop of universal energy a frequency can change, and this was happening to Noor at this precise moment in time. Again.

"I'm sorry Annabelle, so sorry." He put his paintbrush down and extended his arms to hug her. She reluctantly came closer and they squeezed each other chest to chest almost like brother and sister. Age had given Annabelle calmness. In the past, she would have been wailing and projecting herself as an injured soul. He released his grip, kissed her softly on her forehead and said, "I will come back soon, but right now I need to be alone. You can call me anytime Annabelle, I will always be there for you. Always."

Noor did not cry because Christopher's hug helped her stop trembling and the reverberating in her thyroid stopped making music in her neck. As she looked at Christopher with her soft beautiful eyes, she said, once again, in her enchanting Persian tone, "I understand."

They made sweet tender love that night as *Sade* played in the background; her caramel voice and honey sweet tone transported the lovers through a vortex of the divine melody, cascading their thoughts into an abyss of relaxation, release, and pure tender love.

ↂ

In the morning, Christopher was gone.

Noor didn't fuss or fume, or turn into a horrendous dragon. She slowly eased herself out of bed and went about her morning rituals as normal.

She took out her pendulum and asked again: *Is Christopher the right fit for me?*

And like day turns into night, the pendulum swung to the left, indicating no. It had been ten long years of her fighting the pendulum and its answers back to her, but today she let it be right. Her daily question had finally come to fruition with the realisation that she could not go against what destiny had already laid out for her.

As she sat contemplating with the beautiful pendulum in her hand emanating fractals of light, she decided to call Mala.

"*Aunty*, it happened again."

"What happened?"

"We are done."

"Who?"

"Mala… Christopher and I."

"What? Why? Really?" Mala thought back to her days in Boston when the words would cascade from her mouth with wonderment and shock. "Why? What Happened?"

"Mala, will you stop repeating yourself please? It's one of the most irritating traits you have, and every time you get excited or happy or distraught, you're repetitive and it can sound annoying. I'm sure, in the past, Washington appreciated your repetition, in his ear, in bed, but right now your incessant whinging of *why* and *what* is annoying me, so may I please continue?"

Mala caught herself sounding like a lost teenager. She knew exactly what Noor was talking about, so she cleared her throat and spoke with composure and grace. "Sure Noor, tell me, what's going on?"

The weight of the situation with Christopher was beginning to sink in. She suddenly burst into hysteric giggles on the phone until tears were streaming down her face. She had to hold on to her stomach for relief, because she was laughing so hard at Mala's formality.

Mala on the other end was dumbfounded, flabbergasted, and utterly spooked by her friend's strange reaction. She had taken the receiver off her ear while Noor was cackling, and looked at the phone like it was a possessed being. She slowly put the receiver back up to her ear and tried to listen for some semblance of normality in Noor's voice.

"What are you doing Noor, you are scaring the crap out of me. Why are you cackling like a witch? I don't like it."

Noor managed to gain some composure and was wheezing slightly on the phone, trying to return to some sense of "*Noor*-mality." She cleared her throat.

"I have broken up with Christopher."

"Ooooookay... aaaaaand?"

"And I just wanted to tell you."

"Okay..." Mala was confused again. "Are you okay?"

"Absolutely fine."

"Did you know it was coming?" Mala didn't know if she should be concerned or frightened.

"Yes." Noor said still holding on to her pendulum.

"How?"

"Mala, I felt it. I was doing so well for ten years and he followed my lead, maybe because he wanted to travel the world with me and we were each other's ticket for doing that, with no obligations of kids, parents, business plans, it was all so much fun. I felt like a teenager when I was with him. He always made adventure real and heart-warming, he was a true explorer..."

Mala interrupted; she didn't want to hear any more of Noor's airy-fairy explanations. "He got bored, Noor, that is exactly what happened, he got old and bored, just like Washington..."

It was Noor's turn to interrupt, "Can you please stop comparing everyone's break up to yours? Please, for once in your life stop bringing it back to you all the time. This is about my break up, not yours."

Mala was quiet. She didn't mean to be conceited or to hog up the limelight, but she was still not impressed with Noor's very defensive ways.

"Well, what do you want me to say… congratulations… um, you did it again?" Mala had an extremely sarcastic grin smeared across her face.

"Really Mala? Seriously? Is that what you are going to say to me?"

"Well, you were laughing like a hyena just now, who do you think you are? Acting so holier than thou again, how can you cackle like *Glinda* when you have broken up with someone after being with them for ten years? Noor… ten years, and this is how you behave? Do you think this is normal?"

Noor could feel another fight coming on, but she didn't want to get to the point where her thyroid would jiggle and vibrate in her throat, so she replied in a very calm manner, "Yes, this is my new frame of mind and the new normal that I choose to live in, so what is the problem…"

"Consistency. That is the problem, do not fall into a hole after a few weeks and discover that you are all alone. Your giggling and your acceptance has to be real and not jaded until you go running back to your daddy…"

Noor's mood changed and she suddenly found herself fuming, as heat travelled through the centre of her body. She tried to count to ten, but that didn't work, so she tried fifteen, and then twenty. It was only when she got to sixty-eight that she began to feel a little bit calmer. She didn't want to fight with her demons right now, even though she knew that Mala was telling the truth. On the other end of the line, Mala just waited.

"Thank you, Mala Amani, for all of your truths. I am very much done with this conversation and I would love it if you could stop making me irritated and angry."

"I'm not making you irritated and angry, Annabelle, only you can do that, you are the only one who can do that to yourself."

"Really, Mala? I see, you speak like you are all high and mighty and act so holier than thou too, but look at you, and your life. Your husband, the one you thought was the love of your life left you…"

Mala was beginning to feel angry and spoke through her teeth. She hated it when Noor got caught up in jealousy while comparing her world with everyone else's. So, through clenched teeth, she said, "I left him… he didn't leave me, Annabelle Noor."

Both women were quiet. They had no inclination or intuition of what to say to each other. At their old ripened ages, they shouldn't have been fighting like silly school girls.

Noor finally caught herself and said, "I have to go now." She didn't want to start crying, and kept steadfast in her strength.

"Me too. See you tonight." Mala hung up the phone and was fuming at Noor, again. She didn't want to deal with her anymore. Mala felt like Noor was getting more and more insane in her old age. She always had something to say and was never consistent, and lately more fake. That is how Mala felt about Noor presently. Fake.

Chapter 28

London

Mala was finally back to her frame of mind of everyone revealing a self-script at the memorial to Sharon. The "Christophergate scandal" was still fresh in her thoughts, and made her quake. She knew that it was impossible for Noor to be happy about the breakup, because Christopher was a gem.

As Mala put out some snacks, and ripped the plastic off the cheese, the doorbell rang. She wasn't expecting anyone this early. She looked up at the clock, and it was only 6:00 p.m. She put her cutting board down and walked over to the door, and when she opened the door she was surprised – it was Mila's only son Roshan, a statuesque boy with a very chiselled Indian face. He was so handsome, just like his father, and he had the beauty and gentleness of his mother's soul.

"Hey, Rosh, what's up? No call, no nothing… what are you doing here, is everything okay with your mum?" She ushered for him to come inside. Occasionally Mala would get surprise visits from her nieces and nephew, and although she pretended to complain like an Indian aunty, she was always extremely glad to see them. Michael caught Roshan's eye and came hobbling down the stairs to give him a gigantic bear hug; it was always so lovely to see the connections the cousins had with each other. All seven of them had a sacred bond connected by love and the same soul family. It was magical.

"So, what are you doing here lovely?"

"I was just getting bored of Mum and Dad and asked if I could come down to see you, *Masi*, and she asked me several times if I had spoken to you, but I said I didn't need to, so I took the train down and now I'm here."

"Great, and everything is okay? Yes? Your mother, your father?"

"Yep, as good as it gets with so many mouths to feed."

"Well, some of you should be out already."

"Out of where?"

"Your parents' house," Mala said with a true *Masi* face. "I left when I was eighteen, and I never looked back."

"I know, I will leave soon, but dad says it's the money situation and it's so difficult for him to cope with so many of us around, and without his help, I can't afford to leave."

Mala was a bit upset; how could Maneck even think about insinuating something like that to his own children? She shook her head.

"Well, Roshan, the only thing you need to do now is be innovative and steer your own course, and always feel free."

Roshan grinned. "So, may I take your car out tonight? And go for a spin? And feel free?"

Mala sighed. She didn't want to be responsible for any problems, or for his rebellious actions, but she knew that if she said no, he would find a car elsewhere. He was a very resourceful boy, just like his mother. "Sure, you can take it out, but please be back early. I have guests coming over, the last thing I want to do is worry. Also, I need the car to pick up Shania from the library. Maybe you can do that for me too?"

He nodded. "Sure. I'll do all the picking and dropping and then I'll just go out for a bit with my friends."

Mala interrupted again, "And please no drinking, I am very scared of drinking and driving."

"*Masi*, please don't worry. I won't do that again."

"Yes, please don't, you had all of us so scared, and you weren't allowed to drive for how long?"

"…a year."

"Yes, you see, that's horrible, so please… be careful. And be responsible in your life… think of how far you could get as a young handsome man working at a bank."

Roshan looked at her with amusement. "So *Masi*, what makes you think that I want to work in a bank? Maybe I want to work as a chef…"

Mala's eyes brightened. "Do you?"

"No way, *Masi*, I want to be a pilot, and fly around the world, and I've been studying hard. I need to make the scholarship; then I don't have to burden my parents."

Mala felt perturbed, as she didn't want Roshan to feel this way. He and Michael were the only boys out of seven grandchildren, and in keeping with her traditional upbringing, she didn't want them to ever feel insecure about finances. She remembered how her father made her and her sister feel about spending money.

"Listen Roshan, if you don't make promises to yourself, and do things with a whole heart, nothing will come to fruition. This is what I believe. And I also believe that the universe, or God, or whoever you believe in, hears everything, because you are what you attract. It's not rocket science, Roshan. So, my suggestion to you is believe in what you want and manifest it, and what you want will come true. I promise. Look how much I prayed for Michael and his leg? It took four long years until there were any results but look, one day he just started walking… because he, ultimately, believed in himself, Roshan. Michael believed that he would walk one day, because he wanted to. And that is exactly what he did."

Roshan remained silent. After a moment, Mala sighed and handed the car keys from the old Chinese cupboard by the door to her nephew, and kissed him on his forehead. He was taller than her, but with a very high tip-toe, Mala was able to reach his crown *chakra* to place a very firm *aunty* kiss on his head.

Michael overheard the sound of the keys, and re-entered the room. "Can I go with him Mum?"

"No Michael, not tonight, you said you were going to Jason's house to play video games, right?"

"Why?" Michael was acting like a wannabe rebellious teenager again.

"Because you already made plans with Jason."

"Why do I have to do everything you tell me to do?"

Mala was confused; her son had made plans with his friend Jason and was now changing his mind as well as semi blaming it on her, probably because of Roshan's spontaneity. Instead of going around in circles, though, Mala said, "Because I am your mother."

"Whatever." Michael walked away and plopped himself in the living room to read a book, sulking.

Roshan chuckled at his mother's sister and poured himself a glass of water. Mala looked at the clock and was ready for her friends' arrival.

As Roshan got ready to go, the phone rang; it was Sophia.

"Hi Mala!"

"Hey, how are you? I haven't heard from you in a couple of weeks. All good?"

"Well…" Sophia sounded forlorn.

Mala didn't notice, and interrupted, "So good to hear from you. Alister is on the way with his girlfriend, and we are having a memorial night."

"I know, I heard, Alister told me…" Sophia drifted off.

Mala paused, zoning back in. "Is everything okay? How come you called? Is Alister okay?" Mala had to catch herself once more, and wonder why she was blaming Alister again for Sophia's sadness. She could hear that something was not right on the phone.

"It's Dave, Mala…"

Mala interrupted, "Oh god no, is he…"

"Dead?" Sophia asked Mala with sadness coupled with anger in her voice.

"What?" Mala started to tremble; she didn't want to feel the bile reach her throat. She began to imagine the burning sensation in her oesophagus as she tried to calm herself for the unravelling of Sophia's news.

"Sort of."

"What?" Mala was so perplexed. She remembered the feeling in the pit and the bowels of her stomach when Washington told her that Sharon was gone. She felt like the ground had swallowed her whole being into another dimension. It was horrific. "What do you mean sort of?"

"He is dying."

Mala tried to stay calm. "We all are, Sophia."

"...he only has a few months to live." Sophia said slowly and with effort.

Mala felt sad for her friend and didn't know what to say. At least his death wouldn't be sudden or unexpected, and Dave was older. He had already lived a long and prosperous life. Mala felt harsh for thinking this way, but she made a commitment to be strong for Sophia who was now on the other side of the world. She knew Sophia was not okay, and that it would take her years to get over his passing, similar to what she felt with Sharon. She still wasn't over the tragedy, come to think of it.

"What can I do for you, Sophia?" Mala asked with genuine concern.

After a moment, Sophia replied, "Can you... come to Hong Kong?"

Mala was stunned. She had never been to Hong Kong before. The closest she got was Singapore with her friends, but never to Hong Kong. She would be delighted to see the city, but didn't know how she was going to leave her kids. She could ask Washington to look after the kids while she went on a voyage to console Sophia. However, she didn't want them to be around Emilia too much. She couldn't think of anyone else to look in on the children except Alister.

"Me? To Hong Kong?" She would love to see the city where her best friend, Sharon, grew up, and would definitely contact Sharon's mum Sandy to try and find out all the information. Sandy was now at a retirement home and couldn't for the life of her remember who Mala was, poor thing. She kept confusing all of Sharon's friends, and in the end they realised that Sandy was not really in her right mind with them on the same plane. So, Mala always did what she felt was her duty by visiting Sandy once a month to see if she was okay. Mala would take Shania and Michael to see her as well, and they loved to play cards with Mabelle, who was Sandy's best friend and roommate. Mala's thoughts were interrupted by Sophia's tender voice.

"Yes, please, come here, and just be with me." She hesitated, "As much as it pains me to say, you will probably go through it very soon with Aunty Durga, and I need someone in my life right now who understands the implications of age."

Mala felt despondent thinking about Durga, because she knew that her mother was coming closer to the age where she would be passing soon as well. Mala felt a shiver go up and down her spine. The idea of her mother not being around made her feel uncomfortable. She really didn't want her mother to leave just yet, especially after the fact that both mother and daughter had so much lost time between them. Mala began to think about the concept of time and how scenes in her mind had seemingly passed by in an instant. She was touching her fifties and knew that it was time to start letting go of her mother, realising that she would again, very soon, have responsibilities she wouldn't know how to deal with, which came with the pressure of womanhood. As she grew older, she would learn the significance of how to gracefully mature as a person, and it would be her family teaching her this process. Mala tried to hide her sadness as she spoke to Sophia.

"I know what you mean Sophia… I have to find a way to settle the twins, before I get up and leave. Is the situation very bad?"

Sophia swallowed a big lump in her throat, "Yes, it is unbearable…"

Mala interrupted her. She was not good with death. Thinking about it made her want to vomit. She tried to hold back the feeling in her blue *chakra*, which was trembling with fear and concern. "How bad?" Mala was hesitant. She didn't know if this was the right question to be asking, considering she was already feeling queasy.

"Do you want details?"

"Maybe not," Mala thought the wiser.

"Well, he is so frail… he is just disintegrating, put it that way. But apart from the physical meltdown Dave's body is forcing him to go through, he is trying to be in high spirits. He doesn't have long and he knows it."

"How long?"

"Weeks at best."

"Wow," Mala winced, "Ok. I will speak to Washington tonight and find out if we can make some arrangements."

"Thank you so much Mala, I appreciate your friendship, and how you have always stayed connected to me even after Sharon's death," Sophia said, trying to hold her composure.

Mala smiled. "People come together for a reason, and I remember a little old lady telling me one day how with death there is birth, and we all go through a cycle. This is exactly what it is." Mala still thought of the endearing Chinese lady with fortune telling cards she had encountered not long before Sharon's passing.

Sophia began to feel melancholic. While empathising with Mala on a spirited level, she could feel the pangs of pain and loss come and go as she spoke about Dave. Sophia's heart ached realising she was going to miss him and there was absolutely nothing she could do to keep him from passing on into a different veil. Tears started to softly cascade down her face as a mirror of sadness seemed to reflect on the other side of the world in London, in Hammersmith, inside Mala's home.

Mala asked softly, as she could feel Sophia's hurt bleed through the phone, hearing sniffles signify the pain of losing a dear best friend, "Are you okay, Sophia?"

"No, not at all." She was sniffling more into the phone, as hot tears stung the side of her nose, and mucus started to flood her nostrils. She lifted up her arm and wiped her nose with the back of her shirt.

Mala made up her mind. "I will be there Sophia. Just give me a few days. You can count on me. I will definitely be there. I know how it feels… it is very painful. No one can tell you that the pain will go away right away, because that is not true. It's how we handle the pain and how we internalise our thoughts. You have a few more weeks with Dave, and all you need to do for him, before he moves on, is to keep him happy. We are all going to go one day, we never know when… but while we are alive, we need to be surrounded with music, love, harmony, fun and the feeling that we left with abundance. And what you need to do for your best friend in the whole wide world, is to be a big girl now, not cry… enjoy the time you have with him. Look what happened to me – I was unaware how just in a second, the world can change and flip in front of you with one swoop. We have to live for now, and Dave needs you now."

Sophia was trembling, wobbly tears falling from her eyes. She could feel her body scrunch up into a ball on the floor, with her back to the cupboard in her living room. She was glad Craig was not home to see her like this. Mala felt her pain deeply, and whispered softly, "It's okay Sophia… always know you have memories together. You are going to miss him, there's no doubt – but you will be absolutely fine. I promise."

"I know, Mala, you are right, I just have to let it out as well as let it all sink in. I've been keeping it inside for so long…" she said, trying to control herself.

"I will not say it's going to get better, but what I can honestly tell you is that it will get easier, because there will be times that a memory will flood your mind, and you will be transported and start to daydream. It will hit you in a humorous way, or it will hit you in a very emotional way, where you can feel your body tremble."

Sophia thought for a moment, still trembling. "I want to have a party for him in the hospital ward, like we did for Sharon – remember when we did that, and Washington played for her?"

"Of course I remember that Sophia, it feels like it was yesterday." Mala sighed. "Let's definitely plan something for him. Start by making a list of the people you want there, and then think about a theme, and then think of some music, and I'll help you think of the food part, like a real *auntie*…"

Mala was interrupted as she heard a soft chuckle emerge through her tears.

"Thanks Mala, you are really a wonderful friend, and I am so blessed that we were connected."

"Thanks Sophia, now I think you need to get some rest and just dream of all the beautiful and wonderful times you had together."

"I will. Thanks Mala."

"Anytime."

As Mala hung up, she already began to formulate a mission of how to be with Sophia. She began to systemise in her head, like a true parent, how she was going to make sure her children were safe with Washington while she helped one of the most serene friends she had the honour of knowing. But first, she had to devote her attention to Sharon's memorial. Once again, Mala was on a mission to love and heal, channelling Sharon in the process.

On the other side of the world, Sophia picked herself up off the floor and put the receiver back down. She looked at herself in the mirror that hung over a white brick fire place, and then re-diverted her eyes to the mantelpiece, where pictures of her and Craig, on holiday all over the world, and pictures of her with Dave at a multitude of store openings and fashion shows, glistened back at her. Each snapshot interwoven into each other to make a story of people's lives. She had so much to express, and all those pictures made her feel secure, and ultimately satisfied. Her past was filled with humour, delight, consistency, and ultimately love. Tears began to fall again, but this time, she managed an extremely weak smile, knowing that she was in a very important phase in her life – and it occurred to her that her father may be next. She took a deep breath, and made a decision to be strong, calm, and most of all mature. In the process she was going to spend some amazing and humorous days with the love of her life and best friend, Dave.

She looked up at the clock behind her. It was 7:30 and Craig would be coming home soon. She didn't want him to see her in this state. Sophia was going to discuss with Craig how they could do something special for Dave. Craig was Sophia's ear, always listening with intent and poise. Over the years, Sophia also learned to count on Craig, as well as Dave, for good advice and sound judgement.

She picked up Josie, who was by her side the entire time, and they both snuggled up to each other while Josie put her furry white head right in between Sophia's neck and shoulder with a soft purr. Max and Josie had been through a lot with her. Throughout their unusually long feline lives, they brought Sophia serenity. Josie was her most favourite healer. Max moved towards Sophia and, as if by instinct, stretched in front of her feet as if bowing in prayer. As he moved into a straightened position, he wrapped his body around her legs and purred softly, letting Sophia know, once again, that she was never alone.

Chapter 29

South East Asia

As Sophia was contemplating the meaning of friendship, Dave was patiently laying in a hospital bed. His translucent skin on a 50 kilogram skeletal frame ricocheted the severity of his disease and he looked rather like a ghoul. He switched on the TV and an old documentary about *Kai Tak* airport was on. The series was preaching about safety in the sky, while each plane looked as if it was skimming past a building. There were rumours that when the planes flew by Kowloon City, people could literally see faces peering out of airplane windows. *Kai Tak* airport had a reputation of being one of the most difficult runways in the world and the documentary was giving Dave goose bumps as well as feelings of delight.

He thought back to the day he arrived into Hong Kong. He was ravishingly young, a 38-year-old graduate from the London School of Fashion. At his age, Dave looked like George Michael, with his immaculate sense of fashion and style. His beard was cut into a jagged shape on his face, and his slicked back hair epitomised an Italian movie star. His first and only job in Hong Kong at the store became his life – from the first day to his last. The fashion brand had given him purpose and a place where he could create and have fun. Dave never believed that he was ever working because he genuinely loved what he was doing. He was surrounded by colour, fabric, creativity, and of course, class all the time.

Dave began coughing and tried to sit up in bed, but the medication and his loss of appetite were making him more frail every day. He wondered how Sophia would be without him and felt worried. He knew she was in amazing hands with Craig, but he also knew that Sophia needed an elderly point of view to help guide her along the way, on most occasions. He focused on the present moment and gazed at the clock. It was already eleven thirty at night, but he picked up the phone and dialled Sophia anyway. She didn't answer.

He eased back in his bed and remembered the first day he met Sophia.

She was at Dolce Vita with some of her friends, and she caught Dave's eye more than once. The way she was looking at him was very odd, because Dave wasn't sure if Sophia knew who he was. What she did notice is that he was definitely gay and stunning. Dave's boyfriend at the time was with him, by his side and they looked absolutely wonderful. Sophia was intrigued by Dave.

Suddenly, paparazzi lights flashed, and Dave remembered Sophia squinting and then spilling her drink all over her beige sweater because of the bright lights.

When Dave saw Sophia, he could see a Eurasian beauty with beautiful glowing olive skin – and a very immaculate fashion sense. He wouldn't have noticed her if it weren't for her aquamarine Japanese raw silk trousers, with a knitted beige sweater. He walked over to Sophia and tapped her on the shoulder.

"Hi. Dave. Dave Graham," he said, as if he was an international spy.

Sophia turned around to look at Dave, and with a soft chuckle she said, "Hi. Sophia, Sophia Martin." She extended her hand to shake his.

"It is a pleasure to make your acquaintance. I work for Christian Dior, and what do you do?"

"Bloomberg." Sophia said with absolute confidence.

"Lovely. And how long have you been here, in Asia?"

"Oh, I've been here for about 10 years, although I have just started with Bloomberg, and I'm loving it."

"That's wonderful, petal. May I ask what brought you here?"

"My brother. He needs me now." Sophia took a sip of her martini and couldn't look at Dave in the eyes.

"Is he alright? Your brother?" Dave asked with slight concern.

"No, actually he's not alright."

Dave didn't know if he should be concerned or if this woman was being sarcastic. *"I'm sorry, I hope he's okay."*

"He'll be fine." Sophia didn't want to discuss her family with a complete stranger, so she changed the subject and said, *"I have actually seen you in magazines... have you been here long?"*

"Long enough," Dave said with a smile. *"I would love to ask if you could help me with a campaign that is coming up... I'm actually looking for a Eurasian model."*

Sophia was flattered, yet bemused; even with her petite frame and flawless skin, she never thought of herself as model material. Nevertheless, she felt complimented. *"Me? Model for you? For Christian Dior?"*

"Yes. Would you? Be my muse?"

Sophia was now stunned. People had forewarned her that Hong Kong was full of opportunities, and hanging out around Lan Kwai Fong would help her with public relations as well as meet high flying clients for Bloomberg. *"I am so flattered, but why would you ask me right away? You have no idea who I am."*

Dave turned directly to face her, his mesmerizing blue eyes sinking deep into her Asian eyes. He said coolly, *"I know talent when I see it, petal. Believe me. I've been in the business for so long... you, my dear, have a face that's one-of-a-kind. And believe me again when I say that I would never ask a random stranger on the street."*

Sophia was confused. *"But we are random strangers from the street."*

"No, not exactly. Firstly, we are not on the street. Secondly, we are both having drinks at a very reputable establishment, so I think we are on the same wavelength."

"But I'm still a stranger, Mr Graham," Sophia retorted.

"Not anymore, my dear Ms Martin. We have officially met and we are no longer strangers."

Sophia smiled. She liked this intelligent yet flamboyant man who was truthful, while exhibiting clarity and poise when he was talking. "Yes, indeed, Mr Graham, we are no longer strangers."

Dave smiled and kissed the back of her hand. "And one more thing, Sophia, please don't call me Mr Graham. I am not old enough to be addressed like that. Please just call me Dave."

"Okay, Dave. The pleasure is mine."

"And mine."

"So, when would you like me to start?" Sophia asked, her young beautiful smile emulating adventure as well as gratitude.

"Tomorrow."

"Really? ...But I have work. How can I model for you tomorrow?"

"What time do you finish work?"

"I finish at around 6 and then I head off to the gym. You know, my day starts frightfully early because the market opens up at 5:30."

"I see," Dave said, looking quite uninterested. He was never a numbers man, and the thought of the stock market, graphs, and anything associated with counting; absolutely did not interest him in the slightest.

Sophia was wondering if Dave was losing interest, and quickly saved her chance by retorting, "But just let me know what time, and I'll be there."

Dave looked at her and pulled out his name card. "Here is my number. Give me a call tomorrow and we will get you started. How do you feel about being on the cover of a magazine?"

Sophia was not interested in splashing her face all over Hong Kong, especially since she had just started with Bloomberg. She was content to be his model and muse, but not so keen on becoming a celebrity. "I'm not sure about that, Dave. Why don't we go slow and see what happens from there?"

"Sure, but before you leave, would you be so kind as to take a picture with me? The paparazzi are heading over here again... a different lot, and I would love to have you in a picture with me. Plus, you can do some PR for Bloomberg."

"Sure." And as Sophia turned to pose, an ocean of lights engulfed the scene.

As Dave sat in his bed waiting for his time, he reflected and realised that he had lived a very fruitful and prosperous life. He also needed to tell Sophia that she would be the executor of his will and be in charge of distributing his money to his family as well as his estate. Sophia would be left with thirty percent of his money as a gift. He had to find the right moment to give her this information that was percolating in his mind. He needed to tell her; he knew he was ready to go.

Chapter 30

London

While Mala's flat started to fill up with the beautiful scent of vanilla and patchouli, her friends arrived: Washington, Fatima, Alister, and even Noor. Mala's thoughts flashed back to Sophia and their earlier conversation as she welcomed them all to her home.

They made small talk as they prepared for Mala's memorial of their dear friend. Soft music played in the background as they had appetisers and made a little conversation, as if they had met each other for the first time. Everyone in the room had something to say, but were reluctant to begin. After ten long years these friends had made an impact on each other's lives and could not be forgotten, yet they had transformed into more elderly versions of themselves, with somewhat more clarity and deeper feelings of either love or animosity. Their communal visits to Bazica may have decreased in number, but one thing remained constant was their friendship to Sharon, who seemed to be the glue that held the platform of their connection together.

Mala finally spoke up, gently asking everyone to move into the den, where she had laid out bean bags and throw cushions. When everyone was seated and had found a comfortable spot, Mala began to speak.

"Firstly, I want to say thank you for being here today as we all gather to celebrate our friend Sharon. I know it has been over ten long years, but today marks yet another anniversary… of her passing…

Washington interrupted, "As well as our engagement."

Mala glared at Washington, confused while wondering why he would have brought that up. She recalled the day at the church and how her younger self had been overly enamoured by Washington's gesture of marriage. It was a romantic action on his part, possibly an omen for anyone else to never get engaged on the day of anyone's funeral. "Yes, Washington, but we are not here to talk about that."

"Oh, yes we are… that's what I'm here for."

Everyone turned to look at Washington and Mala, waiting for the drama to unfold.

"No, we are not Washington, we're here to pay respect to our friend." Mala said with increasing confusion.

"Yes, I know. And I wonder if she was still alive if all of our lives would be different somehow." Washington looked forlorn.

"I'm sure things would have been different with her around." Noor interjected.

"Yes, I would have never left you, Mala." Washington blurted out quickly.

"We don't need to talk about this now, Washington…"

"Oh yes we do."

"There is a time and place for everything, and tonight is not the time," Mala said, slightly taken aback by Washington's emotional outburst.

"Yes, it is… you asked us to come here so we can share our thoughts, Mala…"

Mala was feeling slightly embarrassed as all eyes were on her. She felt like a character in a musical again who had forgotten all her lines. She cleared her throat. "We came here to reflect about our friendship with a very dear person, not indulge in marriage counselling."

Noor was looking back and forth at Mala and Washington like she was at a tennis match, waiting for someone to drop the ball.

"Mala, if Sharon was around, she would have given you some sense and we would have never split up."

"What?" Anger was beginning to rise in the formerly serene Mala; she was now more than irritated at Washington and his selfish antics.

"He might have a point, Mala. I mean, when she was around she was the only one who could actually talk you into things… or out of things…" Noor said, absentmindedly, as thoughts of Christopher played havoc silently in her mind.

Mala interrupted, "How can both of you sit there talking like this? Tonight is not about me and Washington, it's about Sharon!"

"Yes, and we *are* talking about Sharon, Mala," Noor said curtly. "How do you want us to continue the night? Reading from a *bloody* script? Let's not be pretentious here, and let's just speak from the heart, does everyone agree?" Noor asked the room.

Fatima and Alister nodded slightly; they didn't want to get into the cross fire of these three friends, considering that they had known each other the longest.

Mala looked into Noor's eyes. "I did not invite everyone here to talk about problems, I asked everyone to come over so we could remember a friend."

Noor interrupted again, "So you want us to act like your students, right? Stand up and read a poem, or say a few words and just keep it light and airy-fairy? Is that it? So we can all keep it safe, and in the end never really say what we want to say?"

"No, that was not my intention, Noor. I wanted everyone to write something down so we could commemorate Sharon, that's it… I didn't want this to turn into a therapy session. Did you even write anything down, Noor? Did you Fatima? What about you Alister?" She didn't even bother asking Washington as she scanned the room.

Fatima took out a crumpled piece of paper, and Alister had a notebook with him when he walked in. Noor pointed with her index finger at her temple, and Washington shook his head.

"No one wrote anything down except Fatima and Alister? Come on, Noor and Washington, I expected more from you." Mala began shaking her head in disapproval.

"I don't need to write anything down. I already know what I want to say," Washington retorted.

"Me too," added Noor.

Mala was flustered, and feeling bombarded by her friendships. The evening was not going as she had planned. She suddenly wished one of the children would interrupt the evening so it would just end.

"Mala, we are going to let you begin by reading what is on your mind and begin the night as you intended… and everyone will follow after that." Alister was trying to make the situation lighter.

"Why does Mala have to start first?" Washington asked.

"Because it's her house…" Fatima spoke up.

"Let Mala begin, Washington, and right after, you can say your piece," Noor commanded.

Mala began to tear up and she didn't feel like talking anymore. She actually felt like Noor and Washington were ganging up on her. She took out her writing and couldn't see the words on the paper. Her mind drifted back to her wedding day with Washington. It was the most magical day of her life, and knowing that, on this day, she began to feel empty at all the promises that dissolved between her and Washington. Maybe he was right – if Sharon was alive she would have talked them out of separation, and her feisty nature would have helped them see through the hard times. She looked at the paper again and immaturely realised she didn't want to read what was in front of her, to any of the people in the room. Finally, with a long sigh and then a deep breath, she said, "I think this was a bad idea. It might bring up some things from the past that we're not ready for."

"I'm ready," Washington said quickly. "I'm so ready to talk about the last ten years, and how things have been rough without the true meaning of friendship."

"What does that mean, Washington? And why are you doing this now? What do you want to say... really?" Mala asked with severe agitation.

Fatima and Alister were beginning to look uncomfortable again. Noor, on the other hand, was enjoying every piece of drama that was unfolding right in front of her eyes. This was going to be, yet again, juicy material for her book – she'd get around to actually writing it one day, after all.

"I want to say that I made a big mistake. I should have never left you and the children, and I can't be without you, Mala. The last ten years have been so difficult, and I realise that my obsession with..."

"Emilia?" Noor interrupted.

"No..." Washington interrupted.

Mala's complete annoyance at the whole situation caused her to take charge of the situation, "Can everyone stop, please... Washington, please leave... actually, everyone please leave. This was a bad idea and I don't want to talk about Emilia, or about any of the hurt that went on between us, because it is not the time and place. I'm so sorry, but this is not how I expected the evening to go." Mala was speaking with her eyes shut; as embarrassment started to creep into her, thoughts of the past made her feel tipsy and caroused her body to tremble slightly.

"How can you ask him to leave, Mala?" Noor inquired.

"I asked everyone to leave... not just him. Now if you don't mind, please excuse me."

Mala departed the den, gracefully with long persistent strides out into the patio situated on the other side of the flat, tears now streaming down her face. Waterfalls of regret, disappointment and fear were sinking down her face. *What had ten years done to this group of people*, Mala thought to herself. Instead of forgiveness and hope, there was a looming of exasperation and miscommunication, as well as a disintegration of connections.

In the other room, as Alister and Fatima were trying to pacify the situation while asking Washington to give Mala her space, Noor grabbed Alister's notebook and began scribbling notes for the next chapter of her book.

Without saying goodbye, Washington, Alister and Fatima left Mala's flat. Alister left a note:

Mala, we understand what you are going through, and we are here for you always. Please call me in the morning and let's meet up at Bazica for a quick coffee. We are sorry the night didn't go as planned. A meeting over coffee tomorrow will make it better, I promise.

Love, Al

The door of Mala's flat shut and Noor was left alone in the den scribbling away at a story she was on the verge – in her mind – of selling. Her book was going to be full of delight, and tonight's conversation between the friends had conjured up some creative juices. Finishing up her last sentence, she shut the notebook and walked out onto the patio where Mala was still sitting.

"You're still here Noor?"

"Yes, I'm still here, you can't get rid of me that easily."

"*Why* are you here?" Mala asked with slight distance in her voice.

"I'm here because I care, Mala."

"Care about what, Noor? Gossip?"

Noor paused. "How dare you Mala, I'm not a gossip. I stayed because I am worried about you and the way you handled everyone tonight." Noor was trying to be a sincere as she possibly could, it just wasn't working for Mala.

"I know I was rude to ask everyone to leave, but Washington was totally out of line. How could he even suggest that we would still be together if Sharon was alive? I mean the nerve of him… who does he think he is?"

"He misses you, Mala."

"After almost ten years? Really? After ten years he tells me he misses me? What happened to me and my feelings when he told me he was in love with someone else and he was moving in with her? What happened then?" Mala's annoyance began to crescendo momentarily again.

"Mala, listen, people change and he is getting older, maybe he was going through some kind of self-realisation tonight, reminiscing about our younger days… he just got a bit emotional." Noor, slightly sly about the conversation, decided to tread carefully, especially after the conversation about Christopher. Once again Noor felt estranged from Mala after the heated incident.

Mala could sense something was adrift and said very abruptly, "Its getting late Noor… I think it's time for you to leave as well. I'm getting tired."

Noor picked up Alister's notebook and turned to leave.

Shocked, Mala asked, "What is that, Noor? Did you come here to do research on your supposed book?"

"No, not at all. The research came to me." Noor didn't realise it, but she was smirking.

"How dare you, Annabelle Noor? I'm not your research. And I am absolutely insulted at your behaviour… again!"

"Mala Amani, you have got to be one of the strangest friends I have…"

Mala interrupted, "Me? Strange? What about you? I can't believe how many times we have been through the same arguments, Noor. And I am asking you nicely this time to stop using my struggles as a basis for your story and your stupid book. Write about yourself. Your own story is so discombobulated and FULL of drama. Why do you have to prey on my life?" Mala began to feel off kilter once more.

Noor was in argument mode and began fuming with increasing volume, "I am not preying on your life, Ms Amani. Ever since Sharon's passing I have tried to help you fill the gap, tried to be there for you, but you have done nothing but sulk for the past ten years…"

"Sulk? What do you mean? And who do you think you are to speak to me like that? You know what, Annabelle, I am done. Finished.

Our friendship is based on your renditions and is selfish. You know what? It's over. I don't ever want to speak to you again." Mala, by this point, was seething.

"What?" Noor was stupefied. She and Mala had engaged in numerous arguments throughout their lives, and this one didn't constitute Mala never speaking to her again. It couldn't. "You are so harsh, Mala. Your mother was right when she said that you are rough around the edges."

Mala astonished asked, "When did my mother say that Noor?"

"The last time she was here! She was right, your husband left you and your child is disabled, because you are rough around the edges, unlike your sister who is…"

Mala didn't let her berating friend finish. "Get out of my house. Now."

Noor couldn't believe her friend, and tried to add in another sentence before she left, but Mala didn't let her speak. "You are not welcome here ever again. Now leave!"

Angry yet still composed, Noor turned around silently, walked back to the den to pick up her handbag, looked up at the wall of all the pictures of Mala's life, and left her Hammersmith flat. Her thyroid began to wobble furiously as the farewell of a three-decade friendship melted away from her. Without a single visible tear, Annabelle Noor got into her car and drove away.

Mala, overflowing with dread and resentment, was dumbfounded at the whole turn of events. She peered at the notebook Noor had left on the patio table, picked it up, walked into the kitchen and dumped her writing into the garbage. The kids wouldn't be back for a while, and not quite sure what to do with herself, she proceeded to her computer and began to write.

It was a very dark day when she left, but as she drove away the light began to appear and a feeling of renewal gave way to a peaceful existence. When she began to melt away her fears and realise that she was a burden, the feeling of empowerment and delight started to transform her into a very powerful force of nature.

Death was not only symbolised by the loss of the body, but from the loss of spirit. She was awake, but not alive – especially in the eyes of her friends. She was gone, and nowhere to be found again.

That night, as both women lay in their own bedrooms staring at the ceiling, they felt a sense of relief. Noor took out her pendulum, with the light from the prism highlighting rainbows across her bedroom walls. The fractals of light bouncing playfully on the right side of her bed made her feel absolutely nothing. For the first time she had nothing to ask this mesmerizing object and instead hypnotised herself to sleep, as the background of sobs began to emerge through her dreams.

All Mala could think about was Washington, and his heart, and how he made love to her like no other man had even done in her life. His smell, his voice, the way he caressed her, and as Noor's sobs turned into tears of pain, Mala's soft tears turned into regret, loneliness, and mistrust.

Chapter 31

South East Asia

Sophia and Dave made a pact to refer to Dave's death, as his 'debut' in heaven. Sophia refrained from using words like 'going,' 'passing,' and especially 'death.'

Sophia felt a wave of *déjà vu* as she pottered around Dave's hospital room, reminiscing about Mala looking after Sharon during her 'debut.'

"Listen, petal, you really need to sit down. Please stop fussing." Dave was looking frail but was feeling better spiritually, because he instinctively knew his exit was going to be comfortable.

"I'm alright Dave, I just want to make sure everything is okay. These hospitals do my head in sometimes, they don't know any customer service; look how dirty this is," she exclaimed as she was frantically wiping the top of the fridge.

Dave couldn't help but smile. "Just leave that for a bit and come and sit with me. I need to tell you something."

Sophia had been cleaning tremendously in the last few weeks. She had cleaned up her whole house, gutted the basement, and threw out 19 boxes of old clothes, utensils, cutlery and even some of her paintings. She was definitely off-loading. She reluctantly stopped wiping vigorously and sat down next to Dave.

"What can I do for you today, Mr Graham?" Sophia was trying to make the situation light hearted while sitting at the edge of his bed like a secretary.

"I want to tell you something… I have left some money for my brother's… families… and some for you…"

Sophia interrupted, "Dave, I don't need your money… really.

"I want you to have it, because you are family, Sophia… and I can't think of a better person to give it to," he said softly.

"What am I going to do with the money, Dave?"

"Actually, I wanted you to open up a little boutique in Central… call it *SOPH*… and I have arranged for the first 25 pieces to be delivered to your house in about three weeks…"

Sophia gawked at him.

"And," Dave continued, "the first 25 designs are a tribute to our friendship."

"How so?" Sophia asked with a half-smile on her face, fighting to hold back the tears.

"You will see, Sophia. Starting from the first day I met you at Dolce Vita, when you almost spilt your martini on your sweater, you have been my favourite muse. You have shown me that the human body and spirit can be delicate, fragile, vulnerable, and most of all compassionate."

Sophia leaned into the bed and hugged her best friend, and she began to feel the heat rise from the ground into her body as the warmth of friendship was all around her.

Sophia released her grip and enchantingly inspected Dave. He had aged at an immense speed, with his body mirroring the canvas of movement, change and severe age. He looked decayed and frail. His robust body and sparkling blue eyes were embedded, hidden somewhere in between his longing to be strong again.

That night as Sophia lay in bed, she thought about her own life and how so many twists and turns had made her feel like a human roller coaster. She had been through the hamster-on-the-wheel syndrome for most of her adult life.

Clarity in her life right now was knowing and feeling that no matter what side of polarity her life was in, constant change was the theme. She had to move forward in order to feel like she was going to let go of her past someday, especially with Dave.

Chapter 32

London

The following day after the argument between Noor and Mala, Mala sat down at her computer to write a furious rant of words, spilling over like a raging river. She described one of the female characters with words that were spitting out like furious bullets. After her release of words on the computer, she felt somewhat refreshed, and made her way down to Bazica to meet Alister.

By the time she got to Table Number 8, though, she was once again steaming about her friend – Noor's general lack of understanding, compassion, and truth. She also took it upon herself to dig out Noor's notes, written on Alister's notepad, out of the garbage.

She was livid when she read the passage. It read:

I giggled so hard to see her fly off the handle, with her non-knowing of life, and her meaningless relationship(s)… first the love of her life, and then her friends, and eventually she will ponder about the loss of children; it was too bad she couldn't ever have any, because at the end of the day she never had a heart. She believed that her heart was made of gold, but in the end it had turned into tin. And just like Dorothy, from *The Wizard of Oz*, seeking for all of her worldly truths through cartoon-like characters, she was once again diverting the tornadoes of life to find her way "home."

"Look Alister, look what she wrote. Is she crazy?"

Alister, nonchalantly gazing at the at the notepad while sipping on his coffee, said, "It isn't even about you, Mala; look, it says something profound and creepy here about not having children... I don't understand why you are so angry; she is possibly talking about herself." Alister was patiently pointing out the sentence *and eventually she will ponder about the loss of children; it was too bad she couldn't ever have any, because at the end of the day she never had a heart.* "Do you see this here Mala... you have children... she doesn't... what does that say to you? Look carefully... is this you?"

Mala signed. "No ..."

"Then why are you so angry?" Alister looked even more confused than when the conversation began 30 minutes ago.

"Because I know she was talking about me, using parts of my life to create her story, and make a mockery out of me. I know her, I know what she's like."

"Speculating will get you nowhere. And where is Fatima? Maybe she can help us analyse this writing... honestly Mala, I think you are making a big deal out of nothing. Don't go down that road."

Mala sighed again. "I don't want to speak to her again."

"Then don't!"

"I mean, every time we get things together she always has to bring drama into the situation... it's as if she is creating it just so she can write this *creepy* book of hers."

Alister was now chuckling; living with his sister had turned him into a very patient man, and when they were growing up, his sister was his source of entertainment. Her sudden outbursts of theatre in the house with her friends, studies, and environment were always a beautifully passionate respite from his mundane parents. He was able to handle Mala's antics and thought it very funny how women couldn't understand the concept of letting go.

"Why are you laughing, Al? It seems like everyone is always on her side."

"Aww, come on Mala. That is not true, and let me remind you that it was actually Washington who started the conversation, which lead to the outburst... right?"

It was true. Washington had been the one to instigate the whole situation, and upon reflection, Mala was not so sure whom to blame anymore. She was still annoyed at Noor, and didn't want to continue speaking to her, because she always felt rattled. Mala wondered if going across the world to Asia would help her clear the chatter in her head. She had never been to Hong Kong before, and couldn't wait for the adventure. She wasn't becoming Noor, was she? Absolutely not. She looked up from her mocha and, changing the subject, said, "I am going to Hong Kong to visit your sister, Al."

"That's great. Have you ever been to Hong Kong?" Alister just rolled with it.

"No, and I'm looking forward to it. I'm actually going to contact one of Sharon's aunts who is still alive. Do you want to come too?"

Al thought for a moment, and then reverted his thoughts. "No, I'm okay." The memories of Asia haunted him on occasion still. And even though he knew that reflection was a good process, he decided that Asia was a place he would wait to visit for a long while. "I'm glad you're going. I know my sister needs someone right now. She is going through very fragile times and you would be the best person to console her."

"I know." Mala said calmly, looking around for Fatima. Maybe it was a sign that the beautiful Middle Eastern waitress was not available on this day, because Mala was actually wasting her time talking about Noor, who in actual fact was never her true friend. She couldn't have been. There was always the element of competition rather than creation, and it always gave way to some kind of cosmic flip that would cause Mala to shake with disappointment.

Mala thought back to her days in Boston again, and quickly realised she didn't want to reminisce. She was feeling old and disappointed, and with every memory of her best friends she was feeling sadder and sadder. First Sharon, and now, essentially...

Noor. The past was not assisting in forward thinking, especially with her emotions.

"I have told Washington already, and instead of my mother coming out to help for two weeks, he has asked if you can help to look in on the twins as well."

"Of course, always a pleasure."

"Why do you think Washington did that, Al? Instigate a fragile situation… I mean, you're a man… why?"

"Trouble in paradise, Mala… that's all I can come up with. Trouble with the new girl."

"New girl? What do you mean *new* girl? She's not *new*… is there another *new* girl?"

"Maybe…"

"What? I'm confused, what do you mean? Have you seen him with someone else?"

"No, but maybe there is…"

"You shouldn't speculate like that. That's not nice."

"Well, I don't know what to say… his outburst wasn't from a place of happiness, was it?"

"I really don't think so."

Alister finished his cappuccino and sat back in his chair. "Maybe you should meet him and talk it out." Alister didn't feel like dwelling on the subject anymore. It was getting very womanly for him, and he was getting a little irritated after too much going around in circles. Alister knew in his heart, just like Sharon would have, that Washington and Mala should have never separated. And Durga was not happy with her eldest daughter for so long, again, because of the apparent shame separation as well as being married to a foreigner brought to the family. On top of that, Michael's disability didn't compliment the situation. Alister suggested Mala make time to visit a yoga retreat after her trip to Asia. He promised to help out, committing to looking in on the children.

Mala needed a soul scrubbing as well. The dark circles around her eyes made her look even more tired and weary these days. Her young supple skin now showed signs of maturity, and some lines of regret were beginning to creep up onto her face. Both friends sat in silence; one thinking about the meaning of life and death, and the other thinking of life in Asia.

After Bazica, Mala picked up her daughter from the library and they spoke about Durga.

Shania was born a wise soul. Beautiful skin with long curly hair, she had a petite frame that was overshadowed by her long slim legs. Durga adored Shania and always made her feel like a princess. She adored Michael with all of his feistiness and his willingness to learn and never be a victim, but Shania had Durga's heart, and played on her granddaughter's heartstrings like a perfect melody.

"Why are you going to Asia, Mum?"

"Aunty Sophia needs me there right now," Mala replied, using the endearing yet respectful title her children were accustomed to hearing. "Her friend Dave is not well."

"Is he dying?"

"Yes." Mala was not in the mood for continued conversing.

"Well, you better not tell *Nani*, because she is going to be upset that you left us to go see someone who's dying."

Mala didn't quite understand her daughter's logic and said, "Everyone will die one day, including me and your *Nani*. So what you're saying doesn't make any sense."

"I know, and that's how it helps me not think about it. Mum?" Shania looked at her mother's profile as she was driving and wondered what happened to her over the last few months to look so aged. "Are you okay?"

Mala, still with her eyes on the road answered in a very fake upbeat manner, "Yes of course darling, I am fine."

"Did something happen the night Papa came over with everyone?"

"No, not at all. Why, did Papa say something?"

"No... he just didn't want to come inside when he picked me up the last time he came round, and I didn't know why... did you say something to him again?"

"Not at all... it's all grown up talk, there is no need to get involved."

Shania was not easing up on her inquisitive conversation because she sensed, like a baby lion, that her mother was lying. "Roshan said he saw Papa crying."

"What?" Mala was wondering if her daughter was up to something. "When?"

"The day you and your friends wanted to be Celtic witches." Shania picked up her novel and began to read; she had sparked the fire of curiosity in her mother and that was always enough to get a conversation ignited with her. Sometimes it could become a little explosive, causing Shania to tread carefully.

"Roshan wasn't even home, he dropped your brother to Jason's and then went for a drive before he picked you up."

Shania refused look up from her book. "Yes, he dropped my brother, and then he went back home because he forgot his wallet, and on his way out again he saw Papa."

"What did Papa say to him?" Mala was concerned. After all, that was the father of her beautiful children.

"He said nothing Mum, he was crying and when he saw Roshan he gave him a hug and left... he had no words, Mum. What did you say to him?"

"Nothing. I wasn't there."

Shania put her book delicately on her lap and said, "Mum, don't lie."

Shania's over confident behaviour gave her the feistiness of a lawyer, or perhaps the immaculate perception of an FBI agent. Her prowess for delicate situations catapulted her to always excel in everything she did. She was not boisterous or flighty or even rattled much. She had the stillness and calmness of an apache. Her wisdom was beyond her years and she never let anyone get in the way of her dreams. Like a tiger, she would move swiftly and gracefully through situations, especially delicate life issues, which ultimately made her calm.

Chapter 33

London

It had been two long weeks since the outburst at Mala's Hammersmith apartment, and Noor was ready to move on. She was thinking about Paris, maybe even Spain. All she knew is that she had exhausted her time in London. Again.

Two very painful outbursts from her supposedly closest friends – Christopher and Mala – had made it difficult for Noor to concentrate, and instead of eating, which is what she would have done in the past, she began to starve herself by drinking juice all day long from her local gym. She asked her *Muay Thai* boxing trainer, Boon, to deliver the juice to her house every day.

Noor didn't feel like she had anyone to turn to in her life, ever, and understood that she was destined to be alone. For the time being, she had convinced herself she was content, and on occasion Christopher would call in on her to see if she was okay. The conversation was very brief, always kept on a very friendly and amicable level. They both didn't engage in prolonged conversations with each other because she would start to feel pain and start to relive situations that were beyond her control.

She wondered again why she and Mala had developed so much animosity towards each other over the years. She didn't feel bad at all. As a matter of fact, she was happy to be rid of all the drama in her life. Mala had served a good purpose for a story, but even that was beginning to look mundane in her eyes. She looked at her body in the mirror and wondered where she had been a decade ago, or even a decade before that. Transformation was staring right back at her in the mirror. Progressing into the next stage of her life was going to take some upkeep and cleaning of her social circle.

She took out her pendulum and asked, "Should I get rid of Mala in my life?" She waited as the pendulum swung just the way she didn't want it to go – it swung left, indicating "no."

She threw the pendulum on the bed, turned on some music and looked out of the window feeling rather frustrated. Her vengeful nature was not assisting in the growth of what her peers believed should be an accurate transformation. Pondering if speaking to Durga or even young Shania would help, Noor thought the wiser. How would she open the conversation, by agreeing with Durga that Mala was rough around the edges? Be rude about a parent in front of a daughter by asking Shania to speak to her mother? It wouldn't work, because the ties of family were strong no matter how many differences they had. They were bound by three generations She started to feel the pit of sadness move up through her body, and the only person she could turn to was, once again, her father. Sighing, she picked up the phone and called her *Pitaji*.

"Hello?" Mr Noor sounded rather tired these days and was always happy to hear from his daughter. He could travel less, but with his daughter's help, the whole family always had a way to assist with finances.

"*Pitaji*, how are you?"

"I haven't heard from you in a few weeks Annabelle... how are you?"

"I'm okay... I think I want to come back to Paris for a bit." She tried to hold back the tears, because the person she needed to be strong in front of the most was her father.

"Are you okay Annabelle? What happened now? Did someone hurt you?"

"No... no... not at all, I just need a change again, *Pitaji*."

Although Mr Noor had more patience now than in his younger days with Noor, he sighed. "Again? What happened now?"

"*Pitaji*, I just need you to understand me more now than ever…"

Mr Noor interrupted, knowing that his daughter would always be his little girl. "Come back Annabelle, don't worry about anything. I'm here for you."

"Thank you, Dad. I want you to know that this time, it has come from a place of age, Dad, and a place of feeling like the only person I have left in my life is you."

Mr Noor, feeling slightly overwhelmed, caught himself and cleared his throat. "We are family, Annabelle. We are together for a reason. If you need to come home, I will be here waiting for you, and the restaurant Café Des Artists will always be a family run business.

"Thanks, *Pitaji*. I will not pack up all my things; I'll be back in London again soon, I'm sure, but for now I'm going to get some things organised and see you in a few days."

"Okay Annabelle, I will see you soon."

"I love you, Dad."

"I love you too, Annabelle."

And again, like a cosmic force hit both of them at the same time, Mr Noor and his daughter shook their heads as they put their phones down. This time, it was from a place of relief as well as the bond of family: unconditional and knowing.

Noor felt better, less jittery, and asked her house manager Gloria to help her pack her bags. Although she had told her dad she would be arriving in a few days, she made a decision to leave tomorrow, first thing in the morning. She picked up her pendulum from the bed, but this time did not pack it in her bag; she was going to leave the beautiful fractals of glass energy on her dressing table. Instead, she was going to try and rely utterly on her instincts for once in her life.

Part 4

Never the End

Chapter 34

Paris

Noor's contentment to be in Paris was waning with speed, and it was stifling for her to once again reside in father's house. Annabelle Noor had catapulted herself right back into her old paradigm, one that was immature and completely co-dependent.

Her father's wife Anna Maria and Noor were still not on talking terms; the strain was unbearable for both of them. Noor decided to tell her father that she would be moving out and into a serviced apartment. She was not going to work at Café Des Artistes either, because that was old news. She pondered about her lack of maturity for running away again, to her father, who would someday, very soon, not even be there in the physical world for her.

Once again, Annabelle was all alone in her tiny misguided world. She began to write, and the fire of competition began to jolt her into thinking about how she could make her story into a movie one day. Her story was real, true, but to be quite frank… boring. What did she have to say for herself, apart from the fact that she tried to get married a hundred times, she failed at multiple businesses, and she was the daughter of a very rich man who made his 'transactions' seem legitimate through laundering money with his family members? She immediately blocked the last thought from her mind.

Who would want to read her story anyway? She thought about her friends, and they didn't have a very interesting story either. The three of them together – Mala, Noor and Sharon – were part of the fabric of each other, but not so much anymore. The web of their stories was torn, fragmented and dangling by a simple piece of thread.

Christopher had stopped calling to check up on her for some time now, which made her begin to feel even more lonely. She laughed aloud to herself, the warning signs of hysteria emerging into her sub conscious. She began to write.

> In the Land of Oz, or in the land of her fragile mind, the winds of wanting to be "home" were not as she expected. What was on the horizon for this fragile old lady who mirrored repentance? How was she ever going to find the magic of life again? Her younger days were full of laughter and delight… there was no such thing as the yellow brick road, promising light and fortune at the end of the tunnel. Her obstacles were not the characters she had grown to know and love, but the emotions they represented: her heart, her mind and her courage.

> Without her family she was nothing, yet they happened to be the biggest hindrance in her life even from childhood. And just like Dorothy wanted to go back to "Kansas," she wanted to find another way home where she was not guided by family, but rather by instinct and renewal.

Noor wondered whether she had the time to compose all of her musings into a single story, or if her writing had just become catharsis for an aged woman desperately still trying to find herself.

Chapter 35

En Route to South East Asia

Mala sat on the plane typing on her computer; she knew exactly what Sophia was going through, and the only thing that was assisting her now was the power of writing to heal her fragile feelings. Again, she wrote about the female lead of her story.

The idea of friendship and love shook her foundation; moving to another city, all she could feel was the force of negativity driving through her as the transformation from love to hate made her realise that polarity in life – especially her own life – existed and could not be changed. She wondered how the mighty philosophers, Ghandi, Mother Teresa, Martin Luther King and even presidents, could shift so regularly from one extreme to the other without feeling depleted.

It was a constant battle to keep moving forward and staying consistent. Battle? Why did it all have to come down to the notion of war? She revelled in the opposites, once again realising that one didn't exist without the other. How sad that the world couldn't live in one polarity! Was there a hole in the cosmic force? Why did God have to create humans this way? As she travelled across the globe realising her fate she tried to become more grounded in her way of thinking…

Mala's thoughts were interrupted by the air hostess. "Please fasten your seat belts as we are about to arrive in Hong Kong." She looked out the window, and the city illuminated vibrancy with lights shining high on top of the sky scrapers. She was excited to see Sophia but knew at the same time that the moment was brittle, and love as well as care was paramount at this time.

The airport was bustling with all kinds of people. Mala's *Lonely Planet* guide to Hong Kong was absolutely correct when it revealed that Hong Kong was a microcosm of a thousand different nationalities blended into a tiny city full of buildings, beaches, mountains and nightlife. The airport reflected a hub for business people, tourists with families, backpackers, and entrepreneurs with a variety of nationalities.

As soon as she cleared the doors of customs, Mala spotted Sophia right away, exactly the image she had in her mind of her friend. She had apparently lost a lot of weight from stress as well as preparations for the funeral. Mala smiled bravely as she walked closer to Sophia. The closer she got the more she could see that Sophia was not in good spirits.

They hugged very tightly, and both women felt the warmth of love and friendship encircle their auras.

"How have you been Mala?"

"I'm good, I'm okay… you look so frail, Sophia… when was the last time you had something to eat?"

After a brief pause, Sophia said quietly, "I think it's been about two days, Mala."

"And Dave? How is the situation there?"

Sophia looked down. After a long pause, she finally brought herself to say it: "He's… already gone." She gazed, piercing the floor, trying not to spill any more tears, but it was difficult. The scene of his last moments in the hospital were painfully etched in Sophia's mind as she witnessed Dave take his last breath. She had never seen anyone die before; this was the most horrific life experience she had ever encountered.

For all her planning and intentions, Mala had arrived too late. "I am so sorry Sophia, I thought I would make it on time…"

"I am so happy you are here Mala, I really am. You did come at the right time. There are so many arrangements and so much legal mumbo jumbo that he left me with, and he also left me with clothes and a store, and I just need the strength to get it up and running. I know he would hate to see me like this."

"We will handle it together. I'm here to help. Don't worry about anything."

They walked silently to the car as Sophia remembered the time when Dave visited her in London, and when they went to Paris for Fatima's showcase. It seemed like just yesterday they were all together.

The journey from the airport didn't take long, and when Sophia opened the door to her beautiful house in Deep Water Bay, Mala was in awe. The last time she had seen such a beautiful house was Noor's father's house in London. A stinging pain in her heart pulled on the forefront of her new practise not to reminisce about the past.

"Your house is beautiful," Mala said, as she scanned the view from the living room. The white brick fireplace looked magical, and all the pictures on the mantle and the wall told a story of a woman who was loved – a woman who believed in the foundation of friendship and family.

Both women sat down to have a cup of tea and engaged in small talk about Alister, London, Mala's children, and of course Noor. Mala didn't get into full details of the situation with her, because it was not the time or the place. After they ran out of things to catch up on, Sophia took Mala to the guest room and then to the basement to show her all the clothes Dave had designed for her in order to open her shop called *SOPH*.

"This is amazing Sophia, wow, no one has ever done anything like this for me, and I can't imagine anyone thinking of me in this way. You are blessed."

"I don't know where to start… the shop is already there, bought, ready to go, all I need to do is arrange all of these clothes." She paused and took a deep breath. "He asked me to organise a small party for him with his very close friends at the store, once we have everything set up... can you help me do that while you're here?"

"Of course I will." Mala was still looking at all the clothes Dave had designed, reflecting how much he loved Sophia. Everything was a symbol or metaphor for Sophia's character, and it was displayed through clothes: fabric, colour, and pure imagination. "He really loved you, didn't he?"

"Absolutely, Mala... he really did. I've never known anyone to love me as much as he did."

"You are a very lucky woman, Sophia."

"I know..."

Mala, yearning to make the situation better, even though it had been two raw days of not having Dave with her, knew that the only way to help her friend was to move forward, keep her energy up, or at least help her maintain her mental well-being at a stable level. "Let's start first thing tomorrow. I know Dave would have wanted this for you."

"Okay." Sophia looked tired.

"I think we should both get some rest now, and we will work on this tomorrow first thing in the morning."

"Thank you, Mala," Sophia replied, almost automatically.

"You're welcome." Mala smiled trying to make the best of a bad situation.

Both women, again in silence, walked back up to the living room, as the beautiful view of the water shimmered in the bay. Craig was not home yet. He usually had meetings that ran late, three or four times a week. He didn't feel right leaving Sophia all alone during her fragile time, and he was grateful to have Mala visit.

Later that night, as Mala lay in her bed in the guest room of Sophia's house, she remembered stumbling upon an article, about three weeks before her trip to Asia, about the significance of time and how minutes and hours are our biggest commodities; she couldn't help but agree with the author of the article. She pondered that thought for a moment. The truth in that statement made Mala think of her own children. They were still very young and had so much to offer the world. As she drifted off to sleep, she dreamt of her mother and father again; she dreamt of them often, but this time they were both together, on a similar plane.

This time, when her mother spoke, fractals of light emerged from her speech like a rainbow. And right next to her, Santosh, her deceased father, was humbled by her light and energy.

Mala woke up sweating, feeling the pangs of time as a precious commodity creep up into her life. She knew her mother's turn would be next. In the morning, Mala emailed Durga to let her know she was coming to India with the twins for a few weeks during their holiday. She would call and confirm it soon.

The word endless… was an enigma… there was no such thing… or was there? People were always moving in every direction; Mala's children moved forwards; Sharon and Dave had moved upwards for their 'debuts'; Mala and Washington had unfortunately moved backwards; and Mala and Noor had moved sideways – for what that was worth.

It was all so much to consider; lately, Mala was wondering which way she should turn. And the only place she found some respite was in front of her computer, writing.

Chapter 36

Somewhere in the Universe, Centred at Bazica

Taking a sip of her tea – after so many years being around coffee all the time, she had developed a taste for tea – Fatima began to write.

Each person in the story moves in the right direction towards different aspects of life, trying to live in an endless pattern of learning, unlearning, and then learning all over again. What lessons must be undertaken in order to realise that time is endless, yet has its boundaries?

One thing is for certain: the end of something always brings the beginning of something else; the closing of a window causes the opening of a massive door; with each movement, each person is surged into a vortex of renewal and change.

And with death, there is once again life. Endless life... endless time... and endless bonds.

The journey towards the end is never over, there is no such thing; it is a passing of time and true understanding that limitations come from within. The biggest commodity of life is that time – sometimes seeming to pass one by with speed and precision – gives each in a circle of friends a fragile sense of belonging, knowing that even though time is endless, it indeed has a stop sign for the physical self.

As the years pass with age and renewal again as a continuous cycle, generations, lineage, and basic DNA live on endlessly in the fabric of our lives – ever-changing, ever moving, and constant.

Endless

end • less

/en(d)ləss/

adjective

– Having or seeming to have no end or limit

About the Author

Pashmina P. is author of *Mocha Madness*, the second instalment of the International Best Seller, *The Cappuccino Chronicles*. The third and final instalment of the trilogy series, *Endless Espressos*, is due for release soon, alongside another novel on the horizon entitled *Am I the One*, a collection of nine short stories about nine families from different corners of the globe.

Always having a passion for writing, including several stage plays and short stories, Pashmina has been an international performing arts instructor for 16 years, and has a Master of Education degree in International Teaching. She strongly believes in the values of multicultural learning – something that shines in her teaching as well as writing.

The success of *The Cappuccino Chronicles* has given her the desire to pursue her career as a writer, and to inspire people to feel passionate about their own lives through both the mediums of writing and performance.

Mother of two and self-started entrepreneur, her lifelong ambition and dream is to open her own state-of-the-art theatre in Asia, thus merging her passions for writing, learning, and the arts.

Other Works by Pashmina P.

The Cappuccino Chronicles Trilogy

The Cappuccino Chronicles started out as a story exploring simple conversations between four women who sit at a coffee shop almost every day, discussing the troubles they face in the world. The four women have been friends since university, and as the story progresses, each character evolves as they are forced to learn some hard truths about growing up and transitioning from girls to women.

Mocha Madness, the second book of the trilogy in the series of *The Cappuccino Chronicles*, takes the reader on an ongoing journey as each woman matures. Worldly truths change as work, marriage and children become their central focuses. In the continuation, the reader will see how the fabric of their lives and very existences can in one instant be so intertwined with one another, yet suddenly a swipe of universal energy can throw people out of vibration and frequency. Such changes greatly alter the course of these women's lives – and by extension, our own. The hard truths are revealed in family, friendship and love as the women learn how to move on with their lives with dignity and grace, but this time with a deeper sense and understanding of the knowledge that experience provides.

Endless Espressos is the final instalment of *The Cappuccino Chronicles* trilogy, and although the word "endless" plays a very big role in this story, it helps the reader realise that there are some aspects of our lives that have to come to an end. In *Endless Espressos*, the characters are again faced with the knowledge that age, as well as the process of aging, gives humans a sense of purpose through a reminiscence about days gone by – and coming to terms with this is not a straightforward journey.

All three instalments in the trilogy – *The Cappuccino Chronicles*, *Mocha Madness*, and *Endless Espressos* – are the embodiment of everyday people, placed into fictional characters who continue to entertain, teach, love, and heal through their transformations. Like a good brew of coffee, the taste can sometimes be bittersweet, enchanting, aromatic, yet all the while full of flavour. The trilogy in this series is full of great conversation, and very simple spiritual truths will compel the reader to get lost in a world of four very powerful women who use time as a means of understanding their own life journeys.

Am I the One

Am I the One is another novel Pashmina is working on which focuses on nine short stories centred around nine different families from across the globe. The path towards internationalism has its ups and downs, and the perspectives offered in this unique set of culture-driven vignettes are sure to open one's eyes to possibilities of understanding not yet considered – for better or worse.

Personal Writing Mentorships, Readers' Theatre, and The Arts

Writing has given Pashmina the freedom to become an entrepreneur, while sticking to her lifelong dream of building a state-of-the-art 1,200 seat proscenium style theatre in Asia; she believes that the arts play a fundamental role in the development of our psyche, and allow us to imagine beyond our wildest dreams.

When she is not writing, Pashmina hosts Readers' Theatre and writing workshops for students, which helps build confidence amongst children while teaching them the importance of collaboration and team work. Pashmina also provides personal writing mentorship programmes, and she and *The Cappuccino Chronicles* team have established themselves as a platform for writers to seek advice, editing, and design prior to approaching publishing houses.

For a *one on one personal mentorship* with Pashmina, serious authors wanting to get their names out into the market can schedule a Skype call to discuss the possibilities. All enquiries can be directed to Pashmina through email at **pashmina.p.writer@gmail.com**.

As a working mom, Pashmina realises that time is of the essence; it is one of our biggest commodities in life, equal in weight to the very water we drink and air we breathe. Her calling to be speaker, coach, and international best-selling author is not one she takes lightly, and for those ready and willing to take the leap, she would love to hear from you.

The Literary Fairies

we make your literary wish come true

Pashmina P.

has partnered with

The Literary Fairies

who have a mission to give to those who have
experienced an adversity or disability an opportunity
to become a published author while sharing
a story to uplift, inspire and entertain the world.

Visit TLF website to find out how YOU
could become a published author or where
you can help grant a literary wish.

More details provided at
www.theliteraryfairies.com

81024602R00162

Made in the USA
Columbia, SC
14 November 2017